I0819949

TOUCHED SERIES, BOOK 1

BLOOD DEBT

NANCY STRAIGHT

Book design by Inkstain Interior Book Designing
Available electronically from all major bookstores.
Printed in paperback in 2012.
ISBN-13: 978-1478111047
ISBN-10: 1478111046

BOOKS BY NANCY STRAIGHT

MYTHOLOGY
TOUCHED SERIES

Blood Debt
Centaur Legacy
Centaur Rivalry
Centaur Redemption

Think Centaurs can't be sexy? Think Again!

PARANORMAL ROMANCE
DESTINY SERIES

Meeting Destiny
Destiny's Revenge
Destiny's Wrath

How many lifetimes are enough with your soul mate?

THRILLER/SUSPENSE
BREWER BROTHERS SERIES

His Frozen Heart
Fractured Karma
Shroud of Lies

Award-winning series!

For my sons, Alex and Zack,
whose humor & imaginations
inspire me every day.

CHAPTER 1

Camille Benning – Oceanside, CA

I stared at the phone. I had his number. I had his name. Twenty-two years. . . after twenty-two stinking years of fantasizing about who he was, what he was like, where he was—you'd think I would have dialed by now. The thing is—nobody, anywhere, could live up to my expectations. I'd always envisioned this successful, educated, lead-singer, movie-star, rich kind of father. It was great to think that he was this wonderful, benevolent man, who one day would swoop in and introduce himself, then whisk me away in a limo. Yeah, that never happened.

I can't think of a time when I wasn't dying to meet him. When I would ask my Mom, she would always tell me, "Your father was a wonderful man. We had a few magical days together, and he left me with the most amazing gift to remember him by." Sure, that's what a ten-year-old wants to hear. She would never tell me his name, where he lived, or anything about him other than he didn't live in California.

It didn't matter how hard I pleaded, I think she preferred that he be a mystery. Who would have guessed all those times I said I would trade anything to meet him, I never thought I'd trade my rock, my anchor. . . my mom. Ten minutes before she took her last breath, she grabbed my hand and choked out, "Your father. . .lives in Charleston, South Carolina. His name is William Strayer. He deserves to know you. Tell him . . . tell him I said, 'Goodbye.'"

A few breaths later, she slipped away as death carried her to her final peace. I cried for weeks. No matter how hard I tried, I couldn't process losing my mom and getting the information I'd been begging her for my whole life in the span of ten minutes. All those wagers I'd tried to make with God, to find out who he was—I'd told God I would trade anything—I never meant my mom. I'm not crazy enough to think that God had stolen my mom just so I could find out who my father was, but I had several weeks of erratic thoughts.

I googled him. He was easy to find. He'd been in the same house, in the same job, for better than thirty years. Everything I found out about him on the internet pointed to an average guy, with an average life. He wasn't a rock star. He wasn't famous. *He* wasn't dead.

I took one final breath, steadying myself. I had my phone in one hand and the slip of paper with all his information on my lap. I dialed the number, wondering what I was going to say to him. Before I could press "send," I chickened out and went back to Mom's bedroom to go through more of her things. Peggy, my mom's closest and only friend, had offered to come over to help me, but I was twenty-two. I shouldn't need help with this. Even if Peggy was her best friend, I knew Mom wouldn't want her going through her things. My mom had always been a private person.

Mom knew it was coming. She'd been sick for a long time. Her closet, that normally looked crammed with outfits from the last several decades, wasn't as packed as the last time I'd seen it. Mom must have gone through some of her things before she died because the walk-in closet could actually be walked into.

Tucked in the far back corner, on a shelf, was a treasure box of sorts: a wooden box with the key inserted into the lock. Whatever was inside, Mom wanted me to see it. I found yellowing movie ticket stubs for a title I'd never heard of, an airline ticket from twenty-eight years ago, a crumpled up photograph of my mom holding two babies, and a tourist shot glass from the Crazy Horse Monument in South Dakota. It seemed an odd set of treasures for her to have hidden away. I looked at the old plane ticket: it was for an Angela Chiron—no one I knew. I gently closed the wooden box after I'd returned her "treasures" to their resting place. As I stared at sequined sweaters, stretch pants, dress slacks and dresses, I found myself wanting to make that phone call far more than I wanted to go through my mom's life.

William. Did he even know I existed? He probably had a family of his own. What would they think of me? It had always been just my mom and me. She didn't have any family, at least other than me. Her parents died when she was young, and she'd been an only child. I think her final gift to me – my father's identity—was her way of not leaving me so alone in the world.

I went back to the living room, sat on the sofa, and put my feet up on the coffee table, almost begging Mom to walk into the room and tell me to get my feet off of it. A lonely tear rolled down my cheek. No one would be walking through the doorway to tell me to put my feet down. I hated the idea of being alone.

I took one more deep breath, picked up the slip of paper, and dialed his number again. This time my shaking finger pushed, "Send."

A woman's voice answered the phone, "Hello."

I stammered, terrified of this call, not sure what to say to the woman. "Uh . . . hi . . . is William there?"

"Who's calling?"

"Camille."

"Camille, is this a sales call?"

"Uh, no. Definitely, no. Is William home?"

"Just a minute."

I could only assume that had been William's wife. I wanted to hang up. I saw my hand shaking and prayed that I wouldn't have full-blown convulsions. I had practiced this phone call several times, but realized I should have written things down. My fear began crippling me, and I drew a blank. What would I say? "I'm your love child from twenty-three years ago and wanted to say hi." Not the best approach.

I heard a gruff voice come on the line, "Hello, this is Will."

My voice didn't work. My mouth opened but nothing came out.

"Hello, is anybody there?"

I cleared my throat, closed my eyes and answered, "Uh, yes. Hi, William. I'm Camille."

A friendly voice responded, "Okay. Camille who?"

"Right. I'm Angela Benning's daughter."

"Angela Benning? I'm still not making the connection. Are you sure you have the right William?"

"William Strayer from Charleston, South Carolina?"

"Yes."

"You are the only one I found in information. Have you ever been to San Diego?"

"Well, yes. I travel there, but I don't know an Angela Benning."

"Not even one you knew twenty-three years ago?" Silence answered me back. I wasn't sure if he had hung up the phone, if the connection had been dropped, or if he was too stunned to answer. "William, are you still there?"

"Yes. Yes, I'm still here. I did know an Angela in San Diego. She was a bartender in a hotel."

"That's right."

"Camille, how old are you?"

I did have the right person, and at least I didn't have to draw the connection out for him with big purple crayons. "I'm twenty-two."

"Twenty-two?"

"Yeah, my birthday was last month."

More silence. . . I could feel him doing the math in his head. This was a bad idea. I braced myself for him to deny he was my father, that I was some leech after him for money. His voice spoke softly, "Camille, I don't know what to say. Your mother is an incredible woman."

"Was." I corrected, "She *was* an incredible woman."

"I'm sorry, I didn't know. What happened?" Sincerity was wrapped in his voice.

"She died of breast cancer a few weeks ago. Right before she died, she told me how I could contact you."

"So, you're my. . . I mean she wouldn't have . . . if you weren't mine."

I could almost hear the wheels turning in his head. "Right. I don't need anything. I just . . . I guess I wanted to talk to you."

"Camille, you have to believe me, if I had known I would have . . . I didn't know I had a daughter."

"That's okay, William. I knew I had a father – I mean from a biological perspective, but Mom would never tell me anything about you, well, not until the night she died."

His voice sounded heavy, "Call me Will. Everyone does. So, she didn't want you to contact me?"

"I guess not, well . . . she never told me anything about you. I never knew your name until the night she passed."

"You said that was a few weeks ago?"

"Yeah, she went into the hospital the week after my birthday."

I heard hopefulness in his voice that I didn't expect when he said, "When can I meet you?"

This was a question I wasn't really prepared for. All those practice conversations had more to do with introducing myself and convincing him that I was his daughter. I thought I had prepared for every possible response. I never considered that he would want to meet me. "Uh, maybe the next time you come to California?"

"Camille, I've got a lot going on for the next month. Getting out to the west coast would be hard. Would you consider flying to South Carolina?"

My heart started doing cartwheels. Not only did I have a real father—he wanted to see me! Trying not to gush at his suggestion, "Um, maybe. I've got a bunch of stuff I've got to take care of. You know, estate stuff for Mom, and a job."

"I could arrange for a lawyer to take care of that for you. Camille, I don't want to put this off. I . . . I could make arrangements now. You could be on the red eye tonight."

"Will, you don't know anything about me. I've got a job. I can't just get on a plane."

"You're my blood, Camille. Angela was a magical woman, I . . . I had no idea. If you can't come to me, I'll juggle some things around. I have to meet you."

Huh, that's the same thing Mom had said about him: that he was "magical." I had googled him a few weeks ago. I knew he was somehow involved with finance and investments and ran a firm in Charleston. Since my job was working at a department store as a cashier, reality was that it would be much easier for me to leave my job for a few days. As I looked around the apartment, there was too much of her here. Not that it was a bad thing, but given the last several months, it might be nice to have a change of scenery, for a few days.

I took a deep breath, "Okay, I can call into work and have someone cover my shifts. But I don't have the cash for a plane ticket or motel or anything."

"I'll take care of it. How soon could you be on a plane?"

"I guess tonight. Do you need to talk to your wife or anything?"

"Gretchen will be happy to have you as a guest. She's always wanted a daughter as much as I have." I felt a warm glow in my chest. The emptiness of losing my mom would stay with me forever, but I wasn't alone. I had a father. We exchanged email addresses so we could coordinate the flight. I wondered if this was some sort of a dream. I had run a background investigation on him within days of finding out who he was. All I really knew about him was he paid his taxes, he owned several properties, he had never been arrested, and he hadn't had a traffic ticket or an accident in the last seven years.

I called my best friend in the world to let him know what had just happened. He was so excited for me that he was at my door within twenty minutes. Daniel was like the brother I never had. We looked enough alike that sometimes people assumed I was his sister. He had dark hair, kind of that in between length – it was short, but shaggy. His eyelashes were gorgeous. For a long time I teased him, calling him "Maybelline Eyes," and he had this way of looking at girls that made them all melt – well, all but me. Daniel was on the surf team in high school and even got a scholarship to surf in college, so there was never a shortage of beach babes looking to hang out with him. We'd never been more than friends, and I knew we both liked it that way. We each had a ready-made date for all the big social events, weddings, engagement parties, holiday parties, etc – but none of the romantic attachments that came with it.

Daniel gathered me in a large bear hug and swung me around. "You talked to him? He wants to meet you?"

"I did! He wasn't freaked out about it or anything. He's flying me to South Carolina, tonight, to meet him."

Daniel's enthusiasm diminished in front of me, "Tonight? Why the rush?"

I slapped his shoulder, "I'm his daughter. He wants to meet me."

"Did he say why he never bothered to come see you?"

"I think my mom hid us from each other. He didn't even know that I existed until I called."

"Just like that, he wants you on a plane? What about a DNA test?"

"He didn't ask for any proof. He said he remembered her." I left out the part where he said she was magical – Daniel knew that's what my mom had said about him.

"That must have been some phone call. Are you sure he's all right?"

"I'm not stupid. I did a background check."

"That just means he's never been caught."

I punched Daniel's arm a second time, and he feigned pain. "I'm just saying you don't even know the guy. He could be a serial killer for all you know. There's probably a reason your mom never let the two of you meet."

"She told me who he was right before she died. She must have wanted me to find him."

"Maybe. How about I go with you?"

"Um, I don't know. I think this is something I have to do on my own, but keep your cell phone on you in case I need you."

He frowned with his eyebrows furrowed, "I don't like it. Something doesn't feel right."

"Stop worrying. I'll be back on Sunday. If it gets weird, I'll come back sooner."

"If I don't get a call every day, I'm getting on a plane."

"Right, to fly to South Carolina and do what? I'll be fine. He sounded nice."

"You've wanted to meet this guy forever. Don't get your hopes up. Angela was a smart lady. She must have kept you two apart for a reason."

"Maybe she just didn't want the hassle of sharing custody." This was the lie I'd told myself when I was little. My mom never had boyfriends.

She always told me her life was full, and she didn't have room for one more person in it.

"Maybe, but maybe he's a douche, and she didn't want you to get hurt."

My heart sank. I didn't have the strength to argue with him. I knew he was right. I knew Mom hid his identity from me, but I didn't care why. Everyone needed family, no matter how weird they might be. I was willing to take a chance: one crazy father was better than nobody.

For the next fifteen hours, through two airports and the whole time I was in the air, Daniel's words continued to echo in my mind, *"She must have kept you two apart for a reason."* Why would she have kept us apart? Was she ashamed of him? What did he do that made her not want him in her life? She'd never, for as long as I could remember, had a boyfriend – had he done something to her?

CHAPTER 2

Camille Benning – Charleston, SC

The wheels touched down at the Charleston Airport. Although I wasn't a world traveler, I recognized that it was a very small airport, two whole luggage carousels in baggage claim. I had been to San Diego's airport lots of times; it was like a maze of endless signs and was seriously intimidating even for the locals. Charleston's was small and felt welcoming. I had found pictures of Will on the internet. I knew he was near fifty, with graying hair, distinguished face, brown eyes, and a nose that was slightly larger than his face required. Not unattractive, but I doubt he'd ever been a huge heart-throb. The pictures I found of him were all with suit jackets and ties, so I scanned the baggage claim area for a middle-aged man in a suit. It was 10:30 a.m. on a Wednesday. I saw a few people who had the right attire, but none looked like the picture I'd downloaded of him. I kept checking my phone for a message from him, but nothing.

I felt the nervousness gripping me, wondering if this was a mistake. Daniel's words continued in my head; I tried to shake his warning away and knew I needed to come up with a plan. How would I get to Will's house? I checked my phone again, nothing new. This was a dumb idea. I saw my bag approaching on the carousel. As I reached down to pick it up, a guy my age in a polo shirt, khakis and dress shoes loped through the large double-doors from outside. He was carrying a piece of paper with clear block letters that read, "Camille Benning."

It definitely wasn't Will. I rolled my bag over to the guy and said, "Hi. I'm Camille Benning."

I saw his eyes widen momentarily and felt him look me up and down as a huge toothy smile flashed my way. "Hi, Camille, I'm Brent. Welcome to Charleston!" His brown eyes looked glad to see me, and his cheeks dimpled when he smiled. His dark brown hair was cropped short, and it looked like he was either a sun worshipper or he'd never worked a day in his life – golden bronze skin was hard to come by with a full-time job.

"Uh, thanks." I wasn't expecting a car service. Will was definitely losing cool points by not bothering to meet me at the airport.

"Can I help you with your bag?"

I shook my head, "That's okay, I've got it."

He responded with a startled look, "I must have said that wrong. I'll take your bag for you." He reached for it, but my knuckles didn't budge from the handle.

My voice stern, "No, thanks. I've got it." Years of caution from Mom about strangers, about not looking weak, I wasn't about to let this clown think that I wasn't capable of rolling my own bag. If he kept this up, there was no way I was going to give him a tip.

With a snicker in his voice, "Headstrong just like Dad; he'll be thrilled." I raised my eyebrow, not understanding his comment. He must have seen my confusion because he clarified, "I'm sorry, I assumed Dad mentioned that I would be picking you up. I'm your brother, Brent."

Brother? Holy crap! A father, stepmother, and a brother – all in less than a day. I felt a smile erupting as some of the loneliness I'd felt the last month offered to evaporate. "Oh, uh, no. We didn't talk that long yesterday."

"That figures. Well, the car is this way." Brent led the way through the double doors while I rolled my own suitcase.

Here I was excited to be flying across the country to meet a father I had just found out about. In the back of my mind I assumed he had a family, but I never expected for him to send his son to pick me up. When I ran the background check on him, it didn't say anything about a son. That's something that should definitely show up if you blow forty bucks to dig into someone's past.

As we stepped through the double doors to the outside, the heat nearly took my breath away. It was like stepping into an oven. "Wow, is it always this hot?"

Brent chuckled, "This isn't bad. Wait another couple hours: that's when it starts to get uncomfortable." It felt like a hundred degrees and a hundred percent humidity. I knew July would be hot, but I didn't think I would be slow roasting. We stepped out to the curb where Brent motioned me to a beautiful BMW sedan. It was snowy white with tan interior. A guy waited in the driver's seat and a second in the front passenger seat.

As Brent put my bag in the trunk, I stole a glance at the two men waiting in the car. Neither looked old enough to be Will, either.

Brent stepped back to the passenger side and opened my door for me, holding it while I sat down and then closed it for me—very gentlemanly. He walked around to the other side of the car and sat next to me in the backseat. The two guys in the front seat turned around. They each shared the same big toothy smile and bore a striking resemblance to Brent. As Brent reached for his seat belt he said, "Camille, these are your brothers Bart and Ben."

"Uh, nice to meet you both."

Bart began driving, so it was Ben's turn. "We're glad you're here. I know you flew all night. Did you want to go back to the house and crash or stop for a bite first?"

Until he mentioned food, I hadn't realized I was hungry. "I don't want to be any trouble. Whatever you were going to do was fine."

Bart let out a hearty laugh, "We were told to take care of you for a few hours until Dad can get home from work. There're great restaurants here. Do you like seafood?"

Bart had said the magic word. I loved seafood. "Yeah, if you guys are hungry, I could eat."

Ben turned around in his seat because I was sitting directly behind him. "So, you live in San Diego? Have you lived there your whole life?"

"Yeah. Well, near there. I live in Oceanside; it's a little north of San Diego."

"So, do you surf?"

"Not well. But I've been on a board a few times."

"If you want to go surfing while you're here, you can borrow one of mine."

"Thanks."

"How long are you staying?"

"'Til Sunday."

"Wow, that's a quick trip. So are you on summer break from school?"

"No, I, um . . . I never went to college." It never bothered me before that I couldn't afford college, mainly because I never had any real desire to go. But looking at these three in this car, I, for the first time, felt a little intimidated about my choice.

Ben casually asked, "So, what do you do?"

Wondering if Ben was purposely trying to make me feel uncomfortable, I said confidently, "I'm a cashier."

I could tell Ben sensed that he'd sort of rattled me, and he smoothly tried to make up for it. "I was a cashier all through high school at a grocery store—that was a great job. I'm jealous."

Ben got an "A" for effort, but it was obvious that a mere cashier was not in the same league with these three. I decided I'd try to get the focus off of me. "So, how old are you three?"

Brent answered, "I'm twenty-four, Ben's twenty-five, Bart's twenty-six, Bruce is twenty-seven and Beau's twenty-eight. Bruce and Beau couldn't fit in the car without cramming you in like a sardine. I just texted them to meet us at the Harbor Club."

I looked squarely at Brent. I didn't know any family with five kids, "Five boys?"

Brent nodded enthusiastically. He was notably cautious with his next question, "Um, how old are you, Camille?"

"I'm twenty-two."

No one responded right away, and just before the pause got seriously uncomfortable, Brent's excitement returned, "Well, great, you're legal. We could all go hit a club or something while you're here."

The image of me walking into a bar with five very tall, handsome guys had its merits. "Maybe. Are there good clubs here?"

"Probably not as sophisticated as San Diego, but there're some decent places to dance downtown."

Brent was still pressing me for more info, "So, do you have any brothers or sisters, I mean . . . other than us?"

I shook my head that I didn't. "It was always just Mom and me."

Brent's jovial tone came down a few octaves when he said, "Oh, yeah, I'm sorry about that. Dad said she passed away recently."

I was beyond tearing up every time someone told me they were sorry for my loss, but the sincerity in his voice and eyes struck me tenderly. I didn't want to break into full-fledged tears, so I asked, "So what does your mom do?"

Ben and Bart exchanged looks, but Brent didn't miss a beat, "She's a housewife."

Five boys, all had been born a year apart, and a mom who didn't work outside the house. What were they, Mormon? I only had a few friends growing up whose moms stayed home: they were all wealthy. Judging from the car and the way these three were dressed, maybe my assumption was correct.

"So, when did your parents split up?"

I felt that same tension from before. This time Ben turned around to answer, "Our parents are still together."

The reality of the situation hit me—like a Mack truck. Will, my father, met my mother twenty-three years ago. They had some sort of wild fling, with me as the result. Will was married when he met my mom, and he was still married to the same woman—Brent, Ben and Bart's mother. My stomach cinched tight. No wonder my mom would never tell me who my father was. I could feel the color drain from my face.

Ben, still peering at me over the seat, must have seen my stupor. "It's okay, Camille. Dad called us all together last night and told us. Mom knows."

"And she's okay with me being here?"

Bart, from behind the wheel piped in, "I'm sure she had some words with Dad after we went to bed, but she told us all we were taking the rest of the week off to welcome you to the family."

"Seriously?" All three heads nodded in unison. "So, you all just called your bosses and took the week off?"

Brent leaned in and said, "Yeah, we all work for the same guy. He understood."

Bart said, *after they went to bed.* Did they all still live at home? Who still lives with their parents when they're adults and have the money to live anywhere? Were they a part of some cult? Something felt fishy. I texted Daniel discreetly from the back seat: "Arrived OK. Going 2 lunch w/ 5 brothers. Haven't met Dad yet. Will call soon." If this was some sort of a trick, I wanted Daniel to know where to tell the police to start looking.

Bart pulled the car in front of a restaurant and handed the keys to a valet. I had nearly forgotten we were going to get lunch, and after the last couple minutes, I wasn't sure I could hold any food down. As we stepped out of the car, I was again blasted by the heat. Luckily, it was exactly five steps from the curb to the restaurant's door, and we were again in the cool.

I had always been a little on the tall side for a girl, I was 5'10" – I looked at my newly found brothers: Brent was the tallest of the three and had to be at least 6'3". Ben and Bart were both a couple inches taller than I was. As we walked to the hostess standing behind her podium, I could see the family resemblance with two more tall, slender men waiting right in front of us. Aside from the height and dark hair, I didn't look much like them. Of the two who were waiting with the hostess, the one closest took a couple steps toward me and grabbed me in a strong bear hug, "Hey, little sister! We're glad you're here! I'm Beau."

My mind was working again, and I realized the next brother to take me in a hug was Bruce even before he introduced himself. He gave me a quick hug, sweet, but not bone-crushing like Beau, "Nice to meet you, Camille. I'm Bruce."

"It's nice to meet you both, too." I'd never been shy my whole life, but at this moment, I wasn't feeling like a social butterfly. Luckily, each of my newly discovered brothers was genuinely welcoming and completely over-the-moon charming. As I looked at them, their handsome looks were obvious, the same perfect toothy smiles, warm brown eyes, dark brown hair, and dimples. Conversation had steered clear of me; I'd been worried I'd have a repeat of the awkward conversation in the car with the two new brothers, but Beau and Bruce were more interested in talking about plans for my time here, rather than how I came to be.

After a lunch of appetizers oozing butter, fresh seafood and starches, over an hour of great conversation, I came to a single conclusion: If I never met my father, I wouldn't feel slighted. I'd never dreamed that I would have a sibling, let alone five who were beyond cool, each seeming really excited to have a little sister. Not one of them seemed to care that I was only a half-sister. I'd never been a pessimist, so I refused to give in to the feeling that this was all a little too good to be true. Rather than question whether these guys were really glad to see me or if they were just the world's best actors, I decided I'd just relax and enjoy it.

Bart looked at his watch as a sneaky grin emerged, "It's barely noon. We could buzz over to the club and take the boat out for a couple hours." His suggestion had been made to the group, but he quickly turned and added, "I'm sorry, Camille, I guess I should be asking you. I know these guys are up for it."

The energy these five had was euphoric. I couldn't think of anything I wouldn't want to do so long as they were around. "Sure, okay."

As we were walking out of the restaurant, it occurred to me we had never paid. Having spent plenty of time as a waitress, I put on the brakes and said, "Wait, what about the check?"

Bart shook his head, "We're here a lot. They'll just put it on our membership."

I still felt a little nervous as we approached the hostess, until she called out to Beau, "Mr. Strayer, I trust everything was to your liking?" Beau, the oldest of the group, was leading the way to the door.

Beau shot her a big smile, "Perfect, like always, Janice. Tell Peter he outdid himself today with the Shrimp Pasta."

Janice wasn't wearing a nametag and didn't seem the least bit concerned that we didn't sign a piece of paper. She had star-struck eyes as we filed past her. I was just a few steps away when Brent stopped, looked at Janice and said, "Oh, wait. This is our little sister, Camille.

She's visiting from California. Could you let the staff know she should be added to the membership and has full privileges."

"Yes, Mr. Strayer. I'll take care of it right away. Welcome to Charleston, Miss Strayer."

I felt my heart flutter a little, not because she had called me by the wrong last name, but because Brent took the time to tell her that I belonged. I wasn't some visitor—I was their little sister. I had been in this magical place less than two hours—I had found five brothers who I didn't know I had and was developing a real kinship to them already. I had never been overly emotional, so the wetness in my eyes trying to get out felt completely out of place.

Everyone was standing inside the door when Bart explained to me, "No sense standing in the heat; they're bringing the cars around for us."

As if his words could make beautiful German automobiles appear out of thin air, two identical BMW sedans pulled up in front of the restaurant. I'm sure my mouth was gaping open when I commented to no one in particular, "You have matching Beamers?"

Brent, standing next to me said, "Yeah, that was Dad's idea. He didn't want any of us to feel slighted, so we all got the same car. I tried to talk him into a Camaro, but that was a big no go." I did the math in my head. I knew there was no way to get that model for under $50,000, and Will had bought five of them for his sons. Who does that? My mind flashed to my earlier idea that my family was a part of some religious cult.

We drove just a few short blocks and left the cars with another valet. I looked at the inconspicuous sign indicating that this was the Yacht Club. When Bart suggested we go out on the boat, I was expecting. . . well, a boat. As we walked past the club to the pier behind it, Beau was again in the lead and made his way to the furthest slip. The largest yacht in the harbor was directly in front of us and displayed the name, "Easy Money." Holy moly, this wasn't some little cabin cruiser or something to buzz around the harbor on; we could take this thing to the Bahamas.

I was careful not to suggest it. The little time that I'd spent with the five led me to believe we'd be at Nassau by dinner time if I weren't careful.

Although much more comfortable around them after lunch, I reminded myself that something didn't feel right about them. There was a reason a person had instincts, and I refused to ignore mine. I couldn't put my finger on it, but something felt wrong. I sent another text to Daniel, "Going 4 a ride on the yacht w/ 5 brothers, will call U later." As I put my phone in my purse, the pessimistic part of me wondered how far I could swim if I had to.

CHAPTER 3

Zandra Chiron – San Diego, CA

A granddaughter. How had Angela hidden from me all this time, and how had she found a way to give birth and hide her children as well? Where had they been? I had searched the planet, the far off mountains of Tibet, the vast Sahara desert, the rain forests of South America, and every disgusting third world city in between. Every time I heard a whisper of where she might be, I searched. No stone was left unturned. She couldn't possibly have hidden in plain sight all those years. She had been protected by a magic more powerful than my own – but whose?

Angela had been dead to me, for years—since the day she ran away. She abandoned her family, left us to pay her debt. I knew she still breathed, somewhere, but none of my powers could find her; that could only mean that she was protected by another. Who in our society would be willing to cross me?

That putz she lured in may have been a pure-blood, and the bastard daughter they conceived may be in my lineage, but something was wrong. Had she been born without a twin? Were things changing or had Angela tapped into a new source of magic? Was our bloodline finally diluted? William Strayer was not worthy of Angela. He knew it. He had no idea what he was up against if he intended to keep this granddaughter from me. She and her brother were the last in my line.

When Angela's body died, I could feel her enter the spirit world. Even in death she refused to answer my calls. Angela paid as much attention to me in death as she had in life; that would change soon. Camille was my heir; she would be exactly the leverage I needed. We'll see how long Angela can ignore my calls when her precious daughter is living the life that Angela herself escaped.

Isaac, her father, indulged Angela too much as a child, coddling her, constantly accusing me of abuse. They deserved each other; let her join him in the pasture. Until his death I had always wondered if he had hidden her from me. Once he passed into the spirit world and I still could not locate Angela, I knew that he hadn't betrayed me after all. I never believed Isaac's denial until his death proved his words true.

With that knowledge I was at a loss as to who could have protected her. I wondered if my worthless brother Zethus was involved. He swore the arrow didn't exist. All these years I wondered if it was his arrow that cloaked Angela from me, but if that were true, Camille would still be under its protection. Once Angela passed, I felt Camille, I knew she existed. I had zeroed in on Southern California, and in a few more days, I would have found her apartment. I was close. I knew I was close. But why can't I feel her brother?

I listened to her phone call with William Strayer – she was already in Charleston by now. He would let his guard down. He wasn't a protector. The fool didn't stand a chance against me. It was only a matter of time. I needed to be patient, as patient as I had been the last twenty-eight years—I needed only be patient for a few more days.

CHAPTER 4

Camille Benning – Charleston, SC

As I looked around the yacht, I had to wonder: was Will a billionaire or something? My mom wasn't wealthy. I could remember growing up and for weeks eating nothing but Ramen Noodles, macaroni and cheese, and hot dogs. I could feel a twinge of jealousy in me, not begrudging that they had so much, but disappointed that I came from almost nothing. I wouldn't have traded a day with my mom for all the nice cars and beautiful boats in the world, but I had to wonder why my mom never contacted Will to tell him about me. He could have surely helped enough so that we could have had better food. I couldn't think of any good reason for us to struggle the way we had. Now that she was gone, I'd never be able to ask her why.

We climbed onto the yacht, and an employee from the club untied the ropes and handed them up to Brent. "Mr. Strayer, good to see you again."

"Hi, Josh, any chance you wanna ride along today?"

Josh blushed at the offer, "Thank you, Mr. Strayer, but I'm working today."

"Oh, come on. I'll go in and clear it with your boss. It'll be fun."

"Mr. Strayer, thanks, but I'll have to decline. Besides, you'll need me here to tie her off when you return." Josh gave a kind of salute with his hand, and turned to walk away. We powered out into the harbor, headed for blue water, with Beau at the helm. As stifling hot as it had been when we got out of the car, the breeze out on the open water was wonderful.

I'd gone to school with kids like my brothers – at least from the wealth perspective. But there was something about these five: they were almost magnetic. Aside from their obvious good looks, their demeanor was welcoming, their words to others were thoughtful, and each looked others in the eye when they spoke. In a word, they were "genuine," not at all like the pompous stuffed shirts I'd become accustomed to tuning out.

Everyone seemed to be having a good time, telling stories of stunts they'd pulled when they were younger. Each seemed to tell a story that was more brazen than the last – laughter erupted in all directions with each new story. I tuned out for a while, wondering if any of this could seriously be real. I found myself wishing for a way to let my mom know that I was going to be okay. I'd miss her for the rest of my life – but something I never thought possible, until that moment, I was no longer alone. Beau was the sweetest, his eyes were kind; whenever someone spoke, he looked them square in the eye, giving them his full attention. Bruce seemed to be the comic with an easy smile that reached all the way to his eyes. Bart was the quietest of the five, happy to be Bruce's audience. Ben wore glasses and had an intelligent look about him, but barely spoke more than Bart. Brent was by far the most outspoken; he was the youngest and seemed to be comfortable being the center of attention.

When I tuned back in I heard Bruce saying ". . . then Dad said, 'I'm sorry, Your Honor, I'm sure my son was temporarily insane. He gets it from his mother's side of the family.' Of course, Mom was right there beside him, and she glared at him pretty good. Remember that time when he melted down her best silver to make doubloons for a scavenger hunt at Halloween? Yeah, she glared at him just like that! Then he said to the judge, 'I can assure you, he will not display such poor judgment in the foreseeable future.' I was staring up at the judge, praying it would just be a fine or maybe Dad could buy a fire truck or something for the town and all would be forgiven, you know? The next thing I heard was, 'Mr. Strayer, I understand sons can be a handful, but there are to be no concerts without the proper permits. Even with proper permits, they are not to host, encourage, or sponsor wet t-shirt contests in the courthouse square. Am I clear?'"

Beau jumped in, "You know why you got busted, right? The judge's daughter was one of the girls you sprayed down, and I heard pictures of her got posted on Facebook."

All five brothers were laughing at Bruce's story. I had missed the first part and wasn't sure about asking Bruce to repeat the beginning. It was obvious that these five were no angels. After I don't know how many stories, Beau asked, "So, tell us about California. Do you have a boyfriend?"

I smiled and shook my head, "No, no one special."

He dramatically wiped his forehead, "Well, that's a relief. We were all worried we were going to have to fly out and give him the big brother talk."

I was confused, "Big brother talk?"

"You know the one, 'If you hurt her, I'll hunt you down.' That type of brother talk."

"Well, you can rest easy. No need to hop on a plane anytime soon. I dated a guy for a while, but we broke up a few months ago. No big deal."

Brent looked shocked when he confirmed, "You broke up with a guy?"

"Yeah, it wasn't some epic romance or anything."

Brent asked again, "You dated him and then broke up?"

Surprised by his sudden interest, I could only answer, "Well, yeah."

"What happened to him?"

I laughed, mostly because Brent had a way of looking so serious. "Happened to him? Nothing, it was mutual. We just weren't cut out for each other."

Beau must have noticed the strange reaction in Brent because he said, "Geeze Brent, it isn't a big deal. *People* date." I couldn't help but notice Beau's emphasis on the word *people*, and he gave Brent a look that told them all to leave it alone. I got a weird feeling that there was more to the question that Brent wanted to ask, but after Beau shut him down, he never circled back to the topic.

We spent another hour together before we pulled back into the slip. Josh was waiting on the dock as Brent tossed him the rope, and he had us tied off before Bart had cut the engine. We'd only been out for a couple hours, but the rocking of the water, maybe the sea air, the heat or the sun beating down had me worn out. Josh offered me a hand onto the pier and asked, "Did you have a good time, Miss?"

"I did, thanks for asking." Josh was handsome in a geeky way. He was about my height, just slightly shorter, light green eyes, and deep tanned skin—no doubt his golden bronze skin was the result of working outside all day.

Brent, of the five, was the closest to my age and was the brother who had talked the most to me since my arrival. Brent stepped off the boat behind me as Josh asked, "Miss, which Mr. Strayer was your escort today?"

Josh winked at Brent, logically making the assumption that if he trailed me getting on and off the yacht that I must have been his date. Brent didn't miss a beat, "Josh, I should have introduced you earlier. This is our little sister, Camille. She's visiting this week from California."

Josh gave a slight bow, "Miss Strayer, it's a pleasure to meet you."

I held out my hand, "If I can call you Josh, the least you can do is call me Camille, or better yet, Cami."

"Sorry, Miss Strayer, house rules." A part of me thought I should correct being called, "Strayer," but my new family was obviously well-engrained in the community. I was, after all, the illegitimate little sister: no sense giving people anything to gossip about. I gave Josh an awkward smile and followed Brent down the pier.

As we climbed into the car for the trip to the house, I felt the softness of the leather seats, the cool air blowing on me after being out on the ocean in the heat of the day. I had flown all night and was more tired than I realized. The excitement should have kept me from dozing off, but I must have completely passed out in the car.

I awoke in a brightly colored bedroom, a sunny yellow color on the walls, darkness clouding the windows. I had been sleeping in the softest bed I'd ever felt, wrapped by a four-poster mahogany frame. The room was meticulously decorated, from the beautifully framed prints on the wall to the fresh flowers on the dresser. I looked at my watch and couldn't believe the time: it was 10 p.m.

"Camille?" A low, gentle voice asked.

I looked off to my left to see someone sitting on the other side of the room, on what I was sure was an antique loveseat. I sat up quickly, realizing that today hadn't been some amazing dream. I was really in South Carolina and had spent the day with my five brothers. The room was dimly lit with two lonely lamps illuminating the room. I couldn't be sure who was sitting across the room, as I wiped the sleep from my eyes. Everyone had been so welcoming that I wasn't creeped out by someone sitting there in the dark. I answered, "I guess I was more tired than I realized."

"I'm glad you're here. I trust the boys were tolerable today?"

It was my father, right here in the flesh. I knew from the way he asked the question. My heart began racing, pumping so fast I thought it might beat right out of my chest. I sat up a little straighter, realizing this was really the day I had waited for my whole life. Trying to keep my enthusiasm under control, "They were great. You didn't mention them when we talked yesterday."

We had coordinated every aspect of the trip by email and phone. I'd talked to him several times, but he never once brought up that he had sons, that they would be picking me up, or entertaining me. As I watched him sitting on the love seat, questions flooded into my mind: Why didn't you tell me about them? What's your wife think about me staying in your house? Why did you have an affair with my mom? Why did she never tell me about you?

CHAPTER 5

Camille Benning – Charleston, SC

William looked at a loss, and I knew I couldn't toss all my questions at him at once. He started off apologetically, "I should have prepared you. I was . . . your call was . . . unexpected. I'm sure I neglected to tell you lots of things. They can be a little overwhelming at first, but they're good boys."

I nodded my silent agreement. All those years of badgering my mom for a brother or sister, I had five brothers the entire time and didn't have a clue. Rather than dwelling on the past, I opted to stay firmly planted in the present. "I can't believe I'm here. I've always wondered who you were."

"You must have many questions for me. Ask me anything."

I never knew I even had a father, well, logically I knew he existed. How do you tell someone you don't have the words to even ask the right questions? It was all a little overwhelming. I asked a question that I already knew the answer to, "So, what do you do?"

"By way of profession? I am a financial advisor. Nothing exciting, but it pays the bills."

I caught myself looking around at the room, "You must be good at it."

He nodded, "My clients are all very happy with the services I provide." When I didn't say anything right away, he broke the quiet with, "Your mother. I'm so very sorry, Camille. It is difficult to lose a parent, and I'm sorry you went through her death alone. If I had known, I would have been there for you."

I stiffened a little, "For me. Not for her?"

"If she had wanted me to be there—yes, for her, too."

"She never told me about you, not until just before. . . you know . . . right before she died."

"That makes two of us. I wish I would have known about you, Camille. I don't want to be insensitive, but I have so many things I'd like to know about you."

"Ask away. What do ya wanna know?"

A huge smile enveloped his face, "Everything, Camille. I want to know everything about you."

"Hmmm, well, I work as a cashier in a department store. This is my first trip to a state outside of California, but I've been to Mexico. Today was the first time I had ever been on a yacht and an airplane, and I'm still a little surprised that I was on both in the same day." I stopped, trying to gauge what he was looking for.

"Hobbies?"

"Nothing major. I love California because one day you can be at Big Bear skiing, the next you can be at the beach surfing, and the next you can gamble at Tahoe. I'm usually on the go, but I don't have one big interest that I'm tied to."

"Boyfriend?"

I snickered a little, only because this was the same thing Brent had asked me just a few hours ago. "No. No one special."

"So your mother did tell you?"

I turned my head slightly, "What do you mean?"

"I was worried you might be unaware of your heritage. I didn't know your mother well, but she had abandoned her herd. When I happened on her, she wanted nothing to do with our kind."

What the heck was he talking about? Herd? Mom had never abandoned anyone or anything in her life. We had a stray dog for years that was mean as a snake, but she wouldn't turn her back on it. She kept feeding the vicious thing even when I begged her to let it starve. "Her *herd*? What do you mean *our kind*?"

Will took on a nervous look, like he'd said something he desperately wanted to take back. "Camille, what did your mother tell you about me? About your family?"

"Nothing. . . I mean, she wouldn't tell me anything about you. . . not 'til the night. . . you know. What do you mean she abandoned her family? Her parents died when she was very young."

"Your mother was Angela Chiron. She left her family long ago."

With more resolve than I felt, "Her name was Angela Benning and her parents died when she was still a teenager." Even as I said the words, I remembered the old plane ticket I'd found in my mother's closet, carefully tucked away from prying eyes, but purposely left for me to find after her death. The name on the ticket had been Angela Chiron. I'd dismissed it at the time, but now. . . who had she abandoned? Did she have other kids?

Will abruptly changed the subject, "What about school?"

I answered his question, even though I wanted to know what he meant by *she left her family*. "I graduated high school, but never had the money to get into college. Maybe someday." The fact that I'd opted to skip college had never been a sensitive subject for me. After high school I didn't know what I wanted to do with my life, and Mom had never pushed me.

Will must have thought more of a degree than I did because he immediately volunteered, "Camille, what's mine is yours. If you want an education, money isn't a problem."

I turned my head, not sure how to say it without sounding like a jerk, "I'm not asking you for anything."

His features were warm and his voice thoughtful, "You needn't ask. It's your birthright. I have been blessed with good fortune, and yesterday I found out I was also blessed with a daughter. I'd like a chance to be your father."

"I've only been your daughter for," I looked at my watch, six p.m. on the west coast, "less than twenty-four hours. Maybe offering to pay my way through college is something we can hold off on for a few days?"

Will nodded. I got the feeling that he was just as nervous as and maybe even more excited than I was. He asked, "Are you hungry? We could find something in the kitchen if you are."

I hadn't eaten since lunch. I could only imagine what the kitchen looked like. As we stepped out of my room, I saw this was one doorway in a hall filled with doorways on either side. I didn't want to gawk, but it looked like six rooms lined the hall. The floor was a highly polished wood that felt cool on my feet. Remembering the heat of the day, it felt good to be barefoot on the floor. I was kicking myself for falling asleep on the way back. I had no idea what the house looked like from the outside, where it was or how I got to my room.

We found my brothers all huddled around a television. Brent looked over his shoulder and gave a hearty, "Camille! We were wondering if you were down for the count or what? Glad you got up. Dad thought we'd drugged you or something."

"I don't even remember the ride here. Are you sure you didn't drug me?"

"High on life, little sister, high on life."

Brent and the others turned their attention back to the television as my father motioned me toward the kitchen. I've been to Lowe's, Home

Depot, I've even caught myself looking at some majestic kitchens on the "Do-it-Yourself" channel, but I was not prepared for this: granite countertops, stainless steel appliances, enough cabinets to stock a convenience store, and two sinks. My father's idea of a quick snack and mine weren't the same.

I thought we'd be rummaging around the refrigerator for sliced meat to make a sandwich when he pulled a casserole dish out of the oven that was still warm, poured me a glass of wine, and motioned for me to have a seat at the table.

In awe, I could only ask, "Where'd all this come from?"

"Gretchen makes the best manicotti in the world. When you were still sleeping, she made a second dish for you and kept it warm. I promise you've never tasted anything like it."

He was right. I had had some incredible Italian food in my life, but nothing held a candle to this. Conversation was easy. It turned out my father's parents had lived in this very house. They gave it to him when he started his family. In addition to being a financial wizard of sorts, he was an avid hiker and loved to sail. I was grateful to have some one-on-one time with him, to learn more about him. It seemed odd that my brothers were keeping their distance, and I still hadn't met his wife. No one so much as peeked through a doorway.

After I had eaten enough to feed three heavy-weight boxers, I stood up to rinse my plate. My father asked, "Are you still tired? Or do you have enough energy to keep me company a little longer? We could sit in the den. It's where I spend most of my time."

Another amazing room. An overstuffed leather sofa and matching overstuffed formal chairs greeted us as we walked in. I took a seat in the chair closest to the door, and he sat on the sofa. Bookshelves lined every wall with old leather-bound books tightly lining each shelf. We were both quiet: I don't think either of us knew where to start. What do you say to someone you've fanaticized about your entire life?

My father broke the silence, "Is there anything special you'd like to do while you're here?"

I shook my head, "So far this trip has seriously exceeded my expectations. I just wanna get to know everybody."

"That's great, well, unless you had really low expectations for the trip."

Grinning, "It's just nice to know I have . . ." it was tough to say the word, because it had been theoretical to me, until today, "family."

"It warms my heart to hear you say that, Camille. I always wanted a daughter. It's a little surreal to have you here. I wouldn't have thought it possible."

The basics of Sex-Ed were obviously lost on Will if he didn't think it was possible. I kept my thoughts to myself. No sense being a smart aleck just because he was surprised to know that I existed. "So, how did you meet my mom?"

"She was working at the hotel bar where I was staying. It is uncommon to find. . . well, female. . .you know. . . I was surprised to see her working there."

The more Will stammered, the more weirded out I felt. It was as if he were desperately trying not to tell me something. Will looked away from me and began his explanation while his attention was focused on the wall to my left. "The relationship I had with your mother was not one I am proud of." He turned and looked directly into my eyes as he spoke, "I was prepared to give her anything in the world. All your mother wanted from me was my absence. I pursued her, but she didn't want anything to do with me. I called her a few times in the months that followed, but each time she refused to see or to talk to me. On subsequent business trips, she refused to take my calls or to meet me. At the time, I didn't understand why. Seeing you here gives me a new appreciation for why she shut me out."

"But you were married and you were pursuing my mom?"

He nodded again, "I was. I could never explain the feelings I had for your mother. I would have given anything in the world to her."

I couldn't help but restate the obvious, "But you were married."

"Yes, I was. The truth is, I told your mother I was married with a family, and she was furious with me. She rejected me. She told me to go home to my wife."

"So that's it. You met her, you hooked up, then you told her about Gretchen? I can't imagine why she would have rejected you."

He smiled proudly when he told me, "You have your mother's spirit. I didn't plan to meet your mother. I certainly didn't expect to feel so strongly for a woman I hardly knew. I've always been an honest person. The truth, no matter how terrible, is always better than a lie. I told your mother the truth; she told me to go home."

"And that's it?"

"Until your call yesterday, yes. I've thought about your mother over the years, but any letter I sent was always returned to me with 'Delivery Refused' written on the envelope."

"That sounds like Mom. So, how did Gretchen take it, when you told her about me?"

"I have been married to Gretchen for twenty-nine years. I shared with her that I met your mother the very night I returned from San Diego. I confessed everything. She was as stunned as I that I had met Angela Chiron and had. . . how did you say it? Hooked up? That I had hooked up with her. But I kept your mother's secret, as did Gretchen. Neither of us told a soul."

"What secret?"

"Your mother. . . she was a well-known figure in our community. She disappeared when she was seventeen. Many suspected foul play. When I left your mother, she asked that I not tell anyone where I found her."

"So, she was hiding from someone?"

"Angela never came right out and said it, but she was adamant that I not tell anyone that I had seen her. I told Gretchen, but I knew she would not divulge her whereabouts."

"Did Gretchen kick you out?"

"No. She told me I needed to figure out what my future was and live that life."

"Really? You told her you were unfaithful and she wasn't mad?"

"She wasn't pleased with me, but Gretchen is a wonderful woman. Our relationship has been one of comfortable companionship for nearly three decades. I never set out to hurt her, and I would never lie to her about anything."

"So what was my mother to you? A fling?"

"Not by my choice. As I said, when I met your mother, I felt very strongly for her. She didn't feel the same for me."

"So, how well did you know Mom?"

"I only spent a few days with her, but you could say she made a lasting impression."

Before I got here I was prepared to love this man unconditionally, but the more he spoke, the less I liked him. He'd had a wife and five young sons, he'd been unfaithful, and didn't seem the slightest bit ashamed of his behavior. I didn't know this man in front of me, but I knew my mother: she would never have been able to cope with the guilt of breaking up a family.

He must have sensed my disapproval because I could see the desperation on his face as he tried to explain. "I wanted to be with your mother, but she wouldn't hear of it. Eventually, I stopped calling her. I made peace with her decision. It doesn't mean that I didn't . . . that I wouldn't. . ." Will trailed off, not finishing his sentence.

I decided to ask the obvious question, since I hadn't yet seen his wife. "So, you're sure Gretchen's okay with me being here?"

"Camille, I love Gretchen deeply. She feels the same for me. Because you are a part of me, you are our family. Yes, she's more than okay that you're here."

"This sounds . . . I don't know, odd."

"It's odd that a father wants to make up for lost time with a daughter he never knew?"

"It's odd that your wife is okay with it when you consider how I came to be your daughter."

"Gretchen is an amazing woman. I think once you meet her, you'll agree."

Something had always bothered me. Will might be the only man on the planet who could give me an answer. No matter how calloused it sounded, I needed to ask, "Will, my mom never . . . had a boyfriend, or a husband, or any guy in her life. I don't remember her even once going on a date." I stopped for a second, wondering if I could bring myself to ask the real question. "Why you?"

"You are very much my daughter. I can see it in your eyes. I can hear it in your question. I wish I could give you an answer you'd be happy with. I wish I knew the answer. Maybe she was lonely, maybe the stars were aligned perfectly that night, maybe it was her way of having a family of her own that she didn't have to share with anyone else. I can only speculate. I can't tell you what I don't know."

I still wasn't sure how I felt about my father. I wished that my mother had told me about him, anything. He was as much a stranger to me as I was to him, and I couldn't imagine what kind of wife would welcome me into her home. I didn't know what to think about my mother running away from her family.

"So, what should I call you?"

Will grinned as his chest swelled, "What would you like to call me?"

"I don't know. Is it okay if I just stick with 'Will'?"

I could see the disappointment on his face as he nodded. "You can call me Will if that makes you more comfortable, but I hope that someday you'll come to think of me as your father. I would love for you to call me Dad."

I looked at the floor, as if the carpet were suddenly interesting. "Uh . . . I'll probably have to work up to that."

"I understand." He changed the subject when he noticed my uneasiness. "So, the boys told me they took you out on the boat this afternoon. Did you enjoy it?"

"I did."

"I'm sure they'll have lots of adventures for you this week. Don't let them wear you out. I'm covering the office single-handedly this week, and I'd like to be able to spend time with you in the evenings."

As if Gretchen knew we'd been talking about her, we heard a light tap at the door. Gretchen, the one person I was apprehensive to meet, stepped inside and walked over to my chair. I stood up, still uneasy from the "Dad or Will" conversation and offered my hand as a greeting. Gretchen motioned it away and gave me a welcoming hug, "We're all so glad you're here, Camille." When she released me from her embrace, she took both my hands in hers.

"Thanks." I stammered, "It's a real pleasure to meet you."

"I've already warned the boys to give you a day to get past the jetlag before they start gallivanting all over town showing off their little sister. If you need me to send them to the office so you can get some rest tomorrow, just say the word. If given the opportunity, they'll wear you out." Her eyes twinkled when she spoke. I took her in. Gretchen had short curly red hair – kind of poufy, a wide smile that lit up the room, and the most delicate hands I'd ever felt.

"I had a great time today." I looked at Will, "So they all work for you?"

Will wore a smile that matched Gretchen's, "Yes, they have exceptional financial instincts. Each one has brought in significant profits for their clients, and each has built his own portfolio. Say, you're not interested in finances are you?"

Gretchen answered for me, "William Strayer! You will not try to pressure her into joining you at the office!" Gretchen turned her attention toward me, "Don't let him do that. He convinced each boy to go to work with him in an effort to keep them close. I don't think any one of them wanted to grow up to be a financial advisor, but Will got his hooks in them."

Will's voice raised, in a playful way, "Hooks? You're just jealous because I see them more than you do."

"Maybe, but you're not going to do it to Camille, too." She looked at me, "Camille, you can always go to work with your father, or you can shop all day with me. Which would you prefer?"

"Wow, Will, that's not much of a choice." I got the feeling that they were planning on me staying longer than the five days I had scheduled. That odd feeling I'd had earlier rose to the surface again. Five adult sons still lived at home with their parents, all worked for their father – my father, they all drove the same kind of cars, even Gretchen said he'd pressured them into it. I looked around the room for crucifix on the walls, bibles, religious art hanging – all I found were books and tastefully decorated walls.

Will shook his head, as if exasperated, "Women. Gretchen spends it as fast as I make it."

"William, you know that I'm the reason you are so successful. You can't think that you could do any of this without me?"

I got a strange vibe, like Gretchen was completely serious. The banter between them was fun, but there seemed to be a hint of truth in what Gretchen had just said. Or at least they were both acting like there was truth in her claim. Gretchen was the financial mastermind?

Will stood up and gathered Gretchen in his arms when he sweetly answered, "I couldn't do anything without you. You know I'd be a wreck on my own." His sweetness disappeared when the sarcasm oozed from him, "And I think it's nice that your shopping is single-handedly getting the economy back on its feet." Will's face showed the love he felt for his wife.

I could feel the air of seriousness taking hold. Gretchen turned to me, "Camille, I am happy to have you in my home. I can feel your apprehension around me. Do not fear me. William and I came to terms with his infidelity long ago. At the time, and for many years after, I was displeased with him. But, having you here and having your energy in our family, I forgive him all over again." I couldn't place Gretchen's accent, and I was so overwhelmed with her words that I didn't care where it was from.

"Uh, thanks." I was rendered speechless. There were so many things I should have said at that moment, but I couldn't make my voice work.

Gretchen didn't seem to be someone to mince words. She asked, "How long will you stay with us?"

"My return flight is Sunday."

Gretchen turned to Will, half ignoring me, "William, it looks as though you've got four days. You had better turn on the charm. I don't want Camille to leave us. She should stay here. We're family."

I knew she wasn't talking to me, but I felt like I had to say something, "Gretchen, that's really nice of you. But I have a life and friends in California. I really just wanted to meet Will and get to know him. I'm not ready to uproot and move here."

She turned to me with soft eyes and a thoughtful voice, "Exactly my reason for telling him to step it up a notch. I know you have people who depend on you, but with us, you have a family who loves you and wants you here. We can protect you."

"Protect me? Protect me from what?"

William didn't let Gretchen answer, "Muggers, robbers, thieves. . . lots of shady characters all over the place." He gave her a look, at first I wasn't sure what to make of it – it looked like. . . fear.

Gretchen gave my shoulder a gentle squeeze and walked back out the way she had come in. Will stood, too, not in an effort to trail her out of the room, but in a gentlemanly way as she walked out the door. He took two steps in my direction after the door closed behind her, smiled at me and said, "She's a force of nature."

"I wouldn't have believed it, if I hadn't heard it myself. She really is okay with my being here. But I don't need protecting."

Will knelt down beside my chair, looking directly into my eyes, "I'm not perfect, but I'll never lie to you. She wants you here as much as the boys and I do." Will cradled my face in his hand and caressed my cheek with his thumb. "Camille, you're a part of us. There are things in your mother's past that we need to tidy up before you return."

"But you hardly knew her?"

"We'll talk about it tomorrow. I don't have all the facts, and I don't want to. . . it wouldn't be fair to you for me to . . .we just need to contact your mother's family. I'd better turn in. Goodnight, Camille."

"Talk about what tomorrow?"

"Camille, I don't have all the facts. I promise I'll fill you in on everything as soon as I can."

I wanted to argue with him. I didn't like the idea that he felt I needed protecting. I wasn't some frail flower, but Will had said something that bothered me—something about my mother's family and that she had run away from them at seventeen. Had she been abused? Was he trying to shelter me from them, or was I right to begin with—that William was a part of some manipulative cult my mother had escaped?

CHAPTER 6

Camille Benning – Charleston, SC

I went to my room and had a strange feeling I couldn't shake. Instead of staring at the ceiling after having taken a six hour nap, I thought I'd check in with Daniel. He picked up on the first ring.

"It took you long enough! I've been waiting for you to call for hours!"

"Awww, that's so sweet. Are you worried about me?"

"No, what's there to worry about? You only flew all the way across the country to meet some guy your mom had sex with once and hadn't talked to again your whole life. Then those texts you sent? What the hell?"

"Geeze, cluck or something – you're acting like an old mother hen."

His voice softened when he said, "I was worried, okay? So, how is he, anyway? Is he strange or something?"

"No. . .I mean, I only talked to him for a little while. He seems okay. I also happen to have five half brothers."

"You texted me that much. What're they like?"

"They're like you, but handsome. I wish you could meet them. They took me out on the ocean today."

"You're hysterical. A yacht, huh? Caviar, too?"

"Gross! No, we just went for a bite to eat, then out on the water."

"Cami, be careful. You just met them and they wanted to take you out on the ocean. Did it ever cross your mind they could toss you in the ocean and no one would ever know?"

I pulled the phone away from my ear and looked at the phone – I'm not sure why since there was no way he could see the expression I gave his picture staring back at me on the screen. I would never admit that that was why I sent him the text earlier. "Been watching too many serial killer shows again, Daniel? Why don't you switch back to the Disney Channel?"

"I'm serious, Cami, something isn't right. I can feel it. You shouldn't be there by yourself, and you shouldn't go anywhere without telling someone where you're at first."

He was right, but if I agreed with him, that would just make him double concerned. "Daniel, I'm not on spring break bar hopping in another country! I'm meeting relatives I didn't know I had."

His voice lost any hint of humor it may have had, "Angela kept you from them for a reason, Cami. Be smart."

I didn't want to admit that he was right, so I didn't. "All right. If it'll keep you from having a meltdown, I'll text you whenever I go somewhere."

"I'm serious, Cami."

After I hung up with Daniel, I had a tough time finding sleep. If he could just meet them, he could tell me that everything would be fine. We'd been friends for as long as I knew what a friend was. Daniel thought like me, acted like me, most of the time we finished each other's sentences. I wanted to believe my family was every bit as awesome as they appeared on the surface, but I couldn't shake the nagging feeling that something just wasn't right. Daniel was thousands of miles away, and he was feeling the same thing.

The next morning I showered and dressed, tiptoeing down the hallway. I'm not sure why; I was still on west coast time, so it was after nine a.m. on the east coast. The house was quiet. It reminded me of a library rather than a home filled with eight people.

As I peered into the kitchen, I found Brent sitting at the table looking at some papers. When he saw me enter, I saw his face light up, "Hey, I was just getting ready to write you a note. Glad you're up!"

"Are you going somewhere?"

"We're supposed to go pick up your 'Welcome to the family present' from Mom and Dad, but I was going to go for a swim before it got too hot."

"I don't need a present. Don't let me hold you up."

"Get used to it. Dad likes to make money; Mom likes to spend it. You wanna join me for a swim?"

"That's a consistent theme. Will was giving Gretchen crap last night about her spending habits." I thought about his offer. I loved swimming but had packed a little too quickly, "I didn't bring a swim suit."

"Hmm, well, let's shelf swimming for now and go pick up your gift."

"Brent, that's okay. I'd really rather just hang out."

"You don't even know what it is."

"Seriously, I'd rather not."

"Uh . . . sure, I'll text Dad real quick and let him know there's been a change of plans."

Brent put his phone down and looked back my way hopefully. My question was out before I even realized how rude it was, "So, when money's no object, how do you keep yourself entertained?"

"Entertained? You mean, what do I find fulfilling?"

I didn't want him to think that I thought he was shallow and hoped my question hadn't offended him. "Yeah, are you a workaholic, a big time philanthropist, or what?"

"I work, but it's not that hard. Dad could do it all himself if he wanted to. I think he just keeps the five of us in the office for comic relief. I've never met a charity I didn't like, but I don't think that qualifies me as a philanthropist. I'm pretty simple."

"Girlfriend?"

"Uh . . . no. No girlfriends."

"Now or ever?"

Brent looked like I had struck a nerve, "Ever."

"Oh, sorry." From his reaction I figured he must bat for the other team, "Boyfriend?"

This question made him laugh, "No, Camille, I'm not gay. I'm definitely heterosexual."

That didn't make any sense. Brent was handsome—seriously handsome. He could give up his day job and be a model if he wanted to. He was really tall, deeply tanned, dark, with shaggy but perfectly trimmed hair, a smile that even Colgate would be envious of, and a cool personality. "You're a rich, good-looking guy. Girls probably throw themselves at you."

"Not exactly. Don't get me wrong. I've run across a few that I thought were pretty incredible, but dating isn't necessarily something . . . I mean, it's not . . . you know."

"It's not what?" I could see Brent had touched on something he desperately didn't want to talk about.

"I've just not found Miss Right."

"How are you going to find Miss Right, if you aren't checking out Miss Right-Now?"

"It's just not a good idea."

"Uh, okay. If you want me to set you up or something, I have tons of single friends in California."

Brent's face looked like he was actually contemplating my suggestion. "That would be beyond awesome, but I wouldn't feel right about it. Enough about my love life, what about you?"

"I told you yesterday, I had a boyfriend I broke up with a couple months ago. End of story."

"Your mother didn't mind?"

"Didn't mind what?"

"Did she introduce you two?"

"Well, no. That would be weird."

"But, your mother was . . . I mean . . . you're the same. She wouldn't let you just date anyone."

"Brent, what are you talking about? My mom didn't have a say in any of my boyfriends."

"Boyfriends? You've dated more than one?" I could tell from Brent's expression that he was surprised, but I wasn't sure what he was so offended by. Maybe dating meant something different here?

Gretchen stepped through the door at that moment, her voice full of volume, "Brent, I thought you were taking Camille to pick up her gift?" She leaned down and kissed his cheek and gave my shoulder a comforting squeeze.

"Camille and I were just getting to know each other a little better. I texted Dad. He's going to have it delivered."

"Your brothers are outside clearing the grove for this weekend. Why don't you go give them a hand before it gets too hot?"

I could see the relief on Brent's face. He wasn't at all comfortable with our conversation. "Sure, Mom. See you later, Camille." Brent exited without another word. It was a strange conversation. I'd always been relatively attractive, not a supermodel, but why would he be surprised that I'd had boyfriends? He seemed surprised that anyone was interested in dating me. Talk about a bruise to the ego.

"I can help, too, Gretchen." As much fun as I'd had with them yesterday, I couldn't wait to listen in on more of their stories.

I stood up and was two steps away when Gretchen said, "You and I need to spend some time together. I think there are some things your mother would want you to know."

I felt a twinge of nervousness. It hadn't been that long since my mother's death, and I didn't want to talk about her, not with anyone, but especially with Gretchen.

Gretchen sensed my apprehension, "I'm not trying to make you uncomfortable. I can see your mother's memories are still tender. There are some things she didn't share with you that I think are important you know."

"You knew my mother?" I could feel my eyelids flex as my eyes widened.

"No, Camille. I never met your mother, but I'm certain that she was wonderful."

"Gretchen, I . . . I appreciate it, but . . . I'm not ready to talk about her."

"How would you like to talk *to her*?"

I froze. I felt a rush of heat shoot through my body. My heart skipped. "She died, Gretchen. I was there when it happened."

"Her body died, yes. But her spirit lives on. She's with you now. She's talking to you right this second, but you aren't listening." I froze. I didn't know what kind of game Gretchen was playing, but I didn't like it. They *were* a cult! I was right from the beginning. Gretchen thought she could talk to ghosts. How was I going to get out of here? No way was I getting sucked in.

CHAPTER 7

Camille Benning – Charleston, SC

Gretchen broke eye contact with me and looked over my shoulder. She sounded like she was angry when she said, "You should have told her before you passed. Do you know how hard it must be for her to hear this from me?" Gretchen paused for a second carrying on her imaginary conversation. "I will do my best, but shame on you for not telling her yourself!" Gretchen's eyes focused back on mine. "Camille, I need for you to hear me out. What I'm about to tell you will be difficult to hear, but it's important that you know."

Last night I hadn't been sure how to feel about Will, but I'd liked Gretchen right away. First impressions aren't always infallible. She was nuts, certifiable and likely the ring-leader of this cult – it was always the leaders that were crazy. I needed to decide if I wanted to humor her until Will got home or if I wanted to go outside and call a cab now. I wanted to like Gretchen, but so much had happened in the last month, I couldn't afford to get attached to someone who believed she could talk to spirits

– not just any spirit, but my mother's. It would hurt too much. The only people I'd ever met who'd made those claims were charlatans, thieves and the mentally ill.

"I'm not a charlatan, or mentally ill, and seriously, Camille, what do you have that I'd like to steal?"

For the second time in as many minutes, I could feel my eyes bulging. Did I say that out loud? Oh, my gosh, I'm losing it! "How? . . . What'd you just say?"

The warm smile reappeared, "Yes, Camille. Sometimes I have to *tune in* to retrieve information. I'll not make a habit of it. I'll ask that you give me the same courtesy."

"The same courtesy? What are you talking about? I can't read minds."

"I'm afraid you can. No one has ever taught you how. Your mother is an interesting spirit. She wanted you to have a normal human experience. She thought that if she taught you how to use your gifts you would use them as a crutch."

"Use what as a crutch?"

"In school, knowing what others were selecting for answers on tests would have precluded you from learning the material for yourself. At least, that's what she believed." Gretchen's voice dropped the humor, "For the record, I disagree. You should have understood who you were . . . are."

"You're telling me she's right here and you're communicating with her right now? You're a medium?"

"I've been called many things. I am the Matriarch of this family, and I have pure Centaur blood flowing through my veins. As do you."

Centaur? The half-people, half-horse things? No freakin' way! Mentally ill and delusional. I wonder if Will knew she was a loon. He'd have to know, right?

"Camille, I am not a loon. Before being disrespectful, I suggest you remember I can read your thoughts as easily as I can hear your words. Centaurs are a noble race. We were not half-equestrian as many legends have adopted. Humans were unable to explain the speed of our men and could only describe us in terms of a warrior being carried by a horse. Early paintings showed our kind as a cross between a person and a horse. I can assure you, none of us have hooves."

I started feeling a little woozy. She really could read minds. Centaurs were a different race? I looked just like everyone else. How could I be a Centaur?

"Your mother and father were both full blooded Centaurs, Camille. No human blood is mixed in your lineage. The same is true for your brothers."

"So, what's a Centaur if it isn't a half-person, half-horse?"

"As I said, the speed with which our men have always run was difficult for humans to understand. They began drawing pictograms millennia ago of men with horse bodies to show our speed. The men of our kind have always been fierce warriors. The women are physically strong, but our real strength lies in our minds. Each bloodline carries different skills: some are psychic, some clairvoyant, others can move objects, and some are able to predict the future with uncanny accuracy. There are other talents, too – it depends which bloodline is predominate."

"But I can't do any of those things."

"Yes, you can. You just don't know how. We are not common humans. We have an obligation to keep our race going, to ensure our traits are not lost. You, too, have the same obligation I do. You, too, have the same skills I do. In fact, as a Chiron, you probably have all the skills. Your mother chose not to share with you her talents or develop yours."

"What? My mother couldn't do any of those things."

"I don't know why your mother chose to hide who she was from you or why she kept her secrets from you. This is a critical time in your life, and without your mother to guide you, you could easily make poor decisions. For this reason, I would like for you to extend your trip. There is much for me to teach you, and I cannot do it in just a few days."

I felt like she was waiting for me to say something, but I was still in process mode, so she continued her explanation.

"It is only women of our kind who possess these skills. Men help promulgate the race, but it is the women who are revered. When Will told me he had met your mother, I was floored. We all thought she was dead. She was the last Chiron female heir; her brother never married. Everyone believed the Chiron bloodline would be extinct after this generation."

"What are you talking about?"

"Your mother permitted a union with your father, out of wedlock. She must have done it out of an obligation to all Centaurs, to keep her bloodline alive. But she taught you nothing. You know nothing of our ways or how you fit."

"She allowed a union? That sounds a little antiquated. It takes two to tango."

"I am not belittling your mother. I am merely trying to share with you our beliefs. We are a warrior race, so rather than the 50/50 ratio of male to female that humans have, it is 80/20."

"Why are so many more men born than women?"

"No one knows for sure, but my theory is that from an evolutionary perspective, a significant number of the Centaur male population should have been lost in battle—maybe something like 4 of 5. Because we have known peace for so long, the males significantly outnumber the females."

I couldn't believe I was buying in to her delusion, "Maybe Mom didn't know she was a . . . Centaur?"

"Your mother was the daughter of Zandra. I can assure you Zandra brought your mother up to know our ways. Your mother chose to leave her family and abandon our race."

"My grandparents are dead. My mom told me she'd been on her own since she was seventeen."

Gretchen nodded, "She was indeed on her own from a young age, but I can assure you, your grandmother is very much alive."

I felt my blood pumping again with enough force that I could actually hear my pulse. "Where?"

"Zandra lives in Florida. Your grandfather, Isaac, passed away a few years ago. Neither had seen their daughter in more than a quarter century. They did not know where she was. Zandra only knew of her passing when she sensed your mother's spirit moving on to the spirit world." Gretchen's face took on a strange look when she added, "She was unaware of you."

"Was unaware? Does that mean you've talked to her?"

Gretchen patted my hand, "Yes, I spoke with Zandra late last night. Given the circumstances, she agrees that you should stay with my family. However, she is very anxious to meet you."

She looked over my shoulder again. She spoke in a harsh tone, but not to me. "She is more than capable of handling the truth. Zandra is of no threat to her while she is under my roof. My family will protect her. No blood debt will be paid."

I heard the words echo in my mind, *"Blood debt? What's going on?"*

Gretchen let out a heavy sigh, "It seems your mother had been betrothed to a very powerful Centaur. When she refused to marry him, her family was required to pay a debt of blood, her blood. Your mother ran away and broke contact with her family. Your mother is worried that you may be sought to pay her debt."

"Are you kidding me? There's a price on my head for just being her daughter?"

"It is an old tradition. You are Will's daughter, too. He will try to make amends to the family, monetarily. But, now that people are aware of you, I insist that you extend your stay, at least until you better understand our society. We'll make arrangements to have your things shipped here."

"You're serious. You just spoke with my mom?" I wanted to believe it. I wanted my mother to be right here with me. I couldn't believe the words when I heard them come from me, "Can she hear me?"

Gretchen looked over my shoulder again, then back to me and nodded. "She can hear anything you say to her."

I didn't need any more encouragement, and for some strange reason, I believed Gretchen. "I miss you, Mom. I don't know what to believe." I felt strange talking to her in front of Gretchen. I wondered if this was some sort of trick. In my gut I knew Gretchen had really read my mind; she knew exactly what I was thinking. "Why didn't you tell me any of this?"

Gretchen looked over my shoulder for the answer, then back to me. "She had to make a choice before she died. She didn't want you to know this life, but she feared for your safety if she was no longer able to protect you. Most of all, she says she felt utter loneliness before you came into the world and did not want you to be alone the way she had been."

That sounded like something my mom would say. I caught myself looking in the same direction Gretchen had looked. I asked her, "Will I be able to hear you? Someday?"

Gretchen's voice was barely more than a whisper, "She doesn't belong here, Camille. She will begin to weaken soon. I will work with you so that you may realize your gifts, but know that she won't be able to stay with us for very long. You will need to work hard to learn how to use your skills."

I had kept William's name and phone number for weeks before I finally built up the courage to call him. It was the loneliness that finally made me dial his number. My whole life had revolved around Mom, and it was hard to comprehend that Gretchen was going to give her back to me in some small way, even if just for a short while. I wasn't sure about the things she said about Centaurs, or the idea that it was a different race that I belonged to, but I hoped that I really would be able to hear my mother's voice again.

I looked her square in the eye, nodded and asked, "How do we start?"

CHAPTER 8

Camille Benning – Charleston, SC

Gretchen spent the next several hours trying to help me hear my mother. At 5 o'clock I was frustrated; nothing she had tried worked. I convinced Brent to take me to the store for a soda. While I was standing at the display case, a friendly voice greeted me from behind. "Miss Strayer, good to see you again."

I wasn't used to being addressed with this last name, but the voice was familiar. I turned around and saw the guy who had helped tie off the yacht yesterday. "Hi Josh, good to see you, and it's Cami."

He smirked, "Cami, right. I was expecting to see you and your brothers at the club today. Change of plans?"

"That's the biggest understatement I've ever heard."

Josh gave me a questioning look, but thankfully didn't ask me to explain what I'd said. "So should we expect you tomorrow?"

"I'm not sure. I actually spent most of today with Gretchen."

"Gretchen? Mrs. Strayer?"

I could tell I probably just unleashed a scandal. I had been introduced as their little sister, but I didn't call Gretchen, "Mom." I wasn't sure what to say to keep the rumors from flying rampant. "Right . . . Mrs. Strayer and I spent the day together. The only brother I saw all day was Brent. In fact, he's waiting for me out in the car. I'd better go." I reached into the cabinet, pulled out two sodas, and paid for them.

"All right, well, maybe I'll see ya tomorrow." His voice sounded hopeful—he seemed sweet. When I'd seen him yesterday, I thought he looked a little geeky; today I saw him out of his yacht club uniform, and I was convinced. He stood in front of me with his iPhone in his hand, a blue tooth device on his ear, and a stylus pointed at the screen. I'd always kind of gone for the nerdy guys, but I wasn't interested. Too many other things were going on in my previously simple life to get wrapped up with a guy right now.

I hurried out to the car. When I flung open the door to escape the heat, I heard Brent, "Okay, we'll be back in a few minutes. Yeah, right home." He hung up the phone. "Geeze, I thought I was going to have to go in after you. Everything okay?"

"Yeah, I ran into Josh inside. I might have let it slip that we don't share the same mother. I wasn't thinking."

"Well, we don't share the same mother. Why would that be a problem?"

"I just thought . . . I mean, everyone seems to know your family. How are you going to explain me?"

"We don't have to explain anything. It is what it is. We're just glad you're here."

I shook my head. I kept expecting someone to act normal, and at every turn, each member of my family seemed to be more kind and understanding than the one I had talked to before them. Growing up in California, perception and impressions of others were seriously important. It seemed like everyone I knew cared what others would think. None of my friends in Cali were even close in terms of wealth and clout to the

Strayers, yet they didn't seem to care one little bit that others knew that I was an illegitimate half-sister. So far no one had made that distinction except me. Gretchen had spent the entire day trying to develop psychic skills that I wasn't even sure I possessed, all the while carrying on strange conversations with my invisible mom. It was a little surreal.

I looked over and Brent seemed to be waiting for me to say something, so I asked, "So, what's the plan for tonight?"

"Dinner, dancing, maybe some star-gazing."

"Really? That sounds like a date."

"Date? No, just family. But I already told you, I've never even been on a date, so I hope it doesn't feel like one of those."

"'One of those?' You're too young to be a confirmed bachelor. I never got a legit answer. Why no ex-girlfriends?"

"It's my understanding you have to have a girlfriend for there to be an ex-girlfriend."

"Well, yeah. So why no girls?"

Brent looked at me as if I were the densest person he'd ever talked to, "Easy. It's forbidden."

"By whom? Gretchen and Will?"

"It's the way of our people, Camille. By the time I'm thirty, I will be either married, or betrothed, or I will have to marry a human. If I were willing to settle, I could date. But Centaur women get to choose, and none will choose a man who has shared a bond with another."

"Centaur women choose? Like going shopping? I'd like a six foot-tall, wealthy, smart, funny, garbage-taking-out, chick-flick-watching, football-hating man. Something like that?"

"If that's your list, it'll be pretty easy to find one – well, maybe not the football-hating, but everything else on your list is pretty easy to come by. You could have a husband by this weekend."

I laughed, "So how does she pick you? Do you send in a resume or something?"

"Eligible bachelors are obvious. It's common for courtship to begin at another's wedding. In fact, this Saturday will be your first opportunity to choose."

"This Saturday?"

"Mom didn't tell you? Bruce is marrying Hannah from the Hinman herd."

"Uh, no, she didn't mention it. So Bruce is pretty excited?"

"Excited is an understatement. Hannah's perfect. He was in the running with about fifty others." We pulled into the driveway to see that all the cars were lined up in a row. Brent pulled his white sedan in line with the others; everyone was home. I did a quick count and realized there were six white sedans instead of the normal five – Gretchen must normally keep hers in the garage, because I hadn't noticed it when we left for the store.

As we stepped out of Brent's car, Will came up with a key in his hand. "It's about time!"

I was confused since we'd been gone less than twenty minutes. Brent answered, "Geeze Dad, it's not like we caught a movie; we just went to get a soda."

Will ignored Brent's defense and said, "Never let it be said that I treat any of my children differently. The dealership just delivered it." Will handed me the key to a brand new, Snowy White BMW sedan, identical to the other five parked right beside it.

I was embarrassed to hear myself squeal like a little girl. This couldn't be happening. I had a father and a stepmother who were two of the most amazing people I'd ever met, five brothers who were about as cool as Batman, and a brand new car. I wasn't sure about the whole Centaur thing, but this was better than winning the lottery.

I believed Gretchen, that she really was talking to my mother. I had been on the fence about whether I whole-heartedly believed until Gretchen told me about my second grade play. I had completely dismantled the stage props while I was dancing around like a butterfly. The only way she could have known about it was to hear about it from either my mother or me. In that moment, I knew she was on the level, at least about being able to communicate with my mom. I hadn't thought about that play since I was seven. The only logical explanation was that my mother's spirit had shared the event with her.

Just two days ago I had felt consumed by my grief for my mother. That grief was replaced with a new hopefulness that I'd soon be able to talk to her again, *and* I had a brand new car. I hoped that I wasn't somehow caught in a dream world, or if I were, I wished never to wake up.

I stammered, "Will, I don't know what to say."

"Say you'll stay here. Say that you want to be a part of our family."

I noticed it wasn't just Will standing in front of me with anticipation. Beau, Bruce, Bart, Ben, Brent and Gretchen were all waiting for me to answer. The joy that I felt in that moment rivaled other momentous occasions in my life, like hitting my first homerun when I played softball in high school, seeing a dolphin for the first time in the ocean, and one of my most cherished memories – tasting my very first mint chocolate chip ice cream shake. True, none of these memories could top being accepted into such a tight-knit family, but each of those memories was one that I loved. Without any apprehension, I answered, "I'm in."

Will scooped me up in a tight hug, "Camille, you've just made me the happiest father in the world." While in his embrace, he whispered in my ear, "I'll take care of everything. Don't worry about your grandmother."

I could feel my muscles stiffen. Gretchen must have told him about our conversation about the blood debt. Even though he told me not to worry, the fact that he was whispering to me, out of earshot of everyone else – definitely made me worry. Could someone really want to kill me because my mom had broken off an engagement? I had no reason to doubt Gretchen, but it was all a little hard to swallow.

Things began moving even faster once I had committed to stay. Gretchen took me shopping. In her words, "Your closet is lonely; let's get it some friends."

I noticed that Will and Gretchen were the only people in the house who went anywhere alone. It wasn't anything overt, but it seemed odd that of the eight adults in the house, six of us always went on errands in pairs or better. Having been an only child until this week, by Saturday I was actually craving some alone time. Conversation revolved around Bruce's wedding, although I hadn't seen Hannah, nor had she called. It seemed a little strange. The few friends of mine who had gotten married were all over each other in the days before the wedding, working out seating details, vows, synchronizing last minute schedules. Saturday morning had come and gone and still no sign of the bride.

By mid-afternoon Saturday, Bruce was in exceptionally high spirits. I didn't detect even a hint of nervousness. The backyard had been transformed into a beautiful outdoor cathedral with seating for easily two hundred people.

The brother who I had spent the least amount of time with was the eldest, Beau. I caught Beau straightening seating and smoothing ribbons that had been rearranged by the breeze. Outdoor misting fans were going full throttle, so the grove where the ceremony was to take place was at least ten degrees cooler than the regular air temperature. "Hi, Beau, do you need any help?"

Beau flinched, "Sorry, I didn't realize you were out here, Camille. No, just doing a last minute check before the guests start to arrive. Shouldn't you be inside getting ready?"

"Naw, it's a couple hours before the big event. I just need to get dressed and I'm ready."

"I'm surprised Mom hasn't had you primping and polishing since your eyes opened this morning."

"Why would she? It's not like I'm getting married. I'm not in the ceremony. Nobody knows who I am, and you guys know what I look like."

"But there'll be fifty eligible bachelors here today, maybe more. I've heard news spread pretty fast that you were here. It'll be your first chance to . . . you know . . . find someone."

"Oh c'mon Beau. Who would care that I'm here?"

"Uh, let's see, the Hinmans, the Dixons, the Newtons, the Carltons, the Ivys, just to name a few. Each of those families has an older son who is nearing the end of betrothal age. No one expected for us to have a ready-made sister of age. You'll be pretty popular this evening."

"You're not serious."

"I'm completely serious. I'm in the same boat. Betrothal age for Centaurs is 18-30, so if I'm not picked in the next two years, I'll end up settling for a human."

"Beau, you're great. There are lots of women who would be happy to have you."

"Thanks, Camille. Don't get me wrong. At this point I'm thinking the settling factor could be an improvement over perpetually waiting. It just sucks that I won't be able to carry on our bloodline. At least Bruce will be able to."

"Maybe because I didn't grow up knowing any of this, it's a little hard to take it seriously. I think you love who you love; race shouldn't be a factor."

"That's very 'human' of you, but this is more than just about race. There is magic in our blood, Camille. To let it dilute unnecessarily is akin to wasting the magic. Dad would never let you consider a non-Centaur as a suitor."

"Will doesn't have a say in my decision. When I find the right guy, it won't matter who or what he is. I'm not racing a clock either. It'll happen when it happens."

Beau laughed out loud, a loud throaty snicker, "Camille, you have a lot to learn." Beau shook his head and went back to straightening the wedding decorations.

Brent came up behind me, "What's so funny?"

Beau looked at his younger brother, "Oh nothing. Camille just tells good jokes."

A little miffed that Beau would so easily dismiss my feelings, "Beau seems to think that Will can select a husband for me. I told him that wasn't going to happen, and who I fell in love with and married had nothing to do with Centaur roots or anything else."

Brent took my forearm, squeezing it a little harder than necessary but enough that he had my attention, "Don't say that, Camille."

"Say what? That I don't agree with the courtship ritual that Bruce is going through? Have you noticed Hannah hasn't even talked to him the last couple of days? How can he be marrying a woman he hardly knows?"

Brent looked at me skeptically, "What? That's what's bothering you?"

"Well, a little, yeah. How does he know he'll even like her?"

"It is a great honor to be selected by a Centaur woman. Of course, he'll like her. He'll love her, honor her and cherish her."

"What if they aren't compatible?"

Brent narrowed his eyes, "What have you seen, Camille? Did you receive a vision about them?"

"Whoa, no! No visions. I just think it's odd that they would decide to marry without knowing each other."

"No more odd than dating and unions out of wedlock. Why do people give themselves to others when they know that person isn't going to be with them for the rest of their lives?"

"That's part of finding out who the right person is."

"Then our way should be much preferred. Everyone knows the woman makes her choice. If she can't decide, her family will select the most appropriate match. And who knows her better than her family?"

"You're saying that if I don't pick a husband in the next eight years, Will's going to choose for me?"

"Eight years? Ha! I've never known a woman Centaur to wait until she's thirty to choose. Most choose when they're late teens or early twenties. If you haven't selected someone in the next year or two, yes, Dad will definitely choose for you."

I felt anger welling up within me, not because Brent had made me angry with his words, but because this whole idea was acceptable to them. I could feel my face flush bright red as I readied to set Brent straight when a kind voice came from behind me.

CHAPTER 9

Camille Benning – Charleston, SC

"Miss Strayer, I came early hoping I'd be able to introduce myself." I was getting used to being called "Miss Strayer" and wasn't surprised with myself for turning in the direction of the voice. Before me stood an athletic man. He had light blonde hair, grey eyes, and he stood eye-to-eye with Brent, so he had to be at least 6' 3." It looked like he was wearing a nervous smile. "I'm Chris Carlton. It's an honor to meet you."

I stood dumfounded at this Adonis of a man. I held out my hand in an effort to shake his. He took my palm in his hand, then bowed down to kiss my hand. It was a gesture I'd only seen done in old time movies. Every time I'd seen someone do that, I wanted to gag, so I was beyond surprised when the gesture created instant butterflies in my stomach. Chris held my hand in both of his as he straightened up, "Are you enjoying South Carolina?"

His eyes were mesmerizing, absolutely stunning. I stammered a little, "I'm . . . I like it here, but I'm still not used to the heat."

"Would you like me to walk you to the house so you can cool off a bit before the ceremony?" He spoke with absolutely perfect English, no accent of any kind. This was odd because everyone other than the Centaurs I had met seemed to speak with the southern drawl I'd expected in this area of the country.

I caught Brent out of the corner of my eye, grinning from one ear to the other, and I couldn't help but shoot him a glare. I turned my attention to Chris, "Uh, sure."

We were out of ear-shot from Brent when Chris said, "So, am I the first?"

"The first what?"

"The first to make your acquaintance?"

"Yes, up until now I've just been getting to know my family. I haven't met anyone since I've been here."

We approached the front door, and he nearly shouted, "Excellent! I live on Daniel Island, and I'm finishing up my residency as a family practitioner."

He couldn't possibly be giving me his "husband" resume, could he? Was Chris for real? "That's thoughtful of you to tell me about yourself, but I'm still a little new to the . . . you know." I didn't know how to say I wasn't interested without coming right out and saying it. "Never mind, would you like to come in and cool off, too?" Chris stepped in front of me and reached for the door knob so he could open the door for me. Two points for the tall sexy gentleman with great manners.

As the door opened, Gretchen was in the hallway with a huge smirk that matched the one Brent was wearing in the back yard. Dammit! I needed to keep my thoughts to myself. Gretchen didn't miss a beat. She held out her hand and said, "Hello, Chris, we're so happy you could come today. I spoke with your mother earlier. Glad to hear things are going so well with your practice." Gretchen directed her attention to me, "Camille, did Chris tell you he was a doctor?"

Flushed with embarrassment still, "Yes, he mentioned it."

Chris was gushing with pride when he said, "I'll be joining my family's practice in town very soon."

The embarrassment should have been overwhelming. The idea that a woman could simply pick a suitor and good-looking, educated men would be thrilled to be chosen seemed bizarre. But as I looked at Gretchen and Chris, sure enough—this was exactly what was going on.

Tradition or not, Chris was attractive, had a good job, and seemed to be giving me vibes that he was interested. It wouldn't hurt to get to know him – though I wasn't at all interested in trading in my single status. I motioned for him to step into the family room where the couches were plush, and it seemed a nice place to chat, hopefully away from prying ears. "So, what do you like to do when you aren't working?"

Chris cocked his head to the side momentarily, "I don't understand the question."

"For fun. What do you like to do with your free time?"

"I volunteer at a clinic downtown a few hours per week. Each year I volunteer for two weeks for an organization called Doctors without Borders. I read in my spare time."

Wonderful, a workaholic. "So, no hobbies, like golf or tennis?"

"I've done both. If you enjoy golf and tennis, I'd be happy to take you sometime."

"No. I mean, I don't like either. I just wondered if there was something you enjoyed doing outside of your profession."

"I would be willing to give anything a whirl you felt would be a good use of my time."

That was by far the creepiest answer he could have given me—like a Stepford Wife in reverse. I really took him in for the first time since his arrival: his posture, his eye contact, his non-verbal language all looked—

almost desperate. After replaying the conversation with Brent earlier, one question came to mind. "Chris, how old are you?"

Chris gave me a forced smile, as if his answer were one of shame, "Twenty-nine."

There it was: he was trying hard to make a good impression. If what Brent told me was the truth, and I had no reason to doubt that it was, I was his last chance.

Chris held the unnatural smile when he asked, "You are new to our kind, is that right?"

"That's a great way to put it. Uh, yes . . . I've only been here a few days."

"My mother told me that your mother never told you about your ancestry. Is that true?"

"Yes."

Chris let out a long breath, "This must all be a bit much to take in."

"That's a colossal understatement, Chris."

"Look, if I were in your shoes, I wouldn't be in a hurry to find a husband. You have to make peace with who you are before you can decide whom you want as your partner. I won't pressure you. But don't interpret my lack of pressure as lack of interest. I am my parent's only son. I. . . I would love for you to consider me."

"Uh . . . thanks, I think."

I thought his sales pitch was over and I could relax, until he said, "The truth is, I think you're beautiful. I've known your brothers since I was a kid and would love to be a part of your family. I believe your family would be equally pleased if you joined mine. But it would be a mistake to try to convince you I am the best choice for you before you are ready to accept who you are."

"I know who I am."

"Do you?"

"Yes, and it has nothing to do with being a . . . Centaur." I caught myself – it was the first time I had acknowledged it, out loud, outside my family.

"That's where you're mistaken, Camille. It has everything to do with being one of us."

"What if I just want to be normal?"

"Normal isn't an option when you're extraordinary." Chris put his hand on mine and gave it a gentle squeeze, "You are extraordinary, Camille. Choose wisely."

Chris stood up, bowed his head slightly in my direction, and left me reeling on the chair as he left. A handsome, thoughtful, intelligent, eligible, doctor—no less, just told me I was extraordinary and wanted me to choose him. Five days ago if the same thing had happened, I would have followed him around like a love sick puppy—but it wasn't five days ago. It wasn't left to fate anymore. Finding a husband had never been on the top of my priorities. Sure, growing up, I had always wondered why my mom never found a husband when my friends' mothers rarely seemed to settle on one. Meeting Chris just made me want to ask Gretchen more questions.

I could hear Gretchen's voice in the hallway, "Yes, she's here. Let me see if she has a minute." I was still teetering with reality when she appeared in the doorway. "Camille, you've only got an hour before the ceremony. Do you have time to meet someone before you get ready?"

"I guess so. Who is it?"

She turned away and used her hand to motion someone from the foyer down to the family room. When he appeared in the doorway, I stood to greet him. Gretchen said, "Gus, this is our daughter, Camille."

The fact that Gretchen had used the words, "our daughter," did not go unnoticed by me. The words startled me a little, more than I had expected them to. I was a little unsteady as I looked up at the man towering over Gretchen. I held out my hand, and he took mine in his hand and shook it vigorously. Gretchen excused herself, and I stood with Gus for an uncomfortable moment.

"I know you don't have much time. I just wanted to meet you. I'm Gus Hinman."

My years of etiquette were lost on this hulk of a man as I stared at his six-foot-five frame, dark hair, dark eyes and brutish body. He reminded me of a cage fighter I had known back home. "It's nice to meet you, Gus. I'm Camille."

"I passed Chris on the way out. I can see this may be my only opportunity with you today, and I just wanted to say hi."

I suddenly felt like I had some sort of "USDA Prime Cut" sticker pasted to me. "Well, I'm glad you . . . stopped . . . I mean. . ." Remembering my manners, "Would you like to sit down?"

"I don't want to make you late, but I would like a chance to talk to you later. I play for the Panthers and came back to town for my sister's wedding to your brother. I live a few hours from here in Charlotte but am home during the off-season."

"You're in the NFL?" I could see from his eyes that this was a great source of pride for him, and I'd be lying if I didn't confess I was a little impressed myself.

"Yeah, receiver. I'm not in the area much this time of year, but will be here all week if you've got some free time."

"Uh, sure, okay."

Gretchen popped back in the doorway, "I'm sorry to interrupt, but Camille needs to get ready or she'll be late." Gretchen ushered Gus to the doorway as I bounded up the steps to my room. As I reached for the door knob, I glanced out the window. Everyone arriving, including the two handsome guys I'd just talked to, were seriously dressed to impress. The first pangs of fear grabbed me when I realized I didn't have anything to wear, at least nothing that wouldn't clue everyone in as to how much I really didn't belong here.

As I stared at the few changes of clothes I'd brought with me and the items I'd bought shopping with Gretchen, I decided on a denim skirt, flats and a nice blouse I'd tucked in my bag. My nerves took hold. I'd never been one to want to stand out. My lack of a wardrobe would definitely make me stick out like a sore thumb. I couldn't not attend; I took a seat on the bed, chastising myself for not thinking of this on one of the shopping trips with Gretchen or even earlier this morning. I heard a quiet knock on my door.

Great. Now what? It's bad enough someone must have tweeted that there was a single female Centaur at the wedding tonight. I couldn't imagine what would happen next. Frustrated, I called, "Come in."

Gretchen stepped inside my room, "Camille, I hope you don't mind, but I thought you might be looking for something different to wear. I bought this a few months ago—I didn't know why at the time." She smiled warmly at me, "I believe I bought it for you."

The hair stood at attention on my arms, "You bought it a few months ago?" I looked at the silver and sequined gown she held in her arms, not knowing what to say.

Gretchen sat on my bed beside me, "Many of our kind have premonitions, visions. We can see something significant but aren't able to put it into context at the time. I was out shopping and found this dress. It wasn't my size and it wasn't my taste, but something told me I needed to purchase it. I believe I must have bought it for you. Do you like it?"

It was one of the most beautiful dresses I'd ever seen. Having grown up near Hollywood, I had seen my share of fabulous designer gowns but had never seen one like this one. It was strapless, made of brushed silk, with a thin line of sequins sewn across the bodice, and a sheer fabric flowing from the waist to the floor.

There were no words to describe my feelings for her in that second. How had she been shopping and found a dress for me before she knew me? I knew I had to be a source of pain that she kept masked from me – the illegitimate daughter of her husband. I felt my eyes welling up, wishing I could say to her all the things that my heart felt in that moment.

She must have felt my thoughts because she laid the dress to her other side and grabbed me in a hearty embrace. "You may not be my biological daughter, but you are the daughter I've always wanted." That was it. The misting I was trying to keep under control let loose as tears streamed down my cheeks. I tried to casually wipe them free, but more followed.

In that moment I wished to be a part of the family, not just a sister or a long lost daughter, but a full-fledged member of the Strayer family. Guilt crept into me. My own mother created such a deep hole in my heart when she died; I worried that I'd never find anything or anyone to fill the gap. Less than a month later, I sat in a mansion wishing I had grown up here. The guilt started growing larger as I wondered if this love that I was developing for my new found family somehow minimized my feelings for the center of my universe who had just died.

I released Gretchen, hoping she would ignore the tears, but she didn't. "Loving us doesn't diminish the love that you will always have for your mother. That's the wonderful thing about family: the bigger it is, the larger your heart grows."

I stiffened at her words. I kept forgetting that she could read my mind.

Gretchen's smile never wavered, but she answered my unspoken question, "Only if you do not shield your thoughts – we'll work on that tomorrow."

My body went from stiff to rigid. I felt my eyes widen and my voice refused to cooperate. Gretchen's expression took on a more serious look, "Tomorrow we will continue working on your skills. It won't come as such a surprise when your skills are sharper and you are able to do the same. But for tonight, try not to think about it. You have many young men who anxiously wish to meet you."

I wiped the last couple rogue tears away from my cheeks. As Gretchen stood up, she leaned over and pressed her lips to my forehead. I knew she meant it as a maternal symbol, but as she stood, I felt her body go rigid, a look shot across her face – panic. She was facing a wall so I couldn't imagine what she would have seen to make her eyes so wide, her voice so urgent, "Camille, dress quickly. Don't go outside alone. I need to find your father." She rushed out of my room.

Don't go outside alone. Had she seen something? Did she know something bad was about to happen? I did as I was told, but I felt my stomach cinching itself up into a tight knot.

CHAPTER 10

Camille Benning – Charleston, SC

After I had checked myself in the mirror, I could hardly believe the image staring back. I routinely had bad hair days, and the humidity of Charleston wreaked havoc on me. But in this moment, my dark hair somehow looked perfect. Since I was a little girl, I'd always had long auburn hair, naturally curly, which translated to naturally frizzy and wildly-out-of-control most summers. I happened to be wearing one of the most elegant gowns I'd ever seen and felt almost like a fairy princess. I smirked when I said out loud, "Or maybe a Centaur princess."

A voice called from the other side of my door, "Honey, are you ready?"

I recognized the hesitant voice waiting in the hall, "Hi, Will, you can come in."

The door opened and Will looked a little tentative. His apprehension melted away. He stretched his arms out to me, taking long strides in my direction, and took both my hands in his. "Camille, you are truly a vision. Have I told you today how happy I am that you're here?"

Will stepped over to my bed and sat down, patting the space beside him. I took a seat next to him, a little self-conscious of my "princess" comment, wondering if he'd heard me.

Will took a deep breath and let it out loudly. "Gretchen has filled you in on some aspects of our kind that are less than ideal, yes?"

"What? That I'm supposed to pick a husband the same way someone would pick a new puppy at the pound?"

A nervous chuckle released from Will, "No, actually that was something I thought you might find appealing, but it's related." He cleared his throat, "Your mother had been betrothed to Kyle Richardson of Florida. He was not . . . pleased when your mother broke off the engagement."

"Okay." This much I knew, but he had my attention.

"Our kind, once a woman chooses, she cannot change her mind, at least not without paying a debt to the man she's rejected. There is good reason for this: as men so clearly outnumber the women, if a woman chooses to break off her engagement, it is rare that another woman would consider that man a potential suitor. He is in essence 'black-balled,' and if he is an only child his bloodline is unlikely to continue."

"So when my mom broke off her engagement, Kyle Richardson wasn't able to marry anyone?"

"Actually, he is one of the very few that I have ever heard of to be betrothed a second time to a Centaur woman. The fact that he was given a second chance for his bloodline does not diminish his right to exact a blood debt."

What she'd said had bothered me, but I wanted to hear it from Will. "Gretchen said that he wanted me dead. Is that true?"

"As he is the one that the debt is owed to, he sets the price. Given our circumstances and that so much time has passed, he does not wish for your death."

The pain in my stomach didn't diminish as I waited for Will to get to the bad news. "She said you would pay him, and he'd be fine. I get the feeling that that isn't the case."

"Mr. Richardson has traveled here tonight. He wishes to meet you."

"Meet me? But why?"

"I explained to Mr. Richardson the situation—that I was unaware of you until just this week. You were indeed part of my family. Given your mother's debt, I felt it was my responsibility to pay to ensure there would be no bad blood between our families."

"So, how much am I going to owe you?"

Will shook his head. "You'll owe me nothing, Camille. You're my daughter. If he will accept money as payment, then there's nothing to worry about."

"If?"

"It's complicated, Camille. For right now, he just wants to meet you."

"So he'll be here tonight? I have to meet with him?"

"Yes. I promise, I will be with you the whole time. Nothing will happen to you tonight. But you must talk to him."

I noticed that Will told me everything would be fine "tonight," but he made no mention of tomorrow or the day after. "Uh . . . okay. I feel like I'm missing something?"

"He didn't mention it on the phone, but you know Gretchen sees things. Gretchen shared with me that Mr. Richardson has a son who is of age. He may be unwilling to set a price with an actual dollar value."

"Are you saying I have to marry some guy I don't know because my mother refused to marry his father? You aren't saying that, are you?"

"Camille, the possibility is remote. Gretchen senses that his intentions are pure and that it is better to deal with this immediately rather than delay the meeting. Given the wedding tonight, it's unlikely he'll create any kind of scene."

Our conversation had been calm, but I could feel my blood beginning to boil. I shouldn't have lashed out at Will, but I was furious that this was even possible. "I'm not marrying some guy I don't know. That isn't going to happen!"

"I will never force you to do anything you do not choose. However, since Mr. Richardson has travelled here tonight, I need to insist that you meet with him."

My mouth opened but nothing came out. I started arguing that this was one of the most absurd things I'd ever heard of, but reality was, meeting a man with Will wouldn't be bad. It's not like I was being told I had to marry his son. It was harmless, for now.

As I tried to convince myself that everything would be fine, I realized that knot in my stomach still hadn't eased. Will reached over and took my hand in his. "Camille, I promise no harm will come to you. Do you trust me?"

How do you trust someone you hardly know? I looked in his eyes and nearly melted when I saw love staring back at me through his deep brown eyes. No matter how much I disliked the situation, I did trust him. He may not have been a rock star, he wasn't fixing world hunger, but he was exactly the type of father I had dreamed of. I realized I didn't need a lifetime to know that I loved him unconditionally and trusted him emphatically. He was my father. I was safe with him, and regardless of what a big wheel he was financially, he had given me the one thing I had craved my whole life—a family who loved me back. I reluctantly nodded that I did trust him.

Will took me in an embrace. When he let me go, he took my hands in his again. "I have one last request before we head downstairs." I gave him a quizzical look as I couldn't imagine anything more concerning than what we'd just talked about. "In front of the guests, I need for you to address me as your father." He paused, then added, "Especially, Mr. Richardson. I understand if you aren't comfortable with it, and privately you may address me any way you wish, but tonight, please call me 'Dad.'"

My whole life I had known the word. It had always been in my vocabulary. Never having called anyone that name, my eyes gave him my answer. I could feel the glossiness and used all my willpower to keep them from leaking. I could feel the enormous smile begging to be released along with the tears. I held it all in and simply replied, "Okay."

When we stepped off the front porch together, jitters threatened to envelop me as I looked at all the people I didn't know. Will must have sensed how nervous I was when he confessed, "Having found you is a dream come true for me." It was exactly what I needed to hear. His love for me gave me the strength I needed to face all the strangers on the grounds.

I had been walking on air, floating three feet above the ground. I was going to my brother's wedding with my dad tonight—just a short week ago, an event and a circumstance I would have never dreamed possible. The air I was floating on suddenly got too thin, and I felt my foot miss the bottom step. I instinctively knew I was getting ready to do a face plant on the pavement in front of at least two hundred people I'd never met. My arms flailed out to the sides as if I were a bird about to take flight.

CHAPTER 11

Camille Benning – Charleston, SC

In that single second my mind was able to think clearly about three things: I was going to look like a complete idiot in front of everyone, the impending scab on my face would be both painful and embarrassing, and I was sure I would ruin this amazing dress. It's laughable how quickly my mind had all three complete thoughts as my eyes squinted and my arms flapped in mid-air.

Instead of the rough cement of the sidewalk, I felt two strong, calloused hands. One cradled my face while the other hooked under my abdomen. Those two hands lifted me up from my swan dive and placed me gently on my feet on the sidewalk. Initially I thought Will had caught me, but when I looked up, I saw those hands were attached to a stranger.

I should have been embarrassed with my clumsiness, maybe a little awkward that such a hunk of a man had just saved me from making a complete spectacle of myself in front of hundreds of people – but I didn't. Instead, my eyes took him in. I was wearing shoes with at least a three inch heel, and he still towered over me. His eyes were ice blue – almost turquoise. His dark blonde hair was short, and although impossible to see his frame through his tux, his body took on a "V" shape with broad shoulders and a narrow waist. A great smile spread wide on his face. I waited for some smart-alecky remark about my gracefulness, but he turned to Will and said, "I hope she's all right."

Amazed that I wasn't a bloody mess, "How did you catch me? Where'd you come from?"

His warm smile grew into a Cheshire cat grin, "I, uh, saw her falling. Thought she wouldn't want to spend her brother's wedding in the emergency room."

When Will and I stepped off the porch, no one had been anywhere near us. I knew because I was focused on all the people off in the distance. So unless this guy was the invisible man, he had literally materialized out of nowhere. It was strange, but he was looking at Will, not me. "Well, thanks. I'm Camille." I held out my hand in an effort to shake his.

This handsome stranger looked at my hand, then to Will with a frightened look on his face. Will was standing at my side and casually slid his hand over the top of mine, gently pushing it down from where it hung in mid-air. "Drake, we're so glad you could come tonight and celebrate with us. How is your father?"

Drake angled his body so that I was no longer in his direct line of sight. He answered Will, "His construction business is doing well. He sends his regrets that he couldn't be here." I didn't know what to think. This Drake guy had caught me in mid-air but refused to accept my hand or allow me to thank him properly. Instead he pretended as if I weren't there. After the welcoming I'd received from Gus and Chris earlier, this guy's response to me had me dumbfounded.

Will was all smiles when he said, "I'll make sure to catch up with him soon. Thank you, Drake, for your quick action." Will's eyes darted in my direction, making it clear that he was appreciative of Drake for not letting me swan dive into the cement. Will placed his hand on the small of my back and guided me forward, away from Drake. Once we were several strides away, he leaned down and whispered to me, "I should have warned you. Betrothed men will not address you directly and under no circumstances will they physically come in contact with you."

"But he caught me in mid-air. I was just trying to say thanks."

"It's okay. He's not offended. He knows you aren't familiar with our customs. I am sorry I wasn't paying closer attention. I didn't realize you'd lost your footing until Drake had already caught you."

"I didn't even see him near us until he caught me."

Will smiled and nodded, "Centaur men are very fast."

"Like Superman fast?"

"Pshaw . . . Superman was a comic strip character. . . But I guess that's pretty accurate. Most Centaurs can sprint short distances at the speed of sound."

My mouth opened and my eyes widened. He couldn't be serious. "The speed of sound?"

"Well, I could say 'faster than a speeding bullet,' but depending on the caliber and weapon the bullet is shot from, some bullets travel several times faster than the speed of sound."

"You're serious?"

"Camille, I know this is all new to you. I rather hoped we would have been able to slowly immerse you into our ways, but now I wonder if we shouldn't have assembled a handbook of some kind." Will's smile never wavered, but there must have been something else he desperately wanted me to know. Just as he opened his mouth, he stopped and his posture abruptly changed – his hand still resting on the small of my back was now rigid.

"William, it's so nice to see you again." A tall, thin man, somewhere in his late forties or early fifties was walking directly toward us. He stopped directly in front of Will with what I could only describe as a forced smile. "I'm happy that one of your sons is finally taking his place in the kingdom. I genuinely hope your other four are not forced to settle for a human."

William ignored the snide comment and graciously said, "We're very happy for Bruce, too."

"One is enough for your bloodline, so you have my heartfelt congratulations."

"Thank you." Will was looking around the yard and out to the grove. I recognized the look: he was planning a getaway from this guy.

"I heard the bride's father required a handsome dowry be paid. I hope that's an ugly rumor?"

"Kyle, the negotiations of the heart are not for any of us to speculate on."

"The heart, or the wallet?" Kyle gave a hearty laugh and slapped Will on the back.

I looked at Will, wondering if he had really bribed the bride's father. If it were a lie, he would be screaming right now, defending the honor of the bride and her father. At least I thought so. I didn't know him all that well, but he didn't strike me as someone who would let a verbal assault go unanswered.

The man's eyes roved in my direction. I felt the weight of his stare; I wasn't frightened, but definitely uncomfortable. "So this is Camille Chiron. It is lovely to meet you. You look just like your mother."

I looked at Will, silently asking if I was supposed to shake his hand or not. I didn't want to look like a complete idiot and was desperately hoping for some sort of an indication on what I should or shouldn't do. I wanted to correct him. I'd been Camille Benning my whole life. This week I'd gotten used to being called Camille Strayer, but no one had ever called me Camille Chiron. Still unsure of what was and wasn't acceptable, I simply replied, "Thank you. Did you know her very well?"

"Better than most. We were betrothed." He didn't drop his stare as it went from uncomfortable to excruciating. Then a light bulb went off: this was the man my mother owed her blood debt to.

Will ended the conversation abruptly, "Kyle, I was hoping we could have our discussion after the nuptials." I felt my own nervousness straighten my back and widen my eyes as reality set in that this man believed I owed him my life.

The weight of his stare was nearly painful. The look on his face did not match his words, "I wouldn't dream of delaying such an important event. Of course we can talk after."

He didn't flinch, move, or break eye contact with me. I felt Will's hand urging me forward. I could imagine why my mother had rejected him. Although every person I saw looked like they'd stepped off of a magazine cover, there was something about Mr. Richardson that didn't feel right: a weakness of some kind, as if a part of him were missing. I couldn't put my finger on it, but there was definitely something amiss when I compared him to all others in attendance. I couldn't see what would have ever gained her interest in him to begin with. As I looked at the guests, young and old, there was definitely a common thread—attractiveness. They weren't attractive in a Venice Beach kind of way, but in a Hollywood Movie Star kind of way. Tall, muscular, full heads of hair, charismatic smiles, and thoughtful words greeted me with each new introduction. I wondered silently what was so different about Kyle Richardson.

As we took our seats waiting for the ceremony to begin, I could feel eyes watching me. I worried that Kyle Richardson was staring me down, but when I turned my head, I was just in time to see Drake, the man who had caught me in mid-air, turn away. He sat next to a beautiful lady. Her long blonde hair flowed nearly to her waist; she had high cheek bones, a light complexion and perfect posture. She looked like the poster child for beauty. As I continued looking their way, she turned her gaze toward me and gave me a slight grin in silent greeting and raised her fingers in a casual hello. Wow, I could see why Drake wouldn't want to rock the boat with her. I shared a half-grin with her and moved my gaze to where Bruce stood up front with the minister.

The ceremony was remarkably short. It mirrored every other wedding I'd ever attended until the very last announcement was made, "The two joined here today are now one in our kingdom's eyes. Welcome them into our home. Should one perish before the other, remember Hylonome's sacrifice when Cyllarus was lost in battle against the Lapiths. Neither will now breathe without the other."

Not having a clue who Hylonome or Cyllarus were, I made a mental note to do some research. Will's words echoed in my mind from the other night – that he and Gretchen had been on the outs when he met my mother – everything I'd heard since then sounded like that wasn't really an option. I'd give it some time then ask Gretchen a little more. As thrilled as I was to finally have someone to call "Dad," I still wasn't convinced he was for real. Sure a living, breathing person, you bet – but I had a nagging feeling that something still didn't feel right. This final statement of the wedding vows seemed ominous, unwavering. I wondered if I was taking this vow too literally.

I didn't have long to consider the vows or what my father had done twenty-three years before – because within minutes a full-blown party erupted. The men who had introduced themselves to me in the house, Chris and Gus, and a slew of others after the ceremony each took his turn with me on the dance floor. Although a lot of fun, it wasn't the best venue to get to know potential husbands or even potential boyfriends.

The dance floor had been assembled in a wooded area with lights beautifully strung from the trees. I staggered off the makeshift dance floor after my sixth partner had cut in, introduced himself, told me about his lineage. I decided to find one of my obviously absent brothers, thinking it might be more fun to dance with one of them over a desperate Centaur looking for a wife.

I felt a hand wrap itself around my forearm and pull. The shock of being pulled forward made me stumble as I ended up eye-to-eye with my mother's jilted ex-fiancé. My mouth gaped open, and my eyes were wide. He hissed, "Well, aren't you the little Homecoming Queen?"

CHAPTER 12

Camille Benning – Charleston, SC

My eyes narrowed, and I didn't try to camouflage the venom in my voice, "Get your hand off me before I remove it."

Although his grip loosened, he didn't release my arm. "Show some respect, you wretched little . . ." He didn't finish his sentence as Will was suddenly standing beside us, eyes blazing. He kept his words to himself but stared at Kyle – as if the two men were both considering their next move. When, after a full minute, no words were spoken, you could nearly cut the air with a knife and fork. Finally, Will's eyes fell to Kyle's hand, still wrapped around my forearm.

Kyle's voice was full of hate, "She may belong to you, Will, but remember that I choose her fate."

Will's response was strong and commanding, "Kyle, I told you I would be willing to meet with you and discuss the debt owed to you. You choose nothing."

Kyle's grip tightened on my arm again, and I couldn't imagine what was going though his mind, "I'm sure we'll come up with something that is mutually beneficial."

These two would have continued to talk about me like I wasn't actually there if I'd let them. I wrenched my arm away from Kyle's hand, put my back to Will and glared at Kyle while I spit out, "I owe you nothing. My mother made a choice more than two decades ago that you weren't good enough for her. Get over it already."

I could still feel the burn on my forearm from his grip as Kyle returned my glare. In a calm, hateful voice he said, "You don't know what you're talking about."

My adrenaline was coursing through my blood when I nearly shouted, "I know that if you had been half the man you pretend to be, you'd be my father. Instead you're trying to intimidate me and my father – it's not going to happen, Slick."

The words were no sooner out of my mouth when I felt my feet lifted off the ground and wind against my face. I saw nothing but a blur of trees and bushes for five full seconds until I was gently put back on the ground. The sensation had been so foreign my senses couldn't give me a good explanation of what had just happened. My feet were firmly back on the ground, my body upright, and two warm hands were on each of my shoulders. I looked up into the eyes of the person who had flown with me at ground level. It was the third time I'd seen those light blue eyes tonight: Drake stared down into mine. His hands on my shoulders were warm; he was close enough that I drank in his cologne. I recognized the scent immediately—Calvin Klein's Eternity, the same fragrance I bought for Daniel. It was my favorite.

His eyes held me for longer than they should have: he must have realized when his gaze quickly dropped to the ground. Still furious at Kyle, I didn't have much time to process what had just happened. "What did you do that for? Better yet, what did you just do? Where are we?"

"Camille . . . I'm sorry . . . I was listening."

"And?"

"You aren't accustomed to our ways. Your words might as well have been a sword. Kyle could have struck you down. I just moved you out of his way."

"You moved me? How? Can you fly?"

He shook his head and chuckled, "No, I can't fly. I ran, but it feels a little like flight, doesn't it?"

"Where are we?"

Drake abruptly let go of my shoulders. He must have remembered the no touching policy. "A mile to the west of your home."

"A mile?" I couldn't shield the disbelief from my voice, "So you just snapped your fingers and we're suddenly a mile away?"

Drake shook his head, "I didn't snap my fingers. I just told you, I picked you up and ran."

I couldn't believe he had done that, and I wasn't pleased that he had scooped me up while I was trying to make a point with Kyle Richardson. "Why would you do that? I was in the middle of a conversation."

"I'm not sure. I was. . .I was worried what he might do to you."

"I can take care of myself."

Drake shook his head, "Not against a Centaur. We're all warriors. I had to get you away from him."

"But why?"

"Centaurs are unpredictable when they're angry. I couldn't let him lash out at you. I didn't know if your father would be fast enough to stop Mr. Richardson."

I knew Drake had the best of intentions. He believed I needed his protection and gave it to me willingly, twice. I hadn't asked for his help either time. I didn't even know I needed his help the second time. I couldn't help but acknowledge that his fast action definitely kept me from being a bloody mess earlier, and maybe even a second time at the hand of Kyle Richardson. "Well, thanks." I stretched up on my tip toes and gave him a kiss on his cheek.

Drake took a step back from me and placed his palm over the side of his face, cradling it as if I'd just slapped him. His eyes looked like blue saucers as I made a mental note that it's not okay to shake hands *or* kiss a betrothed Centaur's cheek as a "thank you." He didn't need to say it; I could see how badly I'd offended him written all over his face.

Before he had the chance to chastise me for yet another "Camille misstep," another blur to my right appeared: Brent with a worried look on his face. "Good save, Drake. But you'd better get back. You don't want Bianca to find out you swooped in and saved Camille, twice. I've got her." Drake nodded and took another step away from me. He glanced at me again; it looked like he wanted to say something but changed his mind at the last second. I watched him lower his head and disappear into the night.

"Okay, Brent, what the hell is going on?"

"I think that's pretty obvious. Dad was trying to work a deal with Kyle Richardson to come to terms on your blood debt, and you pretty much sliced the guy wide open and started shoving big fat salt pellets into his wounds. Good job, Camille." His words were harsh but his tone was amused.

"So is Will . . ., I mean, is Dad . . . pissed?"

"Shocked is probably a better description. I doubt you'll be included in any of their discussions anymore."

"Level with me, Brent. Is what my mom did that big of a deal?"

Brent's humor drained in that instant. "Yes. Choosing a partner is sacred. You don't get to choose and then change your mind. I think Mr. Richardson is a certifiable jackass, but your mom broke one of the seven tenants. It is fully within his right to collect a blood debt."

"I keep hearing that, but humor me: what, exactly, is a blood debt?"

Brent motioned to a rock planted on the ground. I sat down while he squatted in the grass beside me. "A blood debt happens when someone in our society has been so incredibly wronged it affects their bloodline. In human terms it is closest to premeditated murder. If I had wronged another Centaur and owed a blood debt, it would literally be a death sentence for me. Lucky for you, there are so few female Centaurs in the world that no one would collect it against a woman. But your mom really did wrong Mr. Richardson. It was within his right to take the life of someone in her family." If I had to pay a blood debt for my mom, could one of my brothers be forced to pay it? I shuddered at the thought.

"But, that was over twenty years ago. Why now?"

"I wish I knew, Camille. When Dad pulled us all together and told us the whole story, no one could believe that he hadn't exacted his revenge when it all happened. Maybe he didn't because your mom went into hiding or something. It doesn't make sense. Reality is that Dad will do everything he can, but, ultimately, it's up to Mr. Richardson."

"But you just said he can't kill me."

Brent shook his head, "It's a negotiation. I think Dad would promise him nearly anything not to lose you. If Mr. Richardson intended to carry out a death sentence, other herds would step in to protect you. It would mean war."

"Isn't there a statute of limitations or something? The person who owes the debt isn't even alive anymore." I caught myself speaking callously of my mother and felt a rush of her envelop me. Gretchen told me that my mother was still with me and that I could communicate with her. I turned away from Brent when I felt my mother's presence. I yelled into the darkness, "Mom, you'd better have a plan because there is no stinkin' way I'm going to owe that man a thing!"

I could smell my mother's perfume. I felt warmth encompass me and saw the slightest outline of her face appear in front of me. She seemed to be saying something, but I couldn't understand. It didn't matter how hard I concentrated, I couldn't make her image sharpen, and I wondered if maybe it was my imagination.

Brent started to say something, but I held my finger to my lips to quiet him. I concentrated on the outline of her face, hoping to bring her better into focus. I could see her figure desperately trying to tell me something, but still no sound. I shook my head at her, "I can't hear you."

Her outline began to diminish. I could still see her in the same spot but no longer with the vibrant colors from just seconds before. Brent held out his elbow, offering to escort me back. Since it was obvious that my psychic sensor was still malfunctioning, I decided to pump Brent for more information. We began a leisurely stroll back when he advised, "If you choose someone right away, Mr. Richardson won't have a chance to force his son on you."

Still reeling from having seen my mother's ghost or spirit or whatever it was, I didn't give Brent's suggestion much weight. I was in my own little world when I realized he'd stopped walking and was staring at me. "Camille, did you hear me?"

Embarrassed at being lost in thought, I uttered, "Uh, what? No, I'm sorry, I wasn't listening."

"I said, if you choose someone soon, he won't have a chance to make you marry his son. He would have to accept a cash payment."

"Brent, I'm not ready to marry anyone, and I don't care who says I have to. I'm for sure not picking someone I've never met who came out of the same gene pool as Kyle Richardson. For that matter, I'm not picking anyone. Maybe I want to be like my mom and just live on my own."

We began walking again, and Brent's strides remained constant. He didn't seem deterred in the slightest that I had no intention of choosing someone quickly. After about ten minutes of walking at a normal pace, I could see the lights of the party coming back into view. Brent's arm tensed and Bruce appeared out of thin air – I had to work on getting used to Centaur speed. Bruce was seriously nervous, "Camille, Mr.

Richardson thinks you took off with the guy you're going to take as your husband. He's flaming mad. If you pick someone right now, Dad's pretty sure he'll leave and not return."

"Have you all lost your minds? I can't just throw a dart at a wall and pick some guy to be married to!"

"I get that it isn't ideal, but if you don't pick someone, you might get stuck with his son. What's worse? Choosing a great guy you don't know that well but who will treat you like a queen, or being forced to marry into the Richardson herd? C'mon, Camille, you met a bunch of guys tonight. Pick one, and I'll go get him and bring him here. Then the two of you can give your announcement directly in front of Mr. Richardson."

"That'll never work."

Bruce must have believed that I was somehow considering his stupid idea. "I'll go get whatever guy you tell me to. The two of you can come back to the party as if you'd been planning this all day. You can have a super-long engagement if you want to."

"What if during this super-long engagement I decide that I don't like him, that he's not the right guy for me?"

Brent and Bruce both froze. Both looked at each other, nearly dumbfounded with my question. Finally Bruce answered, "You aren't serious?"

"It's called dating. You're supposed to test drive a few guys to make sure you pick the right model. Believe it or not – it's a pretty normal concept. Try one on, if he isn't right, you trade him in on a new model."

Bruce looked at me and said, "Camille, I can't tell if you have a warped sense of humor or if you're being serious."

"I didn't ask to be whisked away from the conversation I was having with Kyle. That Drake guy just swooped in and took off with me. Did it ever occur to anyone that what I was saying was important? I didn't ask to be rescued, and I'll be damned if I'm going to marry a guy who I can put up with just to keep Kyle from forcing his son on me. When I find the right guy, it'll be natural, it'll be for love—it won't be selection by the lesser of two evils."

Another blur appeared out of nowhere. "There you guys are! Holy crap, do you know they're tearing the place apart?" Beau had now joined us as well.

Shocked, I asked, "Who's tearing the place apart?"

"Kyle Richardson thinks Dad's hiding you. He's already done a room-to-room search of the house and guest quarters. They're searching the woods now."

I felt my resolve growing ever stronger. "I guess I'd better pick up the pace. I'll go back and I tell him he's nutso again."

Bruce was nearly pleading with his eyes when he said, "Camille . . . don't." We continued forward. I could feel Brent, Bruce and Beau getting more apprehensive with each stride.

As we approached the clearing to the back yard, I saw Hannah pacing under the canopy of trees. Bruce watched her with nothing but love in his eyes. The selfish part of me realized I'd tarnished her wedding whether that had been my intention or not. Trying to be more sensitive and realizing this was absolutely not the right time to throw a tantrum no matter how justified I felt, I said, "Bruce, I'm so sorry. I hope Hannah isn't mad."

Bruce stopped me in my tracks, put both hands on my shoulders and pulled me into a hug, "She's upset, but not with you. None of this is your fault. We handle this as a family. She's as much a part of our family now as you are, and she won't stand for Richardson's games any more than the rest of us."

"You should go to her. Tell her I'm really sorry . . . and Bruce?" His dark eyes looked fully into mine, "Thanks for coming to look for me. It means a lot."

He bobbed his head slightly, acknowledging me without making me feel like some girl who needed protecting. Brent slipped his arm around me, and Beau walked a few strides ahead of us. As the three of us came fully into view, I noticed that Bruce and Hannah were walking behind us, still in her wedding dress and he in his tux. Two blurs arrived on either side of Brent and me, Ben to my left and Bart to Brent's right. The emotion of the moment was not lost on me. My five brothers and my new sister-in-law surrounded me as we walked the last few steps to the driveway.

The music quieted and a hush fell over the guests. Gretchen and Will stood on the porch while Kyle Richardson stood to their side. They watched as the seven of us made our last few steps in their direction. Just before we were at an arm's distance from Mr. Richardson, I saw a silvery shimmering light come into focus, standing at his side. Gretchen's eyes watched the shimmering figure, and she glanced my way to see if I could see it, too. I nodded to her my silent answer. I could feel the strength from the figure, the warmth that emanated from it. It was Mom.

I could see her, really see her, not just her outline as she stood tall beside Mr. Richardson. Whatever she had tried to tell me in the woods was no longer a priority for her. She wasn't trying to say anything to me; she simply stood next to Mr. Richardson. She had always been protective of me, so I expected her to be glaring at him – she wasn't. She seemed to be looking at him in an affectionate way. Why would she be looking at him like that? I was thrilled to see her; maybe she had just positioned herself there to give me strength, to let me know she was there for me.

CHAPTER 13

Camille Benning – Charleston, SC

I wasn't sure what to expect. I felt like Beau was going to march right up to him and start swinging. He didn't. Beau stopped short just feet before the shimmering light. The men all seemed oblivious to it, but Hannah, Gretchen and I could see Mom.

Mr. Richardson spat out his words, fury seething through his pores, "I don't want my son to meet you, not yet. However, I refuse to let my bloodline perish, as your mother nearly extinguished it twenty-eight years ago. My son, Gage, is twenty-four. If he is not betrothed by his twenty-ninth birthday, I will summon you, and you will marry him. You will not take a husband before his twenty-ninth birthday. If he should become married before that date, no debt will be owed to my family. If it is you he marries, your debt will be repaid by your wedding vows. Do you understand my terms?"

In my mind I was silently cheering—five years. I wouldn't have to go through this whole ritual of finding a husband for five years! This was the best possible situation for me. No pressure, no reason for men to introduce themselves to me. I was ready to scream out "Yes!", but I didn't want to make a big mistake. "Mr. Richardson, I'm too new to this life to make this decision without counsel. I need to speak to my father, privately." I saw Will's posture straighten as his chest stretched.

"Of course, Camille, your family should counsel you on my offer."

I stepped through the door and into the front hallway. Will followed me and closed the door behind us. I very nearly squealed, "This is great, right?"

A pleased grin spread across his face, "Yes, this is excellent news. I think he offered the fairest deal he could under the circumstances. I've heard that his son, Gage, is a good man. Without a formal promise to you, other Centaur women may still consider him. If one of them chooses him for her husband before his twenty-ninth birthday, you owe their herd nothing."

I opened the door, not even waiting to be fully out of the house, "Mr. Richardson, I accept your offer."

His words were slow as his eyes nearly burrowed into mine, "You understand the gravity of your words?"

"I do."

"You will not commit yourself to another for the next five years?"

"I won't."

"Do you understand the consequences should you not honor your promise to me this evening?"

"I do."

Mr. Richardson stepped directly in front of me, his hands tight behind his back. I didn't know what it was about him, but he gave me one final threat, "If you dishonor our agreement, I will not hesitate to take my payment."

My eyes narrowed. I didn't need this added reminder. "Mr. Richardson, I am fully aware of the consequences. If at any time in the next five years you threaten my life or the life of someone in my family without justification, I won't hesitate to take yours. Just so we're clear."

There was a collective gasp in all directions. No one expected me to make the threat, but I wanted this man to know my mother had not raised a daughter to be weak, to be submissive, or to be manipulated by anyone. It wasn't an empty threat, and I would not hesitate to make good on it. I had not grown up with the luxury of a family – other than my mom. I grew up where if someone threatened your life, you'd better check their hands for a weapon. In a matter of days I knew there wasn't anything I wouldn't do for my new family, including not allowing this reject of a man to bully them. I put my back to him and walked away, allowing my threat to hang in the air, daring him to test me moments after I had made it.

A little louder than was necessary, but definitely spoken for my benefit, I heard, "William, thank you for allowing me to join in Bruce and Hannah's celebration this evening. It has been my pleasure to be a part of such an enchanting evening."

Brent was the first one to catch up to me. He whispered, "Geeze, remind me never to cross you. I thought Dad was going to have a heart attack back there. I bet your lessons from Mom tomorrow include not threatening the life of Herd Leaders."

"It wasn't a threat, Brent. That was my promise to him."

"Threatening to kill someone isn't something to be done lightly."

"Brent, you ever seen someone murdered right in front of you?"

"Uh. . . no."

"I didn't grow up here. I grew up in the real world: watching drive-bys, robberies and gang retaliation. I saw one guy killed over forty bucks. It can make you a little jaded. I wouldn't have said it if I didn't mean to follow through. Gretchen can give me any lesson she wants. If Kyle threatens you or anyone else in my family – it'll be the last thing he ever does."

"Camille, this is the real world, too. We may put a higher price tag on life than the people you grew up with. It doesn't mean our dangers are any less real or our warnings can be ignored."

"Maybe you're right, but I bet he doesn't try anything that could be construed as threatening. Think of my exchange with him as modern warfare – a pre-emptive strike."

Brent shook his head at me. He seemed unwilling to agree with me, but at least he decided not to argue the point further. Within minutes the party was again in full swing: Kyle Richardson was noticeably absent. As soon as the music returned, the makeshift dance floor was crowded, voices were again chattering loudly, and everyone was having a good time. For as massive as he was, Gus had great rhythm and was by far my favorite dance partner. I couldn't help but wonder how cool it would be to go to all the NFL games. He asked, "So, any chance you'd want to catch a movie this weekend?"

I gushed, "Um, okay. We can do that?" I still wasn't sure what was and wasn't okay.

He beamed back at me, "You bet. You choose someone in your family to escort us."

I thought of the choices. Although I was closest to Brent – he was not in favor of dating for the sake of dating. Maybe Beau? "Give me your number, and I'll send you a text with the *who* and *when*. You're sure no one will think it's a big deal?"

"There's a line-up of other Centaurs waiting to dance with you. You're welcome to tell every one of them that we have plans for next Friday." Gus' smile was all encompassing, and I couldn't help but smile at his jab against the others.

To be fair, I did dance with every other available Centaur. I don't know how many turns I had taken on the dance floor, but enough that I needed to rest. I made my way to a table where Brent was sitting. I desperately wanted to ask him if a movie was okay, but decided to wait and ask Beau when no one else was around.

I had just barely arrived at the table when Drake and his beautiful fiancé, Bianca, came to the same table and sat with us. I was a little nervous given his reaction to me in the woods, but he wasn't glaring at me or anything. The music was still going full tilt. I had seen the two of them dancing on the floor and knew they had to be near exhaustion as well. Brent and Drake seemed to be pretty good friends, immediately engaging in conversation about some sporting event. I lacked the energy to pretend to have interest in their conversation; Bianca's interest mirrored mine.

Bianca looked over at me with a thoughtful smile, "Is it true that you are a long lost Centauride?"

I hadn't heard of this word before. "Centauride? – I'm sure I should already know, but what is it?"

Bianca smiled sweetly, "A female Centaur."

It still felt odd that everyone so openly spoke about creatures I'd considered nothing more than myths until a week ago. "That's what everyone keeps telling me."

"So, it's true. You really had no idea?"

"My mom died recently. I didn't know about my . . ." What was the right word? "ancestry."

"You're lucky to be a Strayer. They are one of the strongest herds."

"Really?"

She smiled sweetly, "I've watched all the eligible Centaurs vying for your attention tonight. It's hard to choose which herd to join. Trust me, I was where you are recently. I just picked Drake a month ago."

"The choosing process still seems so foreign to me, but I guess there isn't a rush."

"I imagine you had people breaking down your door when news spread of your arrival."

"The front door's still intact, but I did meet a bunch of men today." I leaned in and did my best to keep my voice low, "Is it true there's no dating, or was Brent pulling my leg?"

Conspiratorially she answered, "Yeah, you window shop for a while, and you can go on a chaperoned date, but even those are frowned on."

"Why?"

"Because if you go on a couple dates with a guy and then decide he's not the right one, it almost looks like a rejection. If a Centaur is rejected by a Centauride, other Centaurides might not think to give him a chance. Why take someone else's reject when there are so many to choose from."

"And once you choose, then there's no changing your mind?"

"No, it's a final decision."

"How long did it take you to decide?"

Her eyes darted to Drake, I'm sure to see if he was still engrossed in conversation with Brent. "It was the hardest decision of my life. I agonized over it for weeks."

"Weeks? That doesn't seem like a long time." I realized we were whispering, and this was obviously not a conversation she wanted to share with her future husband. I motioned for her to step away from the table, and she quickly followed my lead. Both Brent and Drake stood up when they realized Bianca and I were going for a walk. I shot them both a look and motioned for them to stay at the table. They did.

We strolled across the grounds and were well beyond everyone's earshot before she spoke again. "From the time I was sixteen I had men anxiously hoping I'd choose them. I went to college first. My mom told me she picked my dad at sixteen, and although she loved him and didn't regret her decision, she knew that the things that were important at sixteen were different at twenty-two."

"So you're twenty-two?"

"Yes. These last few months almost killed me. I knew I couldn't put it off any longer. My father had already made it pretty clear that he was going to arrange a marriage. I was terrified of who he might pick. He started bringing Centaur men home for dinner; all of them seemed to look at me like I was a piece of meat. I couldn't take the chance, so I made my decision last month."

"Drake? He's really handsome. That was probably an easy choice." I remembered his calloused hands catching me in mid-air right before I nearly fell off the porch and his quick reaction when I'd ticked off Kyle Richardson. Drake seemed like a great catch: smoking hot, kind, super-fast, and definitely protective. "I could see why you picked him."

Bianca looked around to make sure we were still alone. "He wasn't actually my first choice. Don't get me wrong, I know he'll make a wonderful husband, but I had planned to choose another until my mother disapproved."

"Really? I thought all Centaur men were nearly perfect?"

I could tell Bianca was apprehensive talking about her first choice. "My mother hated the family of the man I wanted to choose, so she wouldn't hear of it. She said it would be a terrible fate, and she would never give me her blessing."

CHAPTER 14

Camille Benning – Charleston, SC

"Don't parents mellow out after a while? I mean, after the wedding she would have been fine with it."

Bianca shook her head, "She's our family's matriarch. I couldn't go against her wishes. Falling out of her favor would have impacted my abilities."

"Abilities? You aren't just automatically psychic and stuff?"

"Oh sure, I can read other's thoughts, but some in my family have telekinetic powers. Those have to be given to the daughter from the mother."

"Wait, like moving objects with your mind?"

"Yeah! My mom's amazing. She's one of the strongest I've ever seen! She can lift a semi-truck while carrying on a conversation." I could tell this was still a sensitive subject with Bianca, and I was more than surprised that she would openly share it with me. After she collected her thoughts again, she said, "I couldn't disappoint her."

I'd never been a fan of idle gossip, but Bianca had piqued my interest, "So, the guy you wanted to marry – did he know?"

She didn't want to talk about it. Her eyes fell from mine when all she said was, "He knew."

"He was an okay guy? It was just his family that your mom didn't approve of?"

She forced a smile at me. I knew there was more to this story that no way would she tell a stranger. "He was. . . is an incredible guy. It's not his fault what his parents or grandparents did, but Mom was convinced that an apple doesn't fall far from the tree. She absolutely hates his grandfather and told me she would never give me her blessing."

"So how did you pick Drake?"

"I'd known him forever. He's sweet and kind. I knew we would mesh okay." I couldn't help but notice that Bianca still wouldn't look at me, and I knew she needed a subject change.

"I wonder if my mom was telekinetic?"

Bianca answered, "She was a Chiron, so I'm sure she was."

Bianca said, "Chiron," with reverence, as if it was a big deal. I didn't want to press her about it, but knew I needed to find out more about my mother's family. "So do you think, since my mom's dead, I won't ever be able to do telekinetic stuff?"

"You can still talk to your mom, right?"

My cheeks flushed. I was defective, and Bianca would be the first person outside my family to know. "I can see her, sometimes, but I can't hear her."

"Really? You know, she's right here with us now."

"How can you tell?"

Bianca giggled at me, "Duh, I can see her."

"Does she want to say anything to me?"

Bianca looked past my shoulder and nodded, "She said she's proud of you. You handled yourself with strength and courage, but there is something she needs to tell you about Mr. Richardson." Bianca paused for a second, looking back at me, "She doesn't want me to know. She's still very strong." Bianca furrowed her eyebrows as if sizing up my invisible mother. "Once someone passes over, their strength seems to diminish by the day until after a while they just leave entirely. Your mom must have been seriously strong while she was alive because she doesn't seem to be weakening."

I chuckled, "I don't know, I never saw her lift a semi-truck in the air, but she was tough – she didn't take crap from anyone." I wasn't sure why I felt such a kinship to Bianca, but I confessed, "I miss her. So if she died before she could teach me all the stuff I'm supposed to know, does that mean I'll never be like everyone else?"

"I bet the two of you find a way. You just need to practice communicating with her."

I was seriously excited that both Gretchen and Bianca believed it was only a matter of time before I'd work out the kinks. Bianca was looking off into the distance, and I wondered if there was something more she wasn't telling me. "So this guy you didn't choose, that you wanted to – why was he on your short list?"

Her face took on a sad look, one foreign to the happy expressions I'd seen up until now. "We went to college together. Centaurs aren't allowed to date, at least not unsupervised. But we pushed the envelope and met each other at movies, football games, the library, none were ever technically a date because we never went together – we just happened to keep meeting each other. He was who I saw in my future."

"If you can tell the future, and you see him there, doesn't that mean you'll end up with him?"

"I wish. I can't see the future. But when I dreamed of the future, he was the one I was tied to."

"But you picked Drake anyway?" This didn't make sense.

"Don't get me wrong, Drake's great. My family approves, and I care about him."

"But you wanted someone else. Does he know?" I felt bad for Drake. This whole concept seemed ludicrous.

"Drake knows." She dropped my stare and seemed ashamed of what she shared next, "They were best friends. We all grew up together."

I felt my eyes widen, "Best friends?"

"Past tense. They haven't spoken since my parents made the announcement."

"I'm sorry." It was all I could say. This Centaur selection process seemed dumb; I looked back at the table and wondered how Drake felt about the whole thing. He may have found a woman to carry on his bloodline, but he'd lost his closest friend in the process. Maybe because I hadn't grown up knowing what I was or because I didn't feel particularly tied to my ancestry, I couldn't imagine the pain the three of them must have gone through. "So do you still talk to him? The other guy?"

"No, it's too painful. He knew it was a possibility. We all knew how my mother felt about his grandfather. We'd hoped that she could let the past be, but it was too much a part of her."

"What'd his grandfather do to your mom?"

"He tried to buy her."

"Buy her?"

"His bloodline was in jeopardy. My family's one of the few Centaur lines that isn't wealthy. He was desperate and made a plea to my grandparents for my mom. When they declined, he went to the bank and bought the note on their farm. He evicted them and humiliated them in front of everyone. My mom's never forgiven him for it."

"Holy crap, that's terrible."

"Centaurs can be ruthless, especially Centaurs who are approaching the end of eligibility. Choose wisely, Camille. My mom isn't the only one that something like this happened to."

"From what I can tell, I don't think money is much of an issue, but thanks for the warning anyway."

"There are lots of other ways families can be manipulated." Bianca whispered, "Like trading."

The hair on the back of my neck suddenly stood on end, "What're you talking about?"

She looked in all directions again. "You didn't hear this from me, but . . . you've got four eligible brothers, right?" I nodded, not know where this was going. "If your parents get desperate for one of their sons to be married, they could trade you to another family in exchange for a wife for one of their sons."

"What? No way!"

"It happens all the time, Camille. If you don't choose someone quickly, your family will choose for you."

I didn't want to bring up the arrangement I'd made with Kyle Richardson. She and Drake weren't anywhere around when it happened, and it wasn't something I wanted others to know about. With that agreement, there was no way I could be auctioned off to the highest bidder, but the idea that this was done to others turned my stomach. I wondered why the family had been so welcoming: it couldn't be for that. I felt a pit forming in my stomach. I didn't want to believe her.

Bianca must have sensed that she had struck a chord because she said, "A friend of mine, Grace, told me about you."

I was still reeling from the fact that maybe my family wasn't as genuine as they had appeared. When I looked back at her, I didn't have the strength for anything more. I was worried I might fold in on myself.

"Grace can see the future. She always tells me that as far as actually seeing someone's future, free will has a lot to do with it. Knowledge of the future has a way of impeding fate, so she rarely tells me anything good." Her wide smile reappeared, her eyes sparkled, "But she did tell me: you and I are going to be best friends. None of the choices either of us makes in this lifetime will drive a wedge between us."

Just like that, I had a new BFF. I had called my best friend in California, Daniel, several times during the week. He was excited that things were going so well and was a little shocked when I told him about the new car and about intending to stay a little while longer – I couldn't wait for the night to be over so I could call and tell him about Bianca.

After Bianca left, I went into the house and sat in my bedroom. I thought about what she'd said—the telekinetic powers. I tried to think of a time my mom did that in front of me and laughed out loud when I remembered – her purse! My mom's purse was always stuffed full, so full, it was impossible for me to find anything in it. Yet she never even looked in the enormous bag: she just reached in and it seemed like whatever she wanted jumped into her fingers. I remembered one time when I had looked in her purse for the car keys for five minutes before dropping it onto the table in frustration. She walked over to the table, put her hand in the bag, didn't even look at the gaping mess, and said, "Here they are," then tossed the keys to me.

I shook my head at the memory. Still chuckling to myself, I looked above the mantle and saw a beautifully framed picture of a white Arabian horse cantering up a rolling hill. Another memory unfolded. The terror from the memory washed over me. I was a little girl, maybe five. We had moved into a second floor apartment that had a high security garage at ground level. My mom had just unloaded the last box. The garage had one of those heavy steel doors, and she said, "Cami, get away from the door. It'll squish you like a bug."

For the first few seconds I did as I was told, but just as the door reached the halfway mark, I saw my stuffed white horse forgotten inside, laying on a box. That white horse had been my constant companion as a child. I didn't want it to be locked inside, so I dashed under the closing door to save it while her back was turned. I had tripped on the return trip out of the garage, and my legs were in the garage door's path. It wasn't one of the new doors that instantly pops back up if something is in the way; all five hundred pounds trapped me and pressed hard on my legs as I screamed.

I could feel the gears trying to turn in an effort to use the door as a guillotine on my legs. She didn't come to me, she didn't scream for help, she stood several feet away and looked at the door, willing it to let me free. As her concentration increased, I felt the pressure of the heavy door subside. Her voice sounded strained when she yelled, "Now, Cami, pull your legs free, now." I did and a second later the steel door crashed to the cement and locked itself into the eyelets securing it in place. When I was free, she wiped the hot tears from my cheeks, lifted me into her arms and carried me upstairs.

As a child, the fear of nearly losing my legs paled in comparison to the shame of disobeying her. Once the tears subsided, I confessed, "I'm sorry, Momma, my horse is scared of the dark."

"It's okay, Cami. Sometimes I'm scared of the dark, too."

"You made the door let me go."

"Shhh, don't tell anyone. It's a secret."

Never once did we talk about it again. I could remember having fuzzy dreams of the incident, but this was the first time the whole event replayed in my mind. Something about the painting of the white horse and the conversation with Bianca made me remember. I wasn't sure if my mom's spirit was still anywhere near me, but I talked to her anyway.

"You moved the door. When I was little – when we moved up to Orange County, you kept the door from crushing my legs." Nothing, I didn't smell her perfume, I didn't see her, but I continued anyway, "You have to teach me how. I know you didn't want this life for me, but you have to help me." Still nothing. I wanted so badly to see her, or know that she was with me. The words were out before I could stop them, "I can't lose you again. Show me how to talk to you."

CHAPTER 15

Camille Benning – Charleston, SC

I walked downstairs to find Brent with a bowl of oatmeal, reading the Sunday funnies. He asked me, "So'd you have fun last night?"

"I guess so. That stuff with Kyle Richardson was a little over the top, right?"

"Which part? The part where you told him you'd marry his son if he couldn't find anyone better, or the part where you threatened to kill him in front of everyone?"

"Yeah, both were a little crazy."

"Camille, you can't go around threatening people, especially Herd Leaders."

"It looks like I can. I did."

Brent rolled his eyes, "Okay, you can't do it without getting in trouble."

"Like what, someone'll take my birthday away?"

"There are worse things than joining the Richardson Herd." I remembered Bianca's warning last night and felt an iciness taking hold toward Brent.

"All right, I'll bite. What are some of the things they can do to me?"

"Send your mother's spirit to the pasture for starters."

"What? Why? They can't do that!"

Brent placed his hand over mine, all the humor drained from him, "Yes, they can. Spirits aren't supposed to stay in our world. If one starts to create problems for living Centaurs, a Herd Leader can have them banished."

"But, I haven't even talked to her yet!"

"Then don't threaten Herd Leaders. If I were you, I'd call Mr. Richardson and apologize. New or not, he won't stand for you threatening him in front of everybody."

I gritted my teeth, "I told you, it wasn't a threat—that was my promise to him."

"Camille, you aren't back in 'the hood.' There are repercussions for your actions here."

"*The hood*? I grew up in Oceanside, you jackass."

Brent let go of my hand, "I know this is hard for you. I'm just trying to help."

"You want to help me? Find Gage Richardson a wife so I'm not stuck with him, and get it out of your head that I'll ever be like everyone else."

"I already know you aren't like anyone else. My issue is the more waves you create, the harder this'll be for everyone."

"The harder what will be?"

Brent looked over his shoulder, after verifying that no prying ears were present, "Centaurides are super powerful. You know why Dad has such a successful business? Because Mom knows what the stock market is going to do. All five of us work with Dad, but no one recommends anything to our clients unless Mom says so."

"How is that powerful?"

"That's how all Centaur women are. The matriarch is in charge of everything." Brent looked over his shoulder again, still satisfied that we were alone, "There's no way Dad met your mom the way he said he did. Mom would have destroyed him."

"I'm not following you, Brent."

"Something more went on, and we aren't going to find out what it is until you can figure out how to communicate with your mom."

"People have affairs, Brent."

"Not Centaurs, not ever." His voice had a finality to it. There was something more that I hadn't been told. Brent asked me, "Can you hear her at all?" I shook my head that I couldn't. "Has Dad said anything to you about the Lost Herd?"

"The what?"

"Never mind. I just wondered."

"No one's told me much of anything. What's the Lost Herd?"

"It's probably nothing . . . I'm not sure." We heard footsteps coming down the steps and Brent visibly tensed.

Will came around the corner wearing plaid pajama pants, fluffy sheepskin slippers and a white t-shirt. His face was unshaven, and he went straight for the coffee pot. "You two're up early today."

Before I could answer, Brent answered for us, "We're just leaving."

Will looked at his watch, "Where to?"

"On the boat with Bianca and Drake."

Will looked disappointed, "A little more notice and I would have tagged along."

"Sorry Dad. Camille and Bianca hit it off last night. Thought they'd like to go catch some sun. We'll be back in a few hours."

"Sounds good. Keep the radio on."

Brent hadn't mentioned going out on the boat, although it sounded like a great idea. I felt much more at ease asking Bianca questions than I did Gretchen, especially after what she told me last night. From what Brent started talking about, I wanted to find out what else he could tell me, too.

CHAPTER 16

Drake Nash – Charleston, SC – Sunday Morning

I heard my phone ringing and groped for my nightstand, trying to make the ringing stop. We'd stayed out pretty late, and I had worked the last thirteen days in a row. Today was my only day off for a while, and I planned to spend it in bed. When I picked up my phone, I saw Brent's smiling face staring back at me from the screen on my Droid, waiting for me to answer. I wanted to push "ignore."

It might be important. I could hear the gravel in my own voice, "This better be good, Brent."

"Good Morning, Drake. Sleep well?"

"Why are you calling so early?"

"Bianca and Camille decided they wanted to make a trip out on the water today. You up for it?"

My blood froze. For a second it felt like it had turned to ice and my heart forgot how to push it through my veins. "Uh, I guess so. When?"

"Camille and I are in the car now. We can pick you up in five minutes."

"Stop for coffee. Make it ten." I pushed "end." My palms were already sweating. I said to no one but myself – *this is a seriously bad idea.*

When my dad told me that Bianca had chosen me, I didn't think I could ever ask for anything more in my life. She was smart, educated, funny, beautiful, and she came from an honorable family. She had her pick of any eligible Centaur out there and had chosen me. I didn't even know I was in the running. My best friend growing up had been in love with her since he was twelve, so in love that he took risks, chances he wasn't supposed to take. None of our kind is allowed to date before betrothal, but he said he didn't care. It was Bianca or no one for him. When she chose me, I didn't know what to say to him. He called as soon as he heard, to tell me congratulations and wish me the best – but that was the last time I talked to him. He hadn't called in over a month, and I assumed our friendship was now officially over.

Bianca was the real deal. I could get a new best friend if it meant that my bloodline was secure. My parents were so proud you'd have thought I single-handedly brought peace to the Middle East. Last night was one of the first times Bianca and I had been together since her parents made the announcement. When I picked her up for Bruce and Hannah's wedding, she was stunning. It was the first unsupervised conversation we'd had since the announcement was made. I had expected her father to accompany us, but her parents followed us in their car. During the car ride to the wedding, she mentioned that she wanted a longer-than-normal engagement. I was so star struck at the time, I think I would have agreed to wait until my deathbed if she had asked me to.

One year. I thought a year would be a piece of cake. When I escorted her to the wedding, I knew that the most beautiful woman at the wedding wasn't wearing white; she was holding my bicep, walking in lock step with me. We were milling around making small talk when she said, "I'm anxious to meet Camille Strayer. I hear she's new to our kind. Tonight will be her first introduction to Centaur society."

I wanted to appear interested, but I couldn't have cared less. "Who's she?"

"Apparently Will Strayer had a Centaur mistress. Camille is his daughter. I hope we get to meet her."

My interest was piqued. "A Centaur mistress? Really?"

"Everyone's talking about it. She just arrived this week and, from what I heard, knew nothing about us."

No sooner had Bianca's words escaped than I saw Will escorting Camille from the house. She looked nervous, pre-occupied, as they stood on the porch and looked out into the crowd. My eyes locked on her, her blood called to me, *screamed* to me. She took her first step down the stairs and something in the distance caught her attention. I saw her take her second step and something wasn't right, her footing looked wrong. I knew she would tumble if no one did anything. Will wasn't paying attention. I could see Brent and Beau were much closer than I was, but neither was watching. I let Bianca's hand go and sprinted to her, stretching both my hands out to catch her before she could miss the last step. She landed squarely in my arms, and I froze.

She would have gone face first onto the ground had I not caught her in mid-air. Her body was light. I supported her with my right hand on her face and my left on her stomach. Time felt as if it had slowed down. I placed her carefully on her feet. In that single second it seemed as though we were the only two in the universe. As she stood there looking at me, I saw the most beautiful, milk-chocolate eyes staring at me. When she thanked me, it was hard to breath. I muttered something in reply, and she held her hand out to thank me. I was horrified. I knew our customs didn't allow for the two of us to touch, and in that second I knew why. Bianca had chosen me. I was betrothed, promised, and I felt an irrational desire for Camille. I couldn't explain it. I wanted to grab her in my arms and never let her go. Somehow my mind found the strength to override my heart's urges.

When I returned to Bianca, I expected her to be furious with me. Not only had I touched another woman, I had touched her in front of two hundred others. Bianca surprised me with a sweet smile and a gentle caress on my cheek. "Thanks so much for catching her. That was such a kind thing to do." I was floored—she wasn't upset in the least. Bianca caught me watching Camille several times through the ceremony. Never once did she show the slightest concern that I was so obviously captivated with the newcomer.

After the ceremony, Bianca prodded me to pay attention to a conversation between William Strayer and Kyle Richardson. The conversation had been strained initially, then Camille said something hateful to Gage's dad. Without thinking it through, I sprinted to her, gathered her in my arms, and ran as fast as my legs would take us. I stopped a mile away, set Camille on her feet, but didn't back away from her. As I stood looking in those milk-chocolate eyes, I felt my world starting to unravel. I tried to tell myself that I would have done the same thing for any woman about to be attacked by a Centaur.

Seconds later, Brent arrived and reminded me of Bianca waiting at the reception. I knew I had screwed up; there would be repercussions. I had touched a Centauride, twice, in front of my fiancé. Without another word, I ran back the way I had come, trying to think of a plausible excuse for my actions. Any other Centauride in the world would have threatened our engagement, or at the very least chastised me, but Bianca seemed both thrilled and approving of my stepping in to help Camille.

Yesterday it had been easier to hide my interest in Camille where there were so many others. But today, on the boat, with Bianca, Camille, and Brent, it would be impossible to conceal. I needed to find a reason not to go, to keep away from Camille, to keep from losing Bianca.

I heard the doorbell ring and knew I was out of time. I'd just let Brent know something had come up. I eased my front door open, fully prepared to tell Brent I couldn't go when I looked down into those same captivating, milk-chocolate eyes.

She wore a wide smile, "Hi, Drake. Brent's on the phone, so I thought I'd let you know we're here. I'm so glad you're going with us today."

My heart leapt trying to escape from my chest, and all excuses I'd found to stay at my apartment evaporated. She stood there in a swimsuit covered by a see-through wrap that left nothing to the imagination. She seemed oblivious to the way she looked, standing an arm's length away. In that moment I didn't care about my bloodline, my engagement to Bianca, my parents, or anything I valued as a Centaur – I was filled with blind lust. My arms ached to pull her to me. I froze, unwilling to say or do anything – I didn't trust myself.

Camille waved her hand in front of my face with an enormous smile. "Hello? Are you feeling okay?"

I could feel beads of sweat forming on my forehead. I was sure my heart had forgotten how to beat. When I hadn't responded quickly enough for her, she placed her palm on my cheek, and whispered, "Drake, do you need to lie down?"

Explosions went off in my head, and electric pulses raced through my body. I stepped away from her, nearly tripping over a pair of shoes patiently waiting by the door. I wasn't at all in control of my motor functions but knew I couldn't possibly trust myself to be near her.

"You know, I think you guys might need to go without me today." I could feel my face flushing bright red.

"Are you sick? Do you need to go to the doctor?"

"I'm sure it's nothing. You have fun today." I closed the door gently while she still stood there. I backed up against the wall and slid to the floor, trying to get a handle on myself. After just a few seconds, I realized I could breathe again, my pulse was slowing, and I squatted there with my back to the wall for support while my body came under control again. What in the hell just happened?

"Drake, we aren't leaving you," Brent's voice called through the closed door. "I'm giving you to the count of three, and I'm coming in."

I shook my head, knowing I could create a decent explanation for my absence to Brent. I opened the door and was fully in control. "Sorry, man, I can't go today."

"Camille said you looked sick. You don't look sick to me." Brent furrowed his brows, his instincts telling him there was more going on than what his eyes saw.

I made an effort to sound normal, "I'm fine. I just have a lot to do today."

"Hello-o-o-o, Bianca's coming. Tell me you don't want to see *her* on a deck chair! Grab your shorts; let's go."

I should have punched him for his comment about my fiancé, but she wasn't the one my eyes were interested in seeing, and I couldn't bear for him to know that I didn't trust myself around Camille. "Yeah, I don't know how her father would feel about us out to sea without an escort."

"What are you, dense? Camille and I will be there. You have an escort. Let's go."

"I've got a ton of work to do around here today. Maybe next time."

Brent knew something was up. He turned his head to the side, considering possibilities. "Drake, is there something you aren't telling me?"

"No, I'm just not a Strayer. I can't go for a sail whenever the mood strikes me."

"Look, you know the rules as well as I do. I can't take your fiancé out on the boat without you. Camille doesn't have any friends, and Bianca was nice to her last night. Do this for me. None of us want Camille to go back to California. If she and Bianca hit it off, she'll be less likely to leave. I promise you can hang out in one of the state rooms and do whatever work you need to. Just come along."

I wasn't accustomed to deceit, but when Brent said it was possible Camille might go back to the west coast, I felt my heart lurch again. Even if she were never to be mine, I knew I would go through withdrawals with her so far away. That was all the coaxing I needed. "Give me two minutes."

Within an hour we had picked up Bianca, made it to the Yacht Club, and were out on blue water. Brent wasn't kidding; Camille and Bianca were fast friends. Although Brent and I had never been extremely tight, he was fun to be around, and it was great to hang out with another guy since I'd lost my closest friend following the news of my engagement to his covert girlfriend. The ladies were tanning on the deck while we talked about the upcoming Clemson / Game Cocks seasons.

"Hey, Drake," Bianca called, "why don't you two come and join us?"

We were on the upper deck, and I waved down my acknowledgement, then said to Brent, "I guess duty calls."

"Maybe for you." Brent said with a smirk.

"You're going down there with me."

"Who's going to drive the boat, Dumb Ass."

I looked in all directions. We were easily five miles from shore with not another boat of any kind within sight. There was no way I was going down there by myself. "Just anchor it and come on." Brent cut the engines, dropped anchor, and turned up the music as the waves rocked the boat gently in the breeze.

The four of us made small talk for about thirty minutes. Then Bianca said, "So Camille, how are you holding up? This is all new for you."

Camille answered, "I love it here. I'm a little in awe of everything. A week ago I thought I was all alone in the world. I'm still a little surprised every morning that I wake up to find out I really do have a family, I'm living on the east coast, and . . . the other stuff."

"The other stuff, you mean – being a magical, mythical being?" Bianca, Brent and I couldn't help but laugh, and Camille looked flustered. I felt bad for her. This was a pretty astronomical shock, but she seemed to be taking it all in stride.

"Yeah, something like that." Camille readjusted on her deck chair. When she did, she stretched her long tanned legs out, pointed her toes, and rested her head on her palms, soaking up every bit of the sun's rays. In my mind I started fantasizing all sorts of things that were grossly inappropriate, and forced myself to look adoringly at Bianca. Although Bianca was absolutely beautiful with her pale blue eyes and blonde hair—my eyes continued to wander to Camille. I was ashamed of myself. I was acting like a hormone-filled teenager – not the way an engaged Centaur should behave.

"Hey, Brent," Bianca asked, "Do you have any video games on this thing?"

"There's an Xbox Kinect in one of the staterooms."

"Oh, I love those. I need to get out of the sun for a little while. Could we go play?"

Brent looked at me as if it were my responsibility to object. I agreed. "We should all go."

"Don't be silly! You stay up here and keep Camille company. She's got the complexion of a Mayan Goddess. It's good for her to keep working on her tan – she's still got a man to find."

Brent stammered, "Bianca, I don't think it's such a great idea for us to be alone in a stateroom."

"Oh, do you have feelings for me, Brent?" she asked sarcastically.

"No! I mean . . . it wouldn't be appropriate. I mean, I don't think Drake would. . ." Brent was stammering and looked like he needed a life preserver.

Bianca's angelic voice asked, "Drake, you don't mind if Brent and I play the Xbox for a little while, do you?"

“Uh, no, that’s okay with me.” I should have objected. I should have insisted we all go below deck together, but I didn’t.

She squealed and leapt from her deck chair, “Great! Okay, here, keep Camille company,” she motioned for me to take the seat she had just vacated. Before I even had a chance to protest, she was through the cabin door with Brent reluctantly following her down the stairs.

I was so nervous I thought I was going to get sea sick. I couldn’t think of anything clever to say, and I couldn’t keep my eyes off of Camille. She must have sensed my vibes because she didn’t seem comfortable making eye contact with me either. I knew I needed to say something before she realized how I ached for her.

“So, do you miss California?”

“I do, but not as bad as I thought I would. Gretchen and Will are pretty amazing. It’s a little like every day’s a vacation.”

“I know it isn’t any of my business, but are you a full-blooded Centaur?” I knew from what Bianca had told me that she was, but I had to keep myself distracted. It was possible for a Centaur and human to marry and have a family, but those children were shunned from our community. Will would have never had Camille at Bruce’s wedding if she weren’t pureblood.

“Yeah,” she answered with a chuckle, “but I think I’m a defective one.”

“Defective?”

“I’m told I’m supposed to be able to communicate with spirits. I can see my mom sometimes, but I can’t hear her. I’m supposed to be able to see the future, but I can’t even tell if that cloud over there is going to produce rain. I definitely can’t read minds either. Too bad I didn’t come with a receipt; Will might want to return me.”

“I doubt that. I think all that just takes practice.”

“I hope so.”

“It’s all still new. Bianca told me you only found out about everything a week ago.”

"Not even a week ago. I called Will Tuesday night and was on a plane a few hours later."

Her eyes were so kind and full of life. I envied her for not having grown up like the rest of us. From the time I was a toddler, I knew what I was, knew that I had to hide my strength and speed from humans, deny who I was. I longed to touch her skin, feel the warmth of her flesh; I shook off my irrational desires and tried to stay on subject. "But you didn't know you were a Centaur?"

"Uh, no. I thought I'd found my long lost father. I wasn't expecting any of this."

"Why didn't your mom tell you, I mean, before. . ." I stopped in mid-sentence when I saw Camille was still sensitive about her mother's death. Her eyes clouded right there in front of me, and she pursed her lips together. I'd struck a bad chord I didn't mean to and wanted to comfort her. "I'm sorry."

"It's okay. I'm not always such a head case. I just miss her." Camille was in so much pain. I tried to reason that if I only had a single parent and lost her, then was tossed into all the complexities of our society, I didn't think I would handle it as well as she was handling it.

In a happier voice, Camille said, "Let me try to read your mind."

"Uh, no. That's okay. I keep mine blocked all the time." Panic swept me. I was able to keep my mind blocked, but I worried about my defenses if I got too close to her. I couldn't let her know how she'd affected me, or how much I wanted her.

Camille laughed, "Even better, so I can practice without worry of seeing some gross guy stuff."

I froze, "Uh, Camille, I don't think that's such a great idea." She ignored me and looked into my eyes; mine refused to look away. I blocked my thoughts with more force than I'd ever used in my life.

She looked a little frustrated with herself, and I breathed a sigh of relief. Camille confessed, "Huh, nothing. Let me try this." She swung her legs over the side of the deck chair so we were seated facing each other. Camille put her hands on either side of my temples; our lips were mere inches apart. I heard the splashing of the waves, a seagull echoing a warning overhead, and breeze whipping the flag at the ship's stern. I continued blocking my thoughts, refusing to let my wall crumble.

Camille repositioned her hands from my temples, sliding them down, cradling my face in her palms. Her gentle touch threw me off guard. In that moment I didn't care if she read every thought in my head. My mind's wall disintegrated in front of both of us. Her eyes widened when she saw a glimpse of my desire for her. I knew I could control my impulses no matter how strong they were to take her in my arms and hold her body to mine. I had just filled her mind with images of the two of us, where I wanted to be and what I wanted to be doing with her: walking in a tall meadow, the sun bearing down; on a snowcapped mountain, the only heat from our intertwined bodies; swimming in the crystal clear waters of the Caribbean near a deserted cove. I savored each of these fantasies and shamelessly shared them with her, each more erotic than the previous.

What I wasn't expecting was her reaction to what was going through my mind. I expected her to slap me, to leap away and scream, to call me hundreds of names that I deserved – I never expected that her mouth would close the gap with mine in an instant.

Her eyes closed, and I felt her soft lips press hard on to mine. My arms did the unthinkable and pulled her seated body off her deck chair and fully onto me. My veins, that last night felt like ice was coursing through them when I saw her, now had molten lava pumping through my body, and I had no recourse but to melt into her. Nothing else in the world mattered beyond the feel of her skin against me, the heat that generated between us, and her mouth on mine. We sat wrapped in each other for a short time before we both came to our senses and released.

As I felt her body go tense, I sputtered out, "I'm so sorry, Camille, I didn't mean for. . .I'm so sorry."

She shook her head, "I wasn't expecting . . . the images." I could see the turmoil on her face. "Drake," she realized she was still wrapped around me and stood up, distancing herself from me, "we can't."

With a heavy heart, threatening to slowly break in this moment, "I know." I hung my head, unable to look into her brown eyes.

"I mean, we can't let that happen again, ever."

"I know."

"You're engaged to Bianca."

"I know."

"If she ever finds out. . ."

I looked up, purposely not making contact with her eyes, "She won't. I'm sorry. I don't know what came over me."

Camille took the towel off of her deck chair, wrapped herself up in it and sat down. I knew I shouldn't, but I felt a longing for Camille. The towel could have been made of kryptonite, and it wouldn't have diminished my hunger. She stammered, "I should apologize to you. You told me not to try . . . you know . . . to read your mind." Her face flushed a deep crimson, and I wondered if she had been reacting to my desire or if she had a yearning of her own.

I knelt down beside her and rested my head on her knees, "I'm an idiot. I knew I shouldn't have come." She didn't make a sound, and I didn't have the courage to look at her. "I swear I didn't plan this."

I felt Camille's fingers running through my hair. Her words were quiet, "I think we should steer clear of each other."

"Yeah," I wrapped my arms around her shins, still not able to let go, "I promise, Camille, I'll never do something like that again. I'll take it to the grave."

"Is Bianca going to, you know – know?"

"Only if you think about it. Do you know how to block your thoughts?" She shook her head that she didn't. Dammit! No matter how strongly I felt for Camille -I couldn't risk my family's bloodline. Camille looked horrified; hopefully her fear of being exposed would keep us both safe. Being this close to her was wrong; I had to let her go. I forced a smile, hoping she couldn't see through it to the emptiness I felt as I moved away from her. I said, "Just don't think about the kiss. If your mind starts to wander, think about a movie or something."

"Okay—think about something else, got it. Gretchen told me only the women Centaurs could read thoughts. You can't read my mind, right?"

I couldn't help but smirk at her, "Technically, you should only be able to read the thoughts I'm not protecting. You caught me a little off guard when you touched me."

"Obviously," she answered.

I couldn't help but laugh at her. I was mortified with my actions, and I knew she shared the same guilt. I could see it. I decided to change the subject before we had any kind of relapse, "I know this is all new to you. Did you find someone you liked last night?" She gave me the strangest look, and I felt the heat rising up again within me. "I mean at Bruce's wedding, you met a bunch of Centaur men. Any of them contenders? You seemed to have hit it off with Gus."

"Ha, that's the one good thing I have to look forward to. I don't have to choose anyone for five years."

Her statement surprised me, and I looked up at her, "What do you mean?"

"It's a really long story, but I'm not going to choose anyone until I'm twenty-seven."

"Your father's okay with that?"

"Sure, why wouldn't he be?"

"I've just never heard of a Centauride waiting so long."

"Good things come to those who wait."

I nodded. I was a lucky man to be chosen by Bianca. I'd find a way to keep Camille out of my thoughts, too. I took Camille's hand, telling myself to savor the few more seconds I had with her before this fantasy was over and my reality kicked back in. "Let's go find Brent and Bianca."

As we walked toward the doorway to go to the lower deck, a large wave rocked the boat hard and Camille fell into me. Steadying her, my arms found her one more time. When I didn't let go, I thought she'd chastise me, but she pulled me into the wall just to the left of the double doors, so no one could see us through the glass. I didn't release her, I couldn't. I could feel my hands shaking. She belonged in them.

Her eyes were wide, her voice accusatory, "Never again, right?"

I couldn't deny the lust I felt for her. My hands refused to release her. My body leaned into hers as I whispered, "Not after this one." This time, it was *me* who closed the distance between us. I knew it was wrong. I knew if we were caught, we'd be screwed, and the shame we'd bring on our families would be unbearable, but I lost myself in Camille anyway. All the things I knew I should care about didn't matter when she was in my arms. I told myself this would absolutely be the last time my arms were able to hold her, and I wanted to drink her in, to consume her, to cherish this memory for the rest of eternity. I didn't hold back. In that moment, I shared every ravenous thought of her. When my eyes opened, I looked down into hers. I could see how she felt. She was torn exactly the same way I was. Our time was over. I confessed, "We always want what is exactly out of our reach."

I let her go and walked through the double doors. I found Brent and Bianca playing Xbox just as they had intended. It was an adventure game where they were jumping, ducking, leaning and—a bi-product of all the activity – laughing. The lightheartedness in the state room was a far cry from the heartbreak up on the deck. Camille never did come in to watch the video games. I was thankful for the separation. I knew it would take some effort before I could be in the same room with her and not have an overwhelming urge to hold her.

CHAPTER 17

Camille Benning – Charleston, SC – Sunday Afternoon

My whole day had been a nightmare. I'd never, ever, had feelings for a friend's boyfriend, let alone fiancé. I'd analyzed the whole situation at least a thousand times – I didn't know how it happened, but I vowed it would never happen again. I wanted to confess, tell her everything, beg her to forgive me, but the selfish part of me wouldn't let me tell her. I was sure the truth would land me on a plane bound for the west coast by the afternoon.

Bianca had been so good to me, my first real friend since I got here, and I'd kissed her fiancé. I was so ashamed of myself. I didn't even try to tell myself that it had anything to do with her feelings for another guy – because it didn't. I couldn't look her in the eye the rest of the day. When Drake went to join Brent and Bianca in the state room, I couldn't follow. The guilt was overwhelming. I wanted to crawl into a corner and hide. I considered taking the dingy back to shore just so I didn't have to face them, to face her. My stomach was tied up in knots, and I was miserable. I could hear my mom's words from my childhood, "Never lie, cheat, or steal, Camille – any other mistake you make can be forgiven, but lying, cheating, or stealing are actions done with malice, with forethought. You invite evil into your heart if you do any of them." Mom was a bartender and a waitress most of my life, so she always had advice for me when I needed it, and in that moment when I needed her words of wisdom, these were the ones that replayed in my head.

When the three came back up on the deck, I couldn't tell Bianca what'd happened. I knew Drake hadn't said anything because she was laughing and carrying on. It was a good thing I'd watched *Titanic* two hundred times over the last ten years. I knew every scene, the entire dialogue for the whole movie. I played it over and over in my head, so Bianca couldn't see what I'd done.

By the time we pulled up in front of Bianca's house, I was sick of the movie and had started going over lyrics to songs in my head. As miserable as I felt, I couldn't bring myself to tell her. I'd never purposely lied to anyone in my life. I knew I'd need to tell her, but I was so distraught I couldn't tell her today. Thankfully, Brent dropped her off first. I pretended to be asleep in the car because I knew I couldn't bear to look her in the eye. I continued with song lyrics in my head until she was safely inside her house. Drake had walked her to the door. He didn't seem to be affected at all – no guilt. What a scum bag.

When he got back to the car, I "woke up" from my pretend nap, but refused to make eye contact with him or speak. The shame began to morph into anger. I felt like I was going to come apart at the seams, and he acted like nothing had happened.

Brent was oblivious to my inner turmoil when he asked Drake, "You and Bianca want to catch a movie later?"

I didn't give Drake a chance to answer, "Brent, I'd rather hang out with Gretchen and Will tonight."

Brent glanced over his shoulder. "Uh, okay. I didn't know you were awake. We can hang out with Mom and Dad today and catch a late showing tonight."

I didn't even glance at Drake in the front passenger seat, "No thanks. Too much sun."

To his credit, Drake agreed. "Yeah, I've got a pretty tough week coming up. I doubt we'll be able to do anything."

I could see Brent looking between Drake and me. He knew something was up but couldn't put his finger on it and shrugged. "Okay. Maybe next weekend?"

I cringed at the thought, but Drake again answered, "Maybe. Oh wait . . . I'm going to a pre-season game in Charlotte next weekend." I was thankful he seemed to want to keep just as much distance from me as I did him. Maybe he felt just as guilty as I did and was just better at hiding it.

When Brent and I walked in the door, we heard voices in the family room, but I didn't have the strength to put on a happy face. I went to my room, shut the door and crawled into bed. It was only a little after 4 p.m., but I couldn't face anyone. It was a fitful sleep; images of Drake kept seeping into my subconscious. Every time I saw those light blue eyes in my head, I startled myself awake – refusing to replay any of the images I'd seen on the yacht today. At midnight, I knew I needed to talk to someone. I picked up the phone and scrolled to Daniel.

He picked up right away, dispensing with the customary, "Hello," and said, "So, tell me about your latest adventure."

"I miss you."

"Oh come on, tired of the private jets and yachts already?"

"Shut up. What're you doing?"

"Beach day. Bonfire in Carlsbad, met a girl."

"You always meet a girl. In two days you'll figure out she's not perfect and you'll meet another girl."

"Naw, I'd give this one a week."

"Wow, she must be special. You're such a man-whore."

"Man-whore? I just love women. So really, what happened today? That mouth freshener girl, did you two do anything today?"

"Mouth freshener girl?"

"Binaca, right?"

"Her name's Bianca, you bonehead!" Daniel sucked at remembering people's names. One time he introduced one of his girlfriends to me as "Anita" when in fact her name was "Benita." She corrected him several times before she decided he wasn't worth her time. Daniel was a great guy but was never big on details.

"Oh, there's such a big difference. Did you two get together?"

"Yeah, Brent took us all out on the boat today. But, I'd much rather hear about your day."

Daniel's tone was accusatory, "What happened, Camille?"

"Nothing happened. Can't I just be homesick and want to know what's going on with you?"

"No. I know you too well. It's midnight there. You didn't call me all day: something happened. Spill it."

"You wouldn't believe me if I told you."

"Try me."

"I can't. I just seriously screwed something up and wanted to hear a friendly voice."

"I hate it when you hide shit. What happened, Camille?"

I took a deep breath. This was why I had called him. I needed to get it off my chest. I had to tell someone before I imploded from the guilt. Daniel was part psychic, at least that's what I'd always told him. He always knew when he wasn't getting the whole story and would drag it out of me, give me advice, and then tell me everything would be fine. "Okay, so there's this guy, who I don't like, that I kind of kissed."

"Why would you kiss a guy you don't like?"

"I don't know. Why do you wear socks to bed?"

"Because I don't like my feet to be cold when I sleep. I'll ask again: why would you kiss a guy you don't like? Do you like him, but you don't want to admit it?"

"I don't know him well enough to like him or not like him. But I know I don't like him."

"Camille, can you hear yourself?"

"Would you shut up and listen?"

"Alright, alright, so you kissed this guy, who you don't like, and it bothered you so badly that you had to call and tell me you don't like him."

"Something like that."

"If you're looking for relationship advice, I say: don't kiss him again."

"You're such a genius. Why didn't I think of that?"

"That's what I'm here for, baby. To help you weed through the complexities of your psyche. This one was a real stumper. I'll put it on your bill."

"So, he's kind of Bianca's fiancé."

"Kind of or he is?"

I took a deep breath, "He is."

"My vote hasn't changed. I still don't think you should kiss him again."

"Thank you, Captain Obvious. Do I tell her?"

"Hmmm, who initiated, you or him?"

"Does it matter?"

"If you initiated, then you have to decide if telling the truth is worth giving up the first friend you made out there. If he initiated it, then he's a snake. He's probably done it before, and he'll more than likely do it again – so tell her."

"I think, maybe, I initiated it. I don't know . . . it all happened so fast."

"Whoa, Cami, you kissed this guy knowing he was Binaca's fiancé?"

"Her name's Bianca, and I didn't mean to."

"You know, I saw that on the news last week. People walking down the street, minding their own business, and BAM their lips turn elastic and wrap themselves around a friend's man. Happens all the time. It's a side-effect from the 'Stupid Pill.' Must have refilled your prescription before you lef' town."

"You're not helping, Daniel."

"Cami, look. You feel bad for a reason. Own up to it with Bianca and it'll make you feel better."

"There's more at stake than me. If I tell her, she'll break off her engagement. Drake says it won't happen again."

"Sounds like you already made up your mind."

"I feel horrible. I needed to tell someone."

"I'm not a priest, so no absolution. I think if it were you, you'd wanna know. If it was just a kiss and nothin' more, she probably won't break it off with him. But if you don't tell her and it is something more, you take responsibility for everything that happens next."

"Nothing else is going to happen."

"Judge and jury, right?"

"What?"

"If you don't say anything, and this guy really is a slime ball, you're acting like the judge and jury by not saying anything—basically forgiving him on Bianca's behalf. You need to decide if you want to be the judge and jury or if you want to be the cop and report it for her to decide."

"And if it backfires and blows up in my face?"

"Then she wasn't that great of a friend to begin with. You can always come back to Cali."

"Thanks, Daniel. Call me and tell me about Day 2 with Miss Wonderful tomorrow."

"Who?"

"Uh. . . the girl you met today?"

"Oh yeah. Get some sleep. You'll feel better tomorrow. Le' me know if I need to pick you up at the airport."

CHAPTER 18

Camille Benning – Charleston, SC

Monday morning was bright and sunny. I had a text from Gus, the Centaur I met at Bruce's wedding, asking if we were still on for Friday night. With everything that had happened yesterday, it had slipped my mind. I needed to talk to Beau.

Since I went to bed Sunday afternoon before dinner, I was well past rested and starving. Daniel was right in a lot of ways, but since I couldn't share any of the Centaur stuff with him, at least without him thinking I was on a new designer hallucinogen, I decided I would be judge and jury. I believed Drake that our encounter was a one-time thing. We'd already agreed to give each other a lot of space. As long as we weren't anywhere near each other, it definitely wouldn't happen again. Something about his reaction yesterday told me this wasn't something he routinely did. I could keep my friendship intact with Bianca, but I'd only see her when there was no possibility of being near Drake.

I would put the incident out of my mind, lock it away, and not think of it again.

When I got down to the kitchen, I was freshly showered, had a healthy glow from the sun yesterday, and was ready for whatever the day had in store for me. Gretchen was seated at the kitchen table with a laptop open. As soon as I walked in, she stood up. "We were worried about you. Is everything okay?"

"I'm fine. I was just spent from being out in the sun all day."

"I checked on you a few times. You're a heavy sleeper."

"Not always, but like I said – yesterday wore me out."

"Fair enough. Well, it's just you and me. Everyone went back to work this morning. What do you want to do today?" She walked over to the oven and pulled out a warm plate of scrambled eggs, bacon, and toast. Gretchen was a true domestic goddess.

"It's okay, Gretchen. You don't have to entertain me or anything. I can find something to do."

"With everyone else gone from the house, now might be a good time to practice some of your Centauride skills." I could sense that she was eager to help me but didn't want to be pushy.

"I'm game. How do we start?"

"Let's try communicating with your mother's spirit. Every Centauride is different. You have five senses; normally one is stronger than the others. For me, my sense of smell is far superior to hearing, sight, touch, or taste. Do you know which of your senses is the strongest?"

"No, not really."

"Have you been able to see your mother's spirit or have you heard her voice?"

"I saw her a little, but it was like watching a grainy television. I could smell her perfume a couple times, though."

"Okay, let's assume your sense of smell is your dominant sense. When you think of your mother, did she have a favorite flower, a favorite meal, a hobby of some kind that has a scent that reminds you of her?"

"All those things. Lavender was her favorite flower, Italian dishes with lots of basil and oregano, and she loved NASCAR, so—exhaust fumes."

"Exhaust fumes remind you of your mother?"

"Yeah, and burning rubber, too."

"If we need to set an old tire on fire we can, but let's try some of the more pleasant scents first."

Gretchen went to work on a lasagna dish, the whole time giving me ideas for how I could try to contact my mom. I got to thinking about the question Brent had asked me about the missing herd. Gretchen stopped in her tracks half way to the oven when she turned to me and asked, "Missing Herd? Are you thinking about the Lost Herd?"

Crap, I forgot Gretchen could read my thoughts. "Uh, yeah, what's the Lost Herd?"

Gretchen placed the pan in the oven and said, "Sit down."

I took a seat at the table but felt strange as Gretchen seemed very uncomfortable. She must have been digging in my thoughts because she uttered, "I see Brent has been doing some speculating of his own." She made a sour face, and I was worried my thoughts might have just gotten him in hot water.

"He didn't mean to. I mean . . . I don't want him to get in trouble."

"I'll speak with Brent later. He obviously piqued your interest. It is nothing you should speak of, to anyone. Do you understand?"

Her voice was so firm I was worried I'd just really screwed up.

"You didn't do anything wrong, Camille. But asking questions about the Lost Herd is dangerous. No one speaks of it. Many your age have never even heard of it. I'm sure Will should be telling you this – but . . . I'll fill you in with what I know. It isn't much. Long ago, there was a fierce Centaur warrior named Rupert, so fierce in fact that he instigated conflict with every Centaur he came in contact with. He was hard on his young; many of his sons were killed by his own hand. Other Centaur warriors tried to intervene and help his sons; each mysteriously disappeared or died very young from seemingly natural causes. There is a blood debt to be paid if any Centaur kills another outside of battle. Many speculated, but none would openly accuse Rupert of taking out his wrath on others. By all accounts, Rupert was more beast than human, and before his thirtieth birthday he had been outcast from the community. The Centaur elders banned him and his descendants from ever returning to Centurion."

"Centurion?"

"It's a city in South Africa. A large community of Centaurs live there, and the elder of each family visits Centurion each year."

"The elders? Who are they?"

"Each herd's eldest male member is an elder and is represented at Centurion."

"So who is our elder?"

"Camille, your father is going to have to answer your ancestry questions. I fear that if I share anything more I'll only put my sons at risk."

"But I don't understand. What's the Lost Herd, and how would my brothers be at risk?"

"The Lost Herd are the descendants of Rupert. Rupert was found guilty of crimes in absentia – he owed many blood debts that were never paid."

It didn't escape me that she didn't share why she thought I would be putting my brothers at risk, but rather than press her for information I knew she didn't want to share, I asked, "Brent seemed to think that I was part of that herd. Why would he think that?"

Gretchen chewed her lower lip. She was trying to answer me, without answering me. "You are unique, Camille. Full-blooded Centaurs can only be born between two married Centaurs. If your mother had been human, no one would give it a second thought: you would be a half-breed.

In our society half-breeds are slightly more desirable than humans but are still not considered Centaur. Most Centaurs forced to marry humans eventually leave our society altogether, and their children are unaware of their ancestry. You are a full-blooded Centaur, born of two Centaur parents who were not married. Until I met you, I would have thought it impossible."

"So, I'm what?"

"We don't know. News of your arrival spread more rapidly than even I anticipated. Men are very anxious to meet you, but their mothers will be cautious. I've asked a friend to look into your future. She can't see it, or when she does, the outcomes are fluid. It's as though your future is not mapped, as though the heavens forgot to write your destiny. It changes from day to day, almost as if your possibilities are endless."

"That's the way everyone's futures are. Bianca told me, free will trumps fate."

"Free will allows people to choose portions of their destiny, but yours won't solidify enough for me to counsel you on any decision. The only thing I do know is your mother has something she must talk to you about. She won't allow me or anyone else to relay the information. You have to practice communicating with her because whatever she needs to tell you – you need to know."

"Do you think she knows why I'm not like everyone else?"

"I hope so, Camille. Promise me you'll not bring up questions to others about the Lost Herd." Her request wasn't a request at all. I liked Gretchen, and I trusted her. I hated that she couldn't just come right out and answer me, but I believed her when she told me I shouldn't ask others about the Lost Herd.

"So no Centaur has ever been born if their parents weren't married?"

"No."

"Not ever?"

Gretchen looked across the table at me. She shook her head. I had come to a quick conclusion, "Maybe Will isn't my father?"

A vase full of flowers flew across the room and landed hard against the leg of the table. Gretchen and I both leaped up in our chairs, avoiding the shards of glass that sprayed in all directions. Gretchen was pissed, "How dare you!"

At first I thought she was screaming at me, as if I'd somehow hurled the vase at her. "You did this to her. You were selfish, and now you're acting like a child!" Gretchen was furious. I couldn't see my mother, but something told me she was in the kitchen. Gretchen started shaking as she fired back, "Maybe you should have asked him while you were alive! What did you expect her to think? What did you expect everyone to think?"

I didn't want to be caught in the crossfire between the two, and only hearing Gretchen's half of the conversation was more confusing than helpful. I reached down and started picking up flowers from the mangled mess on the floor. Gretchen gathered the dustpan from the pantry and squatted down to help me. She didn't seem as angry as before, and this time she addressed me, "Camille, your mother wants you to talk to your father about his bloodline."

We continued trying the remainder of the morning and all afternoon for me to contact my mother. Other than nearly taking a glass vase full of flowers to the shin, I didn't have any contact with her. I can say that the lasagna Gretchen made was absolutely wonderful, and in truth the scent was better than any I'd ever smelled in my past. We tried looking at a picture of my mom. I listened to a full play list of my mom's favorite songs. Her favorite Saturday pastime was being on the beach, so we spent time outside with some sand. None of my senses did anything but stir happy memories of my mother – none made her materialize right in front of me. By the time Will and my brothers arrived, I was exhausted. Gretchen had made a second pan of lasagna, but I knew I wouldn't be able to keep up my end of any conversation. I wanted to talk to Will, but from Gretchen's reaction, I knew I needed to talk to him privately.

I found myself back in my room desperately wanting to talk to Daniel. It was still too early for him to be off work. I picked up my phone and saw I'd missed several calls from Bianca today. The guilt I'd been able to shelve all day reemerged when I saw my phone's call log. I was still so ashamed of what happened yesterday that I couldn't bring myself to call her back. Maybe I really would lose my newest friend to my action on the boat. If I couldn't bring myself to talk to her, eventually she'd stop calling me.

I thought back to the time on the boat with Drake and what I'd told Daniel last night. I *did* initiate the contact, but I never would have if he hadn't shoved all the images of the two of us into my head. Then it hit me – Drake's was the first mind I had read. I hated the idea of revisiting what had happened, but when I put my hands on his face, I wasn't just getting words or emotions, I got images – visions of us together. It was only a few seconds, but when I saw what was on his mind, I couldn't keep my hands to myself – as if I were being magnetically pulled to him. I knew it wasn't rational, it wasn't even something I wanted—it was just a physical reaction. Based on what happened, touch might be my strongest sense.

For thirty minutes I tried to push images of Drake from my head, and thankfully a soft knock on my door finally allowed me to do just that.

CHAPTER 19

Camille Benning – Charleston, SC

It was Brent's voice on the other side of the door, "You okay, Camille?"

"Come on in, I'm just getting some rest."

"You've been doing a lot of resting. Everything okay?"

"Yeah. Gretchen and I were working on stuff today, and I needed a break."

"Do you want to do anything tonight?"

"Like what?"

"That sounded like a yes."

"That sounded like a 'what did you have in mind?'"

"You've been stressed since Bruce's wedding. Let's go blow off some steam."

"Doing what?"

"I'll think of something. Let's get out of here." I was thrilled to see his idea of blowing off steam and mine were one and the same. He pulled up outside Frankie's Fun Park and made a straight line to the Go Karts. This was exactly what I needed.

We took several trips around the track. A guy in a blue Go Kart with shoulder-length hair, wearing a skater t-shirt and a big grin, kept purposely rubbing the side of his Kart against mine at every opportunity. I could tell he was flirting, but it was harmless and kind of cute. Brent was on the other side of the track, but I felt his eyes watching us. A few more turns and I saw the white flag indicating our time was almost up. I took a couple sharp corners and felt my side wheels lift off the track. When I pulled into the pits, the guy from the blue Go Kart caught up to me and said, "What are you, Mario Andretti's daughter?"

"Not unless Andretti doubles as a financial manager."

"Nice moves back there." He held out his hand, "I'm Jack."

"Hi Jack, I'm Camille." Brent emerged from his car and was at my side in seconds. I could see Jack got the wrong idea and thought Brent and I were a couple. I didn't see any reason to contradict the conclusion he'd drawn. With everything else going on in my life, I wasn't looking for a boyfriend – Centaur or human.

I didn't introduce Brent, but Jack opted for a quick getaway, "It was nice to meet you. Maybe I'll see you around." Jack turned around and was gone in a flash.

I pretended to be upset with Brent, "Well, that was a little rude, don't ya think?"

"Guys like that are a dime a dozen. You're a Centauride – you're out of his league."

"I don't know—he was cute." I fished in my pocket and pulled out a coin, "Here's a nickel – I'll take six."

"You drive me crazy, you know it?"

"Oh stop it. It's not like I've never been on a date before, and besides, it was just flirting."

"Camille, you can't date."

"No. I can't marry anyone. There's a big difference. I'm not in the market for a husband. I can date whoever the heck I want."

"Not a human."

"Hello, I've already dated humans. I've never dated a Centaur, but it can't be *that* different."

"Humans? So you weren't kidding? You've dated more than one person?" Brent was not at all impressed.

"Well, not at the same time, but, yeah. Believe it or not, it's pretty common. If you wouldn't have appeared out of thin air, I might have had a date with that guy."

"Well, don't let me cramp your style. Why don't I take you over to the college? You can date the whole football team."

"Cool, do you think I could get better seats that way?" I thought we were joking around, until I noticed Brent was fully pissed off. Most people would have stopped right there, but once I knew how angry he was, I couldn't help but keep pushing his button. "Did I hear on the radio that there's a hockey team here? I bet if I were dating the whole team, I could ride the bus to the away games."

"You aren't funny!"

"Oh, come on, I'm hysterical. You should see yourself right now. It looks like that little vein on the side of your head is getting ready to rupture."

"Don't kid about stuff like that. You can't date humans."

"Brent, I'm an adult. I can date anyone I want. I just can't commit to anyone until Gage Richardson finds someone else to marry him."

"Isn't the whole purpose of dating to find a husband?"

"Uh, no. Dating is about going out and having fun with someone who likes doing the same things you do. Once you get to the point that you can't live without that person – that's when marriage discussions begin."

"You don't have to date. You've got me. We like doing the same things, and you don't have to worry about me having romantic feelings for you."

"That's not dating, that's hanging out with my brother, and no offense, but if that's what I have to look forward to for the next five years, I need to find a fast moving car and a tree. Liking someone in a romantic way isn't a bad thing."

"It is when you can't act on it."

"Wouldn't it be better to do it the normal way? Find a girl you like, regardless of who her grandparents were? Go out and have fun."

"I can't."

"You won't. Do you see her, over there, in the green capris?" There was a gorgeous brunette who was sitting at a table, reading a book and sipping on an Icee, off by herself, oblivious to the action all around her. "Go talk to her. She won't bite you. You might even find that she's fun to hang out with."

"Have you heard anything I've said?"

"Yeah, and I think it's a crock of crap. Love can't be dictated or treated like a business deal. It's in your heart. If you don't follow your heart, how are you ever going to be happy?"

"I'd be so happy to know that I was responsible for our bloodline coming to an end."

"Bruce already took one for the team. You four are free to do whatever you want."

"You're right, and I want to do things the traditional way."

"Okay, but don't look down your nose at me for not buying into the whole bloodline thing."

Brent wasn't as angry as he had been, but I guessed he knew he wasn't going to win this argument, so he stopped trying. As we were walking toward the gate, the girl in the green capris looked up from her book and smiled at Brent; he lost his stride and nearly tripped. I jabbed him in the rib with my elbow and offered to get her number for him.

His only response to me was a glare. Had it come from anyone else, it would have shrunk me two inches on the spot.

Brent didn't want to go anywhere else. We got into the car; he turned up the stereo and headed straight back to the house. I tried to read his mind, not certain that I wanted to know what he was thinking, but I kept coming up empty. I got the feeling that he was going to say something important, but we were in the driveway, and he still hadn't said a word. I wondered if I touched him, like I did Drake, maybe I could read his mind, too. I lost my nerve – I wasn't sure what he'd think of me purposely trying to read his mind. Tomorrow I'd have to ask Gretchen about etiquette when it came to listening to other's thoughts.

As he shut off the car, I broke the silence, "I asked Gretchen about the Lost Herd today."

"You what?!"

"You didn't tell me I wasn't supposed to."

Brent let out a heavy sigh, "What'd she say?"

"She told me I wasn't supposed to ask and some stuff about a Centaur named Rupert that killed his own kids."

"Rupert? She said his name was Rupert?"

"Yeah, why?"

"I need to show you something."

CHAPTER 20

Camille Benning – Charleston, SC

We were standing in Brent's room. His was masculine, no flowers or vases on any of the surfaces, but one thing caught my attention. He, too, had a fireplace in his room, and above the mantle hung an identical print to the one in my room: the same white mare set on rolling hills. It felt like it was significant, but this wasn't what he'd brought me in to see. A large tapestry hung on the wall with a family tree embroidered on it. The trunk of the tree showed two names, Rupert and Genève, with hundreds of branches. I noticed one near the top left bore William and Gretchen Strayer's names and each of their sons branched out from them.

"That could just be a coincidence."

"Oh yeah? Mom hides it every time we have guests at the house. It's like she doesn't want anyone to see it or something. Here look at this." Brent rolled the tapestry up. When it was rolled to the top, little ties hung down to secure it in place. It looked like an enormous scroll, and a print of a dog asleep hung on the wall underneath the tapestry.

"That doesn't prove anything."

"The Lost Herd didn't become human the way all the other Centaurs did."

"Are you nuts?"

"What's so nuts about it? It explains a lot."

"Gretchen told me Centaurs were never really part horse. They were just super fast, so people drew our ancestors as part horse."

"You believed her?"

"Why wouldn't I?"

"I already told you."

"Because I was born? Did it ever occur to you that maybe most Centaur men don't have affairs? The ones that do are probably smart enough to wear condoms."

We both heard footsteps outside his door and froze. It didn't seem like we were doing anything covert, but Brent got nervous and motioned for us to stay silent. We heard the footsteps walking further down the hall, and Brent pointed to the door, covertly trying to sneak out of his own room. He, more so than any other person I'd ever met, needed to find a girl – he was a borderline freak.

Monday night was a night with the whole family, even Bruce and Hannah. I was surprised to see Brent pull out board games, and everyone decided on Cranium. I'd never played, but it was fun, and we played three rounds before I started to see yawns around the table.

I'd left my phone out in Brent's car and went out to retrieve it. As I locked the door to the car, Hannah surprised me by clearing her throat; she'd been just a few feet away. "Oh, geeze, I didn't realize you were right there. How's married life treating you?"

"Good so far, two days down, another fifty or so years to go." When she smiled she had this way about her, like she carried a few rays of sunshine with her just in case she needed them.

"So where are you and Bruce living?"

"A house just a few miles down the road. You should stop by and visit tomorrow."

"Uh, okay. Sounds good."

"Camille, it's none of my business, but – I . . . you know. . . never mind."

"Is everything okay?"

"I'm not sure. I keep getting strange visions about you. Be careful, okay?"

"Strange visions, like what?"

"They're different every time I try to see your future."

"Ha, that's the same thing Gretchen told me. I've always been a free spirit. Gretchen says it's like the heavens forgot to write my destiny."

Hannah gave me a nervous smile, "Yeah, I can't describe it. Maybe it's because this life is so new to you or something. I woke up this morning and had a vision of you in a garden crying. I'd never seen the garden before. It looked a little like the one at Middleton Plantation, but it wasn't one I'd ever been to before."

"Why was I crying?"

She chewed her lower lip as if deciding whether she could tell me. "I'm not sure. It seemed like someone important had died or something. Like I said, it was just a quick flash. Once I see a vision, I can usually recall it and try to make it more vivid, but . . . when I did that with this one, it changed. I can't describe it, but I feel like something bad might happen to you. Just be careful, okay?"

"Thanks, Hannah. Do you know who died?"

"That's the thing, I don't know. There was this big guy standing there watching you. It was just weird."

Goosebumps formed on my arm. I felt tingles all over and wanted to press her for more information. Some of the Centaur nonsense seemed like a bunch of old traditions just for the sake of having traditions, but Hannah's warning gave me pause. I wondered who it could have been who died. If it had been someone in my family, she'd be warning them, not me, right?

As I reached for the front door, my phone rang. It was Daniel. Hannah waved and went back to the house without me as I answered the phone, "Hi, Daniel."

"Hey, Hot Lips. You didn't call me for a ride from the airport. Everything must have turned out okay."

Brent stepped out on the porch where I was talking to Daniel. "I didn't talk to her today."

"Uh huh. Bad news doesn't get better with age. Stop avoiding her."

"I'm not avoiding her." Brent gave me a strange look. I wished there was an international hand signal for GO BACK INTO THE HOUSE!

"Lying to both of us isn't the best choice either."

"I'm not lying to her. I haven't talked to her!"

"Did you try calling her?"

"I haven't had a minute to myself all day. I will."

"Call her now, Cami."

"This isn't something I can say over the phone."

"Why not? You told me over the phone."

I lowered my voice, "It wasn't your fiancé." I saw Brent listening to my half of the conversation. It wouldn't take long for him to piece it together. "Look, I gotta go. I'll call you tomorrow, okay?"

"Don't chicken out, Cami." I hung up before he could get anything else out. Great, if Brent puts this together, I'll never hear the end of it. I put my head down and walked straight through the door, up the stairs, and to my room, so I could avoid Brent. As I lay there looking at the ceiling, I thought about what Hannah had said. The more I thought about it, the less plausible it became. I didn't know anyone with a big garden. Even if I did, the only person I ever thought I couldn't live without was already dead. Maybe that was it. Maybe it would be like Brent told me and someone would send my mother's spirit away. Losing her for good after I was so close to having her again would destroy me.

My phone rang again. I looked at the screen and saw it was Bianca calling. I took a deep breath, ready to answer, but chickened out at the last second. I pushed ignore, then plugged it in to the charger and turned the ringer off.

"Mom, if you can hear me, I need to know what I'm doing wrong. Gretchen said you were right there the whole time today. Why can't I see you? Did I do something wrong? Are you mad at me for finding Will? I need to know if this Centaur stuff is for real." I didn't move. I tried using all my senses just like Gretchen told me to, but nothing. "I need some answers. My whole life I never asked you for anything. I'm asking you for this now." My voice broke; I could barely hear my own words when I whispered, "Please just let me see you." I looked in every corner of the room and saw nothing. "Dammit, Mom. Hannah said I'm going to lose someone," I felt tears threatening to erupt. I choked them back, "If it's you, before I find you . . . then . . . it's game over. I can't lose you twice. Help me."

Absolute silence was all I heard. The scent of the fresh flowers from the dresser was all I could smell. I saw nothing. I cried myself to sleep as my mind replayed Hannah's warning. Somehow, someway, I would find a way – no matter how long it took.

I woke up Tuesday morning to sunshine peeking through my window. I took a deep breath and smelled warm cinnamon rolls: they coaxed me out of bed and to another full day of wasted trying. I may not have been able to communicate with my mom, but I found that I totally liked Gretchen. She had the patience of a saint, and every time she'd see me start to get frustrated, she'd find a way to lighten the mood.

When my brothers arrived home Tuesday night, I steered clear of Brent. I just didn't want a repeat of last night. Beau offered to take me for a walk. We were outside and several hundred feet away from the house before he said anything.

"So, I get the feeling you aren't very happy here."

"I'm fine."

"You know, I'd believe you if you had any acting ability at all. Didn't you grow up in California? Don't they teach acting classes there in school?"

I couldn't help but smile at his attempt at humor. "I'm just frustrated with myself."

"Anything I can do?"

"Yeah, tell me what I'm doing wrong. Gretchen's tried everything under the sun, and I still can't talk to my mom's spirit."

"Maybe you're trying too hard."

"Maybe I'm not really a Centauride."

Beau looked me straight in the eye. "Camille, it takes some time. You can't snap your fingers and expect twenty-two years of repressing your gifts to suddenly disappear. They won't materialize out of thin air."

"That's the thing, Beau. I don't know that I ever repressed anything. I've never had any special powers. I wouldn't care that I didn't have them if every woman around me couldn't easily do the one thing I can't."

"Awww, that's not true. There's lots of Centauride things you can't do." Beau mock punched me in the shoulder, "Even if you stay broken forever, we'll always claim you."

"If you're trying to cheer me up, newsflash: You suck at it!"

"I'm not used to these little sister pep talks. Maybe I need more practice, too." Beau took me in a tight bear hug and whispered, "Things'll work out for ya'. Hang in there. It's only been a couple days."

My left eye leaked at his encouraging words. I wiped it away hard. "Yeah, you're right. I think I'm going to turn in early, see if maybe I have better luck tomorrow."

Beau nodded, "If you ever need someone to vent to, I'm always here for you, Cami." It struck me tenderly; Beau was the first person in my family to call me "Cami." Camille always felt so formal. I'd used it more and more as I'd gotten older, but still preferred "Cami."

I found myself staring at my ceiling for the third night in a row. Both Daniel and Bianca had called today, but I didn't call either of them back. I couldn't call Bianca because I still didn't have a clue about how to tell her or even if I should tell her about what happened on the boat. I couldn't call Daniel because he would be furious with me for not calling Bianca. Tomorrow would be better. It had to be.

CHAPTER 21

Bianca – Charleston, SC – Wednesday Morning

My plan had worked, better than I could have ever hoped. Although I had chosen Drake, I knew fate had chosen another for him. Grace told me of their intertwined futures. She cautioned me not to interfere, to let them find each other. I just needed to make sure Camille and Drake were given enough opportunities alone together to realize the same destiny. I genuinely liked Camille, and my words to her the night of Bruce and Hannah's wedding were absolutely true. No matter what choices she or I made in life, we would remain best friends. If I could just get her to meet with me, I could do a little more nudging in Drake's direction. I looked at my phone. I was getting close to being a stalker. I'd left her seven voice messages and not one was returned.

I made up my mind that if she wouldn't pick up the phone today, I'd go see her. I hated pretending that I didn't know they were destined for one another. When I was forced to make my decision and I couldn't have the man I loved, I did the next best thing. I chose his closest friend, knowing if anyone were to back out on a wedding, Drake would be the most likely. Truthfully, I was a little surprised that he accepted my parents' offer to begin with. It was sheer luck that Camille appeared out of thin air, and more fortunate still when Grace called me in a panic Saturday morning to tell me not to let Camille and Drake meet at the wedding. In Grace's words, "If the two touch, their fates will be sealed. The two are destined for each other." Little did Grace know that I had no desire to settle down with Drake and only too happily would arrange for the two of them to meet.

Drake was handsome and everything, but I really only chose him because of his friendship with the love of my life. I didn't know Camille that well, but Grace was adamant that the two of us would become the closest of friends. Saturday night, I'd shared with Camille that Drake hadn't been my first choice. After I'd told her, I began to wonder if I may have shared too much – she was the only person in the world that I had shared the truth with.

Even without Camille in the picture, I knew I could string Drake along for years if I had to, to come up with a way to make the destiny that I wanted work. Drake would never pressure me, nor would he feel it necessary to begin our relationship before our marriage.

The ache I felt for Gage was too much. I couldn't put it off any longer. I needed to hear his voice. I hadn't heard it in a month. He answered my call in a gruff voice, "You shouldn't be calling me, Bianca."

"Hello, Sweetheart, do you miss me?"

"Don't call me Sweetheart. You're engaged, Bianca, remember? Why are you calling me, anyway?"

"It's just one old friend calling another."

"It's cheating, that's what it is. I'm not having any part of it."

"I just wanted to hear your voice. It seems like forever."

There was a really long pause, then he finally whispered, "Why?" I could hear it in his voice; his feelings for me were as strong as ever.

"Why, what?"

"Don't play dumb. Why Drake? He was my best friend. You couldn't have picked some schmuck? You had to choose Drake?"

"I had to choose, and I'd been forbidden from you. I didn't want someone who I could ever have feelings for. We're going to work this out, I promise. It's still you."

"I can't do that to him, Bianca." His words stung. The month since news spread of my engagement to Drake had to have been hard on him, but no harder than it had been on me.

I tried to reassure him, "It'll work out, I promise."

His words were clear, concise, and full of pain, "You can't call me anymore, Bianca. It's over. We're over."

"It's not over. I won't let it be over."

"You've already chosen. If you reject him now, his bloodline's finished. No one will ever have him and you'll owe him a blood debt. You can't do that to him, Bianca. This thing between you and me—we're done."

"Let me worry about that. Just don't go strutting around where another Centauride can see you. If another chose you, my heart would break."

"Yeah, that's not going to happen. It's always been you, Bianca. My whole life, all I ever wanted was you." He hung up. It felt like he had reached into my chest, pulled out my heart and squeezed it like Play Doh. He was right. I should never have chosen Drake. I should have stood my ground against my mother's wishes, but it was too late to undo what I'd already done.

I wanted to buy time, figure out a way to be with Gage. I had refused to consider what would happen to Drake once I announced I'd changed my mind. I knew Drake well enough to know that if I backed out, he wouldn't demand a blood debt because of his friendship with my real first choice. But if I could just get Camille to convince Drake to break our engagement, everything would work out perfectly. My mother would give me her blessing no matter whom I chose, to avoid the embarrassment of a jilted daughter.

My next call was to Camille. Thankfully, she picked up right away, "Hello?"

"Hi Cami, what're we doing today?"

"Bianca?"

"Well, duh. How many other people call you for a girl's day out?"

"Yeah, I'm not really up for anything today. Maybe tomorrow?" Her voice was strained with distress.

"How about I come over to your house and help you practice?"

"No! I mean . . . I've been working with Gretchen, and I'm a little spent."

I smiled to myself. Camille was too much of a rookie to know I could tap into her thoughts when she wasn't blocking. I cringed when I thought that Gretchen might know what had happened Sunday between Camille and Drake on the boat. I'd been thrilled that things went as well as they did on the deck between the two of them, but I should have warned her about "broadcasting" her thoughts.

She and Drake just needed a little more prodding. "Oh, come on. If you don't practice, you'll never be proficient. I'll be over in an hour." I hung up the phone before she had a chance to argue.

When Camille ushered me into her family room, I could see she was a nervous wreck. She avoided my eyes like a guilty child. I pretended not to know why. "Camille, I get the sense that you're upset about something. Are you okay?"

"Call me Cami. All my friends do. I'm fine, just worn out from working with Gretchen this morning." She was lying to me. I wasn't offended because I knew why – she was so worried I'd find out she had feelings for Drake. I was nearly bursting to tell her that nothing could make me happier. I knew I couldn't share with her what Grace had told me, but I could let her in on my plan.

"Can I share something with you, Cami?"

Still disturbed, she answered, "Uh . . . sure."

"Promise you won't tell anyone?"

"Sure. Cross my heart." Cami made an invisible cross over her heart. That was cute; I hadn't seen anyone do that since I was a kid.

"You broadcast your thoughts really loudly. Has anyone taught you how to block them?"

I saw her eyes turn into saucers, "Uh . . . no. No one has told me how not to broadcast."

"Would it be okay if we worked on that for a few minutes?"

"Uh sure. Will you be able to read my thoughts while you're teaching me to block them?" I kept seeing images of Drake flicker in her mind only to be replaced by images from *Titanic*. She was trying hard to keep the Drake images to herself, intentionally thinking about something else. I could see the anguish on her face. I would have to let her in on my plan sooner rather than later. Her guilt over her feelings for Drake was tearing her up, and if she didn't get this under control, she'd kill my whole plan in the process.

"Imagine a brick wall. Can you see it?" Cami closed her eyes, and I saw it through her mind. "Good, do you see all the different colored bricks you used, the thick mortar closing in all the gaps between the bricks?" She nodded again that she could see this image. "Perfect, now keep that image of the brick wall in front of your thoughts." I waited a minute or so and saw the fortress Cami had built in her mind, thick and tall, keeping her thoughts carefully stored behind it. "Okay, Brent told me about your new Beamer. Imagine that sedan, what it looks like, how the leather feels, the new car scent, but keep all of it behind the wall." It was working. I couldn't see anything but her wall.

We tried several other things: mashed potatoes and gravy with a thick cut of beef, the sun on her face as she lay out by the ocean. Each of these images, I knew, was dear to her, and she was able to keep each of them from me. I hated to do it to her, but I needed to be sure she could keep her defenses up. "Now think of sitting on the deck of the yacht Sunday with Drake." Her brick wall crumbled, and I saw the image she'd been trying to hide from me. I pretended not to know it was there and instructed, "Rebuild the wall, Cami. You can do it. Envision the bricks, all the different colors, its height, its depth, the mortar. Can you see it again?"

I could see her brick wall a second time, but it wasn't as sturdy as it had been a few minutes ago. I could feel Gretchen in the house. I knew she wasn't paying attention to what we were doing, but I also knew her curiosity would get the better of her soon, so we needed to practice elsewhere. "Come on, let's try this outside for a while." Cami was horrified. She was pretty sure I'd seen the image in her mind and was worried what I would do. I could feel her fear, not the fear of physical harm but of losing her only friend. I tried to reassure her, "It's okay, Cami. Remember when I told you there is no decision either of us will make that will ever come between us? I meant it. Let's go."

Reluctantly, Cami stepped out into the sunshine. We walked to the far corner of the property where a lonely wooden gazebo stood off by itself. It was flanked by wildflowers that seemed to grow in every direction, inviting us to share their breeze. The setting was a perfect place to continue practicing her brick wall. After an hour she was nearly exhausted, but she was able to maintain it no matter what I said to her.

I leaned against the wall, not sure how to begin. "You know how I said telling someone too much of their future had a way of interfering with fate?"

"Sure."

"I know how you feel about Drake." Camille wouldn't look at me, so I kept talking. "Cami, I'm not mad. Drake's a great guy. I think I know how both of us can get exactly what we want." She eyed me cautiously, and if the tables were turned, I would probably have the same skepticism. "If you can get Drake to break our engagement, my mother would be mortified—so mortified that she would let me choose the man I have wanted all along."

"Drake wouldn't do that to you. He promised me, never again, Bianca. I'm so sorry. I didn't mean to kiss him. I would take it back if I could."

"You aren't listening to me, Cami. If you can convince him to break the engagement, you can choose him."

"I can't."

"You could try."

"No, you don't understand. I can't choose anyone for five years."

"What are you talking about? You can choose anyone you want, whenever you want – that's every Centauride's prerogative."

"Not after the night of Bruce and Hannah's wedding. I owe a blood debt to Kyle Richardson. He isn't going to force me to marry his son, at least not right away, but if his son hasn't been chosen by a Centauride by his twenty-ninth birthday, I have to choose him."

"Gage Richardson? You're Gage Richardson's backup?"

"Yeah, I never thought of myself as a 'Plan B,' but I guess that's fair. So my convincing Drake to break the engagement with you wouldn't guarantee that I could choose him. Besides I hardly know him, so even if I could—I don't know that I would. I don't even like him."

"You don't like Drake?"

"No!" I couldn't tell if she said it more to convince herself or me. "Bianca, I swear, I don't know how it happened on Sunday. I. . . it wasn't something. . . he just. . ." She couldn't finish her thought, and I couldn't finish it for her.

I didn't want to put her on the defense, so I asked gently, "What don't you like about Drake?"

"I hardly know him. He's *your* fiancé."

I realized I rolled my eyes at her, but I couldn't help it. "Cami, I told you Saturday, I only chose Drake because I couldn't choose the Centaur I wanted."

Cami told me in a not so empathetic way, "Then you must not have loved him, either. If you did, nothing would have stopped you."

"You have no idea how much pressure was put on me. I had to make a decision, and I know I made the wrong one. Drake's handsome, he's strong, he's honest, and if you give him a chance, you might decide that you do like him."

"Yeah, right. I want a guy who goes around putting the moves on other women? No, thanks. If I wanted someone like that, I'd still be dating my last boyfriend. If you don't want to marry him, call it off – but leave me out of it."

This was the point when I wanted to strangle Cami. "Right, I know you still have this idea that you're human and can go roll in the hay with any guy who catches your fancy, but that isn't your reality anymore. I can't just break the engagement with him, either."

Cami stood up straighter, looked me square in the eye and blasted, "I don't care who my parents are or what the traditions are. Other than potentially getting stuck with Gage Richardson, I'll see who I want, when I want, and nobody is going to force me to be or not to be with anyone."

I tried to diffuse her frustration, "Cami, I'm not forcing Drake on you. I'm asking you to give him a chance."

Her stance softened a little, "What's the point? Even if I did like him, or better yet, even if I fell madly in love with him – then what? I think the whole idea of choosing is stupid, but I couldn't choose him even if I wanted to. Remember, Gage Richardson?"

"Gage is who I chose, but my mother wouldn't give me her blessing. Do you see how perfect this is? If you can get Drake to break the engagement, I can choose Gage, I'll get my mom's blessing, and you would be free to choose Drake."

"Have you listened to anything I said? I'm not choosing anyone. If he breaks his engagement with you and I don't choose him, then his bloodline is lost. That's not going to be on me. I'm not signing on for any of this."

I wanted to smack her at that moment. I wanted to tell her I knew she was destined for him, that Grace could see the future and had seen the two of them together, but doing so could screw up everything. "Maybe if you got to know Drake a little better? No pressure. Just give him a chance."

"Bianca, you want me to spend time with your fiancé, to see if he's the guy that I want to marry? Do you know how idiotic that sounds?"

"Don't you see? This is perfect. We couldn't have planned it better if we tried!"

"I don't think this is such a great idea. I think this whole process is stupid. Unless I'm forced to marry Gage, I may stay single my whole life. My mom did. It worked okay for her."

This was going to be harder than I thought. Now was a perfect time for a late lunch. I picked up my cell phone and called Gage back. When he answered, he didn't sound all that happy with me; he started with, "I've already told you to stop calling me."

"Oh, stop it. A friend and I are going to go to Andolini's for pizza. We're leaving now."

"I hope you two have fun."

"I know Andolini's is your favorite."

"So."

Cami eyed me suspiciously; she could only hear my half of the conversation. I turned to make my conversation as private as possible, "I miss you. You don't have to talk to us. I just want to see you. Please?" I heard his sigh, "Gage, it's just pizza."

"All right, but this is it. This is the last time, Bianca."

Cami was watching me when I hung up. I smiled and dialed Drake. He worked crazy hours and told me he usually threw himself into his work and would forget to stop to eat lunch. "Have you had lunch yet?"

"Uh, no, not yet."

"Do you want to meet for lunch at Andolini's?"

"Do we have an escort?"

"All taken care of. Can you meet us there in thirty minutes?"

"Sure, okay."

When I hung up, Cami's tone was accusatory, "What're you up to?"

"There is no better way to get to know someone than to have pizza with them. Let's go. We need to get there before either one of them does."

"You just invited your fiancé and your boyfriend to lunch with us? Aren't you the least bit worried?"

"You just said you needed to get to know Drake better. I'm making that happen."

"No, I didn't. I said this whole thing is dumb."

"Cami, I know you have feelings for him. Don't you want to find out what those feelings are?"

"He's your fiancé!"

"Not if you can convince him to dump me. Let's go." The car ride over was hard. While Cami drove, I tried to tell her Drake was exactly the right guy for her. She just kept telling me that she wasn't husband hunting or something like that. I still felt if I could just get the two of them to know each other a little better – convincing them would be easy.

CHAPTER 22

Camille Benning – Charleston, SC – Wednesday Noon

We found a table in the furthest corner of the place. Music was going, the place was full, and the aroma of marinara, basil and bread baking filled the air. I felt utterly terrified. Still new to the Centaur world, I asked Bianca, "Are you sure it's okay for us to meet Gage and Drake?"

"We just can't go anywhere alone with a guy. Look around you: there are at least a hundred people here." Bianca ordered the pizza at the counter, then came back to take a seat.

Drake was the first to arrive. His jeans were covered in a white powder. Drake had told Will that his dad's construction business was going well; maybe he worked with his father, too. His bright blue eyes were wide when he realized I was their escort. I did my best not to make eye contact with him, but my eyes refused to cooperate, and I stole more glances than I'd like to admit as he approached our table.

Bianca, still maintaining the façade that she was here to spend time with her fiancé, welcomed him with, "Hello, Darling, I'm so glad you could break away and meet us."

Drake mumbled something, but my heart was racing so fast I didn't hear him. This was an awful idea, one of the worst I'd ever been a part of. My stomach was slowly knotting itself. I wanted to blend into the wall, disappear into the background, or better yet—go outside and wait in the car.

Without warning, Bianca stood up and excused herself. She told us she was going to the ladies room, but I knew she wanted to leave us alone. It was strained silence initially before Drake murmured, "About Sunday, I . . . I. . .we shouldn't. . .you two are. . .I'm sorry." When he looked at me, I could see the sorrow in his eyes. I couldn't be angry with him no matter how hard I tried.

He couldn't get a coherent sentence out, and I wasn't confident I'd be able to either. Instead, I simply told him, "She knows."

Alarm spread across his face, "She knows? What's she know?"

"She knows we kissed on the yacht."

His alarm turned to panic, "What'd she say?"

"Ha! You wouldn't believe me if I told you."

Drake looked toward the ladies room, willing her to emerge. "Is she going to break off the engagement?" I didn't say a word, and Drake reached across the table, putting his hand on my wrist, "Seriously, Camille, is she dumping me?"

Before I could answer, I saw a tall, slender, light complexioned man come through the front door. He had dark hair, and a nicely trimmed goatee and mustache; his eyes scanned the room looking in all directions. I couldn't be sure, but if I were a betting person, it was probably Gage. Drake saw that I was watching the door, and when he saw the man who had just arrived, he confirmed my suspicion, "I guess I got my answer: there's Gage. Dammit! . . . I'm screwed. I am so screwed."

I didn't see Bianca come out of the restroom, but within a few seconds she had met Gage at the door. The two stepped to the side and took a seat in a small booth on the opposite side of the room. When it was clear that Drake and I had been given some privacy, I thought it best to clue him in. "Okay, you're screwed, but so are Gage, Bianca and I."

His elbows were on the table, and his hands propped up his head as if it weighed thirty pounds. "How do you figure?"

"Bianca wants you to break your engagement off with her. She wants it to be a fairly elaborate break up, enough so her mother is embarrassed enough to overlook the fact that she dislikes Gage's grandfather. Then she thinks her mother will let her choose Gage."

"And then what? I break the engagement, and then I'm forced to marry a human. The Nash bloodline comes to an abrupt end. I'd be lucky if my parents ever speak to me again."

"Yeah, I didn't say it was a great plan."

Drake's eyes narrowed, "You're leaving something out. How are Gage, Bianca and you screwed in this scenario?"

"Bianca is in love with Gage." I watched to see if he flinched with this little news flash – he didn't, so he must have already known. "She won't break off the engagement with you because her mother doesn't approve of him. If Gage isn't chosen by a Centauride before his twenty-ninth birthday, I have to marry him as payment of my mother's blood debt to Gage's dad. So yes – if you marry Bianca, you do it knowing she's in love with another guy. If you marry her, I'll more than likely get jammed into marrying the man my best friend is in love with. Clear enough picture for you?"

"Wait, when did you agree to marry Gage?"

"Saturday night, but I don't know if there was much of a choice. I've never met Gage, but his dad said if he didn't get married by the time he was twenty-nine, I would have to marry him."

"But if Bianca marries Gage, you're in the clear. You can choose anyone you want, right?"

"Yes." I could feel my face growing warmer. I *wanted* to shout, "But I don't want to choose anyone!" No matter how badly I wanted to shout it out, I said nothing. My "yes" hung in the air, and I saw that Drake had jumped to the same conclusion that Bianca had.

The full weight of his eyes was unleashed, and his stare stopped my breathing. I felt Drake's hand under the table as his fingertips gently wound around mine. His light touch caressing my knuckles instantly brought a flashback of Sunday afternoon in my mind. At first I thought it was me reliving those few forbidden minutes, but I realized it was his memory of it that was pushed to me through his touch.

"Drake, don't."

He whispered conspiratorially, "Tell me you haven't thought about me, and I'll stop." I wanted to look away, but I couldn't. His fingertips continued lightly caressing my knuckles. My heart was still racing; I pulled my hand away from him and put them both on top of the table.

Feigning a resolve I didn't feel, "I haven't thought of you."

"Not at all?" He didn't look wounded—more like he didn't believe me.

I straightened my back, and shook my head. "Not on purpose." Holy crap, I'm an idiot.

Drake leaned way over the table. He was only inches away from me, his voice low, "That's too bad. Every time I shut my eyes, I see you stretched out on the deck chair."

My resolve started to seep from my voice when I reminded him, "You do realize you're still engaged to Bianca, right?"

"From what you said—not for long."

"I'm not going to be a rebound. Whatever you decide is between you two. Leave me out of it."

"Rebound? I'm not in love with her, Camille."

"Then you shouldn't be marrying her."

"Not to state the obvious, but I think that plan will be off the table soon."

"Look, I don't know what happened on Sunday or why, but I'm not looking for anyone right now."

"I know what happened on Sunday. You felt the same sparks I did. You acted without thinking first – probably for the first time in your life. You've been beating yourself up about it ever since."

"You haven't?"

"Sure, until a couple minutes ago. Things happen for a reason, Camille." Drake reached across the table and took both my hands in his. His hands were calloused and weathered, strong, yet his thumbs caressed the top of my hands as light as a feather. I could feel my frozen sensibility thawing "As much as you hate that you lost control for a few amazing seconds, maybe it was supposed to happen."

We sat there watching each other. I'd noticed his eyes before; it was impossible not to: the light blue pierced me, my resolve ebbing away. I had always had a thing for guys with long hair: Drake's was short, definitely too short for my liking. I'd do nearly anything in the world for a big smile with dimples: Drake wasn't even giving me a grin. It creeped me out when men stared at me, but Drake wouldn't drop my gaze. With all this, I should have heard warning bells, an internal siren telling me to hightail it out of there, but I didn't. I knew that my face mirrored the same irrational longing that he had for me.

I remembered my conversation with Daniel from Sunday night, my confession of everything and his warning that no man only cheats once. "So what happens if you're sitting next to another woman and you get the urge to kiss her? Losing control is okay as long as it's supposed to happen?"

Drake was still holding my hands, still caressing the top of them with his thumbs. He pulled both of them across the table toward him, closed his eyes, as his soft lips grazed my knuckles. When his eyes opened, he still held my hands to his lips. I waited for him to deny it, to tell me that he'd never be unfaithful, that he was a decent guy. Instead, he pushed an image of the two of us to me without words.

We were again on the yacht, no one with us. I was wrapped in a towel staring out into the ocean. Drake came up behind me, circled his arms around me and pressed his body to mine. His lips swept my neck, our skin only separated by the towel covering me. His strong arms glistened in the sun, and I heard him whisper in my ear, "I want you, Camille." I pulled my hands away from him, and the fantasy evaporated instantly.

I tried to shoot him a fiery response, but I couldn't do it. The best I could do was, "That wasn't an answer."

"Anyone can tell you what you want to hear. I thought you'd rather see how I felt."

"It still wasn't an answer."

Drake shook his head and confessed, "You're the only person I've ever lost control with. You're the only person who I've dreamt about while I was awake. I can't get you out of my head, and if I could, I wouldn't want you out."

So he wasn't a poet, but my willpower wasn't as strong as it had been. His back was to the approaching Bianca and Gage. I knew she had let Gage in on her little plan, too—they were both all smiles. Gage, Drake, and Bianca seemed nearly giddy with the idea. I still wasn't convinced. When the two sat down to join us, I moved to the seat to the right of Drake. We ate our pizza chatting about everything but Bianca's plan.

I couldn't get the image Drake had pushed to me out of my head. It was as if it was on a continuous loop in my mind, and I had trouble keeping up with the conversation. I figured out that Drake was purposely touching his knee to mine. Every time our knees touched, the fantasy he shared with me went a little further. When the "Fantasy Drake" whispered in my ear, "You're beautiful, Camille. Tell me you want me, too," I abruptly pulled my knee away from him. The three talked about football, the beach, Bruce's wedding, and I don't know how many subjects I couldn't pay attention to. Every few minutes Drake would touch his knee to mine, and I'd be back on the yacht, alone in his arms. I figured with all the talking going on at the table, eventually someone would bring up Bianca's plan—not a word.

I felt Drake's hand under the table. He discreetly wove his fingers with mine, and just as before, lightly caressed my hand with his thumb. This time the image he pushed had changed. It was evening, the stars were out, not a single cloud blocked the night's sky. The grass was cool and wet; we lay on a blanket overlooking a pond. A single candle's light glowed beside us, a bottle of wine chilled off to our side. "Fantasy Drake" combed his fingers through my hair, his lips skimmed my neck, his breath was warm in my ear as he whispered, "Give me a chance, Camille." I let his hand go, and once again I found myself back to reality, seated at Andolini's with Bianca, Gage and Drake. I was embarrassed, wondering if the other two could see what he'd been doing, but they were still chatting about nothing I was interested in. My eyes met Drake's in disbelief. He returned a shy grin before turning his attention back to Gage, who was still talking about a baseball game.

As the waitress cleared the table, Drake leaned over and quietly whispered directly into my ear, "Can you meet me tonight?"

I caught myself starting to feel the same excitement that it looked like the others were feeling. I should have said no. I should have told him I needed to think about it, but the desire I felt for him wouldn't let me. "Where?"

"The pond, just to the south of your parent's estate. Meet me at ten."

I nodded my silent consent, wondering if his image had been pushed to me to ensure I'd say yes. Despite the logical part of my brain screaming that I needed to get to know him better, the illogical, hormone-infested part began pumping adrenaline steadily through my body. I needed the gentle kick under the table from Bianca to remind me to block my thoughts! When lunch was over, it was clear that Bianca and Gage were ready to rekindle the romance that neither wanted to give up on a month ago. I was sure public displays while dating were way over the line, but Bianca left with Gage, and Drake followed me to my car.

I sat in my car's driver's seat. Drake stood outside my door and motioned for me to roll the window down. As the window rolled into the door, I saw Drake look from left to right through the parking lot. He was satisfied that no eyes were watching, at least none he was concerned with. He reached his left hand through the window and gently pulled my face toward his. I thought his lips would seek mine out, but instead he moved his lips to my ear. In a heavy whisper, "Don't be late tonight. If I don't see you soon, I may combust." His lips kissed my ear lobe gently before he pulled away. Tingles ripped through my whole body as I watched him walk to his car.

I hated it when my girlfriends got overly infatuated with guys they hardly knew. I didn't believe in, nor was I ever someone who wanted to hear about love-at-first-sight: the whole idea was a crock of crap. There was something different about Drake, seriously different from anyone I'd dated, or for that matter – ever met before. The way he could push a fantasy to my consciousness and it be so vivid made my toes curl. I couldn't imagine what would happen with the two of us alone, experimenting with this particular skill. I shook my head at myself as I looked in the rear view mirror; I knew I couldn't wait to find out.

I was still new to the area. I was on a street that was vaguely familiar, but I wasn't a hundred percent sure I would find Will and Gretchen's house immediately. Normally Brent drove when we went anywhere. When Bianca and I left for the restaurant, she had been navigating. I felt like I was in the general vicinity of the estate, but I was equally certain I had taken the long way back. I told myself it didn't matter: the long way back would give me a chance to think through everything – in reality it just got me more excited for tonight.

CHAPTER 23

Camille Benning – Charleston, SC

I turned a corner and saw a classic Bentley along the side of the road. It looked like a 1970-something, beautifully polished, all black, with flared fenders. As I approached, I saw a metal jack hooked to the rear of the car, the trunk propped open, and an older woman waving for help. The woman was standing behind the car, her hair white and flowing with what little breeze the day offered. I slowed down and saw the sweat drenching her long floral print dress. This wasn't a well-traveled road; if I didn't help her, she'd have a heat stroke soon.

I pulled up behind her car, leaving a couple of car lengths between us. Her relief spread wide on her face as she started walking toward me. "Car trouble?" I called through the window.

She gave me an exhausted smile, "My tire is flat." I reached in my purse to fish out my cell phone when I realized I hadn't brought it with me. It was still at the house. It felt like an oven outside, so I considered driving her to Will and Gretchen's house so she could call someone to change her tire. Just as I was about to offer, it hit me – I'd only seen Centaurs at their house. What would they think of me coming back with a sweaty old woman?

Helping the lady would help me get my mind off my meeting with Drake tonight. I knew how to change a tire, and I didn't want for this lady to be in the heat any longer than necessary. It had been months since I'd done something kind for a stranger. The last time I'd helped pay for someone's groceries when they were short at the cash register.

I walked past the old woman to the passenger side of the vehicle. As I looked at her tires, both were fully inflated. I started to walk toward the other side of the car when a man who had been crouching low to the ground leaped at me from near the front fender and put a white cloth over my nose and mouth. Before my mind registered what was happening, everything around me went dark.

I came to and knew I was in the car's trunk. I silently swore at myself for stopping to help. I knew better. When I didn't have my phone with me, I should have offered to go to my house and call someone for her. What the hell was I thinking? Newer cars had glow-in-the-dark trunk releases installed; that hadn't been a consideration thirty years ago when this one was new. I could hear the rhythm of the road: thump thump, thump thump, thump thump. It felt like I would suffocate. Sweat dripped off me; the air was hot and heavy. My head throbbed. I felt all around it to see if he'd given me a concussion after he knocked me out. Satisfied that I didn't have a head injury and the splitting headache had to be a hangover from whatever substance was on the cloth he put on my face, I started kicking at the back seat to try to get air. It was futile. I couldn't make the seat cave in, and if the driver heard me, he ignored my pleas for help.

After I don't know how many kicks, I remembered a television show where someone was locked in the trunk, and they'd messed with the wires and somehow shut off the car. I started pawing in the darkness looking for wires, a fuse panel, anything. I turned my body over to the other corner, still nearly suffocating from the heat and did the same panic search for something that would stop the car. My search was fruitless, and I felt myself losing consciousness. My last words were, "Mom, help me." The darkness swallowed me a second time, and I believed the trunk had run out of air. I told myself I'd see her soon.

I awoke again, still in the darkness. The car was driving slower; I could hear gravel under the tires. I assumed we were nearly to our destination, and I searched for a tire iron or anything I could use as a weapon. The car's trunk was empty except for me. I cursed myself again for stopping to help the stranger. I'd seen enough television shows to know abductions rarely turn out well if the victim isn't found in the first twelve hours. I didn't know how long I'd been in the trunk but vowed silently not to be a victim. I wouldn't go down without a fight. It didn't matter that I was a giant sweat ball who desperately needed air – I'd be ready to spring as soon as the car stopped and the trunk opened.

I felt my mind clouding again. I tried counting silently in my head – anything to keep my mind occupied so I wouldn't lose consciousness again. I got to 326 when the car came to an abrupt stop. I slammed up against the car's wheel well but refused to release a whimper. I heard the car shut off, two doors open and close, then footsteps walking away on the gravel. They were leaving me in the trunk! I knew I couldn't hang on much longer. I started screaming with what was left of my energy, hoping a passerby might hear me. "HELP!! LET ME OUT!! HELP ME!! HELP!! LET ME OUT!! HELP ME!!" More silence was all that answered. I continued screaming for help until my voice refused and my body went limp.

I felt air on my face and looked up into the darkening sky. The same man who had ambushed me stood looking down at me. I couldn't focus on his face; my body was too busy sucking in the fresh air. He held out his hand to me; I refused to take it. I lay there in the trunk, immobile from fear, unwilling to move. When I didn't accept his hand to climb out, his gruff voice said, "You don't want out? Fine, sleep in there tonight!" He reached for the trunk's lid and every muscle in my body flexed; my arms and legs flailed trying to get out before the coffin closed on me.

My reaction pleased him; an evil grin emerged on his face as he held out his hand to me a second time. I looked at his hand but instead wrapped both of mine around the lip of the trunk while I swung my leg out onto the ground.

I stood propped up against the car, taking in my surroundings. It was a fortress that stood in stark contrast to the environment around it. It was in a swamp – literally: tall grass, Cypress trees with their knees protruding from the water, and Spanish Moss everywhere. It was dusk, and the life all around us seemed to be waking up. Even in the diminishing light I could see bright blossoms from nearly every plant that lined the flowerbeds around the house. It looked like a welcoming plantation house, a large two story front porch with eight pillars across the front, and big windows to catch the marsh breezes. It looked like something from *Gone with the Wind*, until I put my back to it and saw the swamp and foreboding trees that surrounded it. I saw a one lane bridge with enormous metal gates deterring visitors further down the lane.

I looked for a second route onto the estate, but in the diminishing light, I didn't find one. There was a beautiful garden suitable for an English castle to the rear of the house – I immediately thought of Hannah's warning to me a few nights ago. A woman's voice brought me back to the present when she said, "There's no use looking for a way out. You'll be here for a while." It was the same old woman who had flagged me down for help earlier.

I glared at her, "Who are you?"

"Zandra Chiron. I'm your grandmother."

My eyes widened. Gretchen had mentioned her in a conversation with Will. I hadn't been paying attention. "You kidnapped me?"

"Your father was being difficult. He told me you would be escorted at all times, yet my driver and I found you without an escort. No Centauride of age should be left unguarded. You're lucky we found you."

I answered her but moved my glare to her driver, "He put me in the trunk! I could have died!"

"Watch your tone, Camille. Aragon did what he thought was best."

"Putting me in the trunk and driving me. . . where the hell am I?!"

"I'll not warn you again. Watch your tone. You will not be the pampered princess at my estate. You are here for your protection and education. Aragon will show you to your room." Without an apology, a thoughtful word or a kindness of any measure, she turned and walked away. I could see a vague resemblance to my mother, but she was so vile to me that I didn't want to see any part of my mother in her features.

The chauffer pointed toward the house. As we stepped into the foyer, I demanded, "Where's the phone? I need to call my father!" Aragon neither responded nor acknowledged that I'd even spoken. I hated myself for it, but I stamped my foot like a child and screeched, "Where's the phone?!"

He put a firm grip on my shoulder and physically moved me to the stairs. I didn't know where this man was from, but judging from his size, he had to be part Samoan or maybe a retired Sumo Wrestler. When I still refused to give up my ground, he picked me up like a sack of potatoes and carried me up the steps. When we reached the upstairs landing, he glared at me, as if daring me to continue to be difficult. I wasn't.

Aragon pointed to the last room on the right and followed me into it. I didn't have any luggage, so I wasn't certain what his purpose was. The room was dimly lit; the paint on the wall was old and peeling near the ceiling's edge. I spotted a long forgotten spider web on the window. It looked like no one had been in this room for a very long time. Rather than continuing to stare at Aragon, I explored the room. It was the size of a large studio apartment, with four windows that had to be at least seven feet tall spaced evenly along the east wall overlooking the front of the property. There was a sitting area with sofa and winged chairs just inside the room. A bathroom was attached to the room that was not accessible from the hallway; a closet was full of dusty clothes that looked to be long forgotten. I dug through the drawers in the closet and found an old pair of shorts and a t-shirt that seemed not to have absorbed the dust I saw everywhere else. As I stepped out of the closet, I announced, "I need a shower."

The chauffer didn't flinch. He stood with his back to the door, a menacing look on his face but no response. As I looked in the bathroom, it, too, needed a good cleaning. Did she think I was going to be Cinderella? I dug around and found some soap and some shampoo whose contents had long since separated. "Great. Hey, Aragon, where can I get some shampoo and conditioner?"

I peeked through the doorway when I still didn't get a response from him. "Hello-o-o-o, you're going to have to talk to me eventually. Where can I find something to wash all the sweat off of me?"

Miffed at his lack of response, I walked toward him and reached around him for the door handle. A single hand shoved me backward. "What the hell? I get that you aren't talking to me, but I need something to get cleaned up with!" I started to wonder, maybe he was mute? No, he had spoken when he offered to let me spend the night in the trunk.

I heard a tap on the door. Aragon opened it, and a petite woman walked in with a serving tray piled high with sandwiches, chips, and OHMYSWEETGOODNESS—cold water! As she set the tray down on a coffee table beside the couch, she didn't make eye contact with me. I immediately reached for the water and emptied the glass in seconds. As I was pouring more water into the glass from a pitcher off the tray, a second knock at the door echoed, and Aragon let in a middle-aged man who had a basket of toiletries, a pair of satin pajamas, and a change of clothes. Both the woman with the food and the man left without saying a word or even making eye contact with me. I was grateful and thanked them both, though neither acknowledged me.

As I towel dried my hair, I sat in the bathroom, wondering: What had I done to deserve this? Just hours ago my mind raced with the possibilities of the future. I had silently hoped to slow down the "Drake Freight Train," but I had never anticipated completely derailing it. Having satisfied my physical need for water, food and hygiene, I let my mind wander back to our lunch today. I thought of the fantasies he kept sharing with me through his touch. It had been a foreign experience and one that still gave me butterflies thinking about it.

Drake would think I stood him up tonight. I still wasn't convinced that Bianca's plan had merit, and I hated the idea of being responsible for whether someone's bloodline continued—especially when I didn't know anything about him or his family. Sure he was handsome, and I'd be lying if I said I wasn't attracted to him, but this whole Centaur relationship thing seemed to be for keeps. No matter how great he was, I wasn't ready to commit myself to him or anyone.

I wondered how long it was before people realized I'd been taken? I hadn't locked my car, and it had been abandoned close to Will's house. Hopefully someone was looking for me by now.

I needed to push thoughts of Drake out of my mind and focus on the problem at hand. How was I going to get out of here? Where was here?

CHAPTER 24

Camille Benning – Florida- Thursday Morning

The next morning, sun peeked in around the window shades. I woke up and looked at the door. Aragon still stood in the same place he had been when I fell asleep. I decided I'd try a different approach: using my brightest smile and sweetest voice, I called, "Good morning, Aragon."

Still nothing. I went to the bathroom, threw my hair in a quick braid, and changed quickly into the clothes I'd been given last night: underwear, Capri pants, a white t-shirt, and flops—all were precisely my size. As I approached the door to the hallway, Aragon opened it for me. The house looked interesting, but I needed to see how far Aragon would let me go. I was surprised when he trailed me wordlessly into the garden.

Zandra joined me shortly after I arrived. She stood a few feet away from me but addressed Aragon, "You may go find your relief. I'll expect you back promptly at 9 p.m." Aragon nodded and walked away. Zandra turned her attention toward me.

"I trust you're well rested?" Her words were friendly enough, but the tone she used was less than heartwarming.

"Uh. . . yes. I was just admiring your estate. . ." Crap, I didn't know what to call her. These were the first words spoken to me since my arrival, and they took me by surprise. "It's very . . . big."

She furrowed her eyebrows at me, obviously stunned with my impressive vocabulary. Her response was curt, "Right. While you're here, you will have a guard at all times. Do not speak to any of them. They're here for your safety, not your entertainment. You'll be guarded around the clock."

"Is that necessary? Am I in danger?"

"Danger? Danger from yourself. They won't let you make a stupid mistake like your mother. There's no phone, no television and no internet. No visitors will be allowed until I can trust you. Do you understand?"

I didn't answer – she must have taken my silence as consent. She started to walk away when I blurted out – "What about my father? How will he know I'm okay?"

"You are my responsibility now. He has been notified."

A little more abrasive than I meant for it to be, I told her, "I need to call a friend of mine in California. He'll be worried if he doesn't hear from me."

"Camille, you've had far too many distractions in your life. I intend to simplify it for you, teach you things your mother neglected. I do not have the patience or the desire to cater to your every whim."

She put her back to me and made a straight line for the house. When she did, Aragon's replacement arrived: another large man unwilling to make eye contact with me. The mosquitoes were the size of small birds, so I didn't stay outside long. When I got into the house, Zandra was nowhere to be seen. The guard pointed to the staircase, and he followed me to my room.

When I returned, a plate of pastries, a thermos of coffee, and a pitcher of juice were waiting for me on the coffee table in the sitting area of the bedroom. It looked like more than enough food for the two of us, and I motioned for the new guard to take a seat beside me. He wouldn't make eye contact with me. I gave a heavy sigh, "I won't be able to eat it all myself; you could at least eat with me."

I watched him closely: his eyes didn't even dart in my direction, and, if anything, his posture became more rigid as he stood against the door. He pretended not to have heard a word.

The pastries were all of my favorites: warm cinnamon rolls, donuts with colorful sprinkles on them, and onion bagels with cream cheese. It seemed odd that anyone would know that this combination would be such a welcomed surprise. After I had filled myself with breakfast, I wondered how I would occupy my time. I decided to go for another stroll outside. I reached around the new guard for the door handle, but he merely held his position in front of it.

I looked at him, frustrated, wondering how in the heck I was going to figure out how to get out of this place if I was confined to this room. "I just need some air. I want to go for a walk." He didn't budge. "Are you deaf? I said I'm going outside to get some air."

Still as a statue, he didn't so much as blink in my direction. When I didn't let go of the door handle, and yanked on it a second time, the man put one hand on my wrist and inflicted more pain than I thought possible with just his thumb and middle finger. I remembered a stupid self-defense class I had taken in middle school that had taught about pressure points on the body. This man should have been teaching *that* class.

I can't say that he did any real damage to anything other than my ego, but if he could subdue me that quickly with two fingers, I doubted I would stand a chance trying to force myself through a door he was protecting. My earlier inspection of the windows on the wall of my room showed they'd been painted shut for decades.

I took another look around. If this was where I was staying, the dust was going to have to go. I began in the bathroom; just as I had finished the last of the scrubbing and the whole place sparkled, I heard a soft knock at the door.

The guard opened it and the same petite woman from last night stepped inside with another tray of food. I didn't need to get close to know exactly what it was: potato soup with spicy Italian sausage. It couldn't have been better timed, and it was another favorite meal. I was too pleased with the aroma for my mind to realize how impossible it was for me to again have one of my most prized meals.

During lunch, a box of cleaning supplies had been delivered to the room. The guard hadn't spoken a word all morning, so I wasn't sure how anyone would have known I was doing my Cinderella impression, but I was thankful for the items. By dinner time, my bedroom was spotless. I half expected a tray of food to be delivered again, but the knock on my door was from a man who had brought a change of clothes for me. Clothes may not have been the best description; a black evening gown with shoes that were appropriate for a movie release or a charity ball had been delivered. I showered and dressed quickly, my mind racing with the possibilities. When I emerged from the bathroom, the guard opened the door to the hallway and ushered me down to the dining room.

A meal that could have served twenty people waited for me. I took a seat in the middle of the long table and waited to see who would join me. It was a full five minutes as the food began to cool before I realized there was only one place setting and no one else was coming. The dinner was wonderful, but I could feel the first real pangs of loneliness. After I had eaten, the guard took me to a library where I was allowed to select a book to read. It was a tough decision; all the books were old, really old. Some were written in different languages; several were handwritten. I searched for a romance of some kind and finally settled on *Wives and*

Daughters written by Elizabeth Gaskell. Once I'd made my choice, I was escorted back to my room.

Aragon arrived at promptly 9 p.m., just as he had been instructed to earlier. I didn't try to speak to him, and he didn't acknowledge that he even saw me as he assumed his post inside my room, directly in front of my door. I hated his watchful eyes; I could feel them on me all night long, but he never stepped closer to me than the one step just inside my bedroom.

DAY 2

I awoke to bright sunlight again. I ducked into the closet, turned on the light, pulled some clothes on that had been delivered the previous night, and dressed quickly. The closet was roughly nine feet by five feet; I knew this closet and my bathroom were the only places that I would have some sense of privacy. I used my time in the closet to feel around for any secret passageways. One of the baseboards was loose. It looked like something was jammed behind it into the plaster, but I didn't want to disassemble the closet my second morning here.

Zandra's home may have been a pseudo prison, but was surprisingly pleasant to explore – at least as much as I was permitted to see. The walls were adorned with equestrian paintings, statues of horses, centaurs, and ornate wooden finishing. The floors were wood accented with lush rugs in every room. As I walked outside to the gardens, I really took them in for the first time. I was not expecting the meticulously manicured plants, the stone walkways that shimmered in the sun, and the life-sized, marble Centaurs sprinkled throughout. When Zandra found me meandering through the expanse, my education began.

Zandra came up to me, patted her shirt down with her palms as if to brush away any stray pollen that may have landed on her. We were stopped in front of a statue of Zeus. I had seen images of him many times, so when she asked me, "Camille, quickly, who is this?"

I answered without hesitation, "Zeus."

"And do you recognize the woman beside him?"

I knew it was his wife, but for the life of me I couldn't remember her name. I shook my head, and she answered, "She was Hera." I hadn't studied Greek mythology, ever. I think the only reason I recognized Zeus was because of Saturday morning cartoons as a kid.

"Hera was very beautiful. Zeus was proud of her beauty and loved having a handsome wife. But occasionally someone would admire Hera too fondly, and Zeus would take out his vengeance. Have you heard the story of Ixion?"

I shook my head that I hadn't, so she continued. "Ixion was a god Zeus thought was a close friend. Zeus suspected that Ixion had romantic feelings for Hera, but he wanted to be certain of Ixion's intentions with Hera before he passed judgment on this friend. Zeus sent a cloud, Nephele, disguised as Hera to learn Ixion's trustworthiness. The cloud bore a child for Ixion, who was named Kentaros."

"A cloud, like a cloud in the sky?"

"This was Zeus. His power was limitless, so making a cloud take the form of Hera was not difficult for him. When Kentaros was born, he was shunned by the gods as well as humans and was forced to live out his days, utterly alone. Eventually, Kentaros moved to the beautiful pastures of Thessaly and bred himself with the mares that lived in the pasture. Kentaros is the father of all Centaurs."

"But, I thought that Centaurs that were half horse were all just a myth?"

"No, we are all children of Kentaros."

I knew using Will's first name diminished his position in front of Zandra, so I purposely included "Dad" in my response. "Dad told me we were descended from warriors. Gretchen said that humans described the warriors' speed as fast as horses, so they began drawing our race as both man and horse."

"Camille, you don't really believe that, do you? Where does the magic in your veins come from?"

I answered cautiously, hoping not to infuriate her and not wanting to let on that I had my doubts about magic in my blood, "From my mom and dad."

"Exactly. They were both descendents of Kentaros and his mares. Most of the herds from that original pasture are still represented, their magic unabated, their blood pulsating with that of a god."

"Our ancestors really were half horse?" The notion still sounded absurd to me, but she continued.

"My given name is Zandra Chiron. Have you heard of Chiron?"

"No."

She furrowed her brow at me. "Chiron was the noblest of Centaurs. Had there been royalty among Centaurs, he would have surely worn a crown. He was unlike many of the other Centaurs born on that pasture. Most Centaurs were fierce warriors, more prone to battle than civility. Chiron was different: he was gentle and kind. He was a musician, a physician, and even a teacher of gods. One of his prized pupils was Zeus' son, Hercules."

"So Chiron was a teacher?"

"As I said, he was a Centaur of many talents. During a class where Hercules was paying more attention to his lessons than to his weapons, he inadvertently shot Chiron with an arrow that had been dipped in the blood of the Lernaean Hydra."

"A Hydra, that's the snake that you cut off its head and two more grow in its place, right?"

"It is similar to a snake, but it was a sea creature. Its blood was poisonous and brought instant death to humans. Chiron was an immortal since Zeus himself had shared his immortal nectar with him, so the blood-tipped arrow only brought suffering and pain to Chiron."

"But you just said Chiron was a physician. If he was an immortal and a doctor, why didn't he just cure himself?"

"He tried unsuccessfully for years to cure himself. He begged the other gods to kill him to end his suffering, but none would kill him, and he couldn't be comforted."

I looked around, a little worried because Zandra seemed to take all of this as reality, and a small part of me wondered if a suffering immortal Centaur was around the corner. "So what happened?"

"Prometheus was a Titan who stole fire from Zeus and gave it to man. Fire was a substance for use by the gods and was not intended to provide warmth to the lowly humans. As punishment for giving fire to mankind, Prometheus was chained to a rock in Tartarus. Each day as the sun came up, an enormous vulture would come to the rock and gnaw his liver. Each night the liver would grow back."

"That's awful!"

"For him, immortality was a fate worse than death – an eternity of physical anguish. Hercules, despite his accidental poisoning of Chiron, was good. He watched day after day the suffering that Prometheus was subjected to and asked Zeus to release him from his punishment." She saw my interest and asked me, "Camille, have you not heard this before? Did you learn nothing in school?"

Ashamed that I'd never heard these stories, I was intrigued and hoped silently that she would continue. "I don't remember any of this."

"And your mother never shared any of these stories?"

"No, never."

She kept her contempt masked, but I could see it was there. "Zeus believed in harsh punishments but was persuaded by the young Hercules to show mercy. He agreed to let Prometheus free of his punishment if another would take his place. Hercules wanted to offer himself up in place of Prometheus, but Chiron wouldn't allow it. Chiron gave up his immortality and released Prometheus from the rock in Tartarus."

"But how was he allowed to give up his immortality in Tartarus, if Prometheus couldn't?"

"Prometheus knew he was being punished and chose to hold on to his immortality. He believed eventually he would be forgiven by Zeus and his punishment would be over."

"But Chiron took his place before Prometheus was forgiven?"

"Yes, but Chiron's liver was never eaten by the giant vulture. Zeus was so moved by Chiron's selflessness that he placed Chiron in the stars. You know him as Sagittarius."

"So you're a direct descendent of a constellation?"

"No, I am a direct descendant of Chiron who was so loved by Zeus that he was permitted an eternal place in the heavens to look down on and to guide his children. In that moment Zeus forgave Ixion for his desires for Hera and forgave Kentaros for being born. Zeus bestowed many gifts on the Centaurs. The men he allowed to keep their warrior instincts and speed. The women Centaurs, he gave the gifts of communicating with the spirits so that they could always receive guidance from Chiron, the gift of seeing the future so they might guide their husbands, and telekinesis so that no object would ever stand in their way. For all Centaurs, he gave the gift of mortality and allowed us to take human form."

"Dying was a gift?"

"Mortality is one of the greatest gifts ever bestowed. After a long and fruitful life, we are able to rest." She looked at peace as she finished her story. In a slightly more brusque tone she said, "That's enough for today. Tomorrow we'll talk about why Chiron's bow is always pointed toward Scorpius."

Zandra stood to walk away. "Wait, that's it?" She nodded, and took two steps before I yelled, "Look, I've been here for two nights. I need to call my father."

"I have no use for telephones. If you want to speak to him so badly, project your thoughts."

My teeth were clenched, "I don't know how."

Her mouth curled up in an evil twist, "Then you obviously need the education I am offering you."

Zandra walked out of the garden, leaving only my guard and me. Forgetting that he couldn't speak to me, I asked, "So have you heard all of that before?" He neither spoke nor acknowledged that I'd uttered a syllable. "I'm, Camille. What's your name?" Again, not even an acknowledgement that I'd spoken. I could feel my eyebrows furrow, "What's next on today's agenda?" I got my answer—more silence.

CHAPTER 25

Daniel – Oceanside, CA – Thursday Afternoon

Three days had passed since I heard from her. The call Sunday night had me concerned. It wasn't like Cami. She always put her friends before everyone else. As stoked as she was about meeting Bianca Saturday night, I couldn't imagine what would have possessed her to put the moves on Bianca's fiancé Sunday. Something wasn't right. I dialed again. "Damn voicemail," I said to no one in particular. No fricken way I'm leaving another voicemail.

Something was wrong. I could feel it. No way would she not return one of my calls in three days. I got on the internet and found William Strayer. I scratched his number on the back of a receipt and called him.

A lady answered the phonc, "Hello."

"Hi, this is Daniel. I'm a friend of Cami's. Could I talk to her?"

"Uh. . . Camille isn't here right now. Could I take a message?"

"When will she be back?"

"She's visiting her grandmother in Florida. I'm afraid I don't know when she'll return."

"Since when does Cami have a grandmother?"

"I'll give her your message when she returns." Her voice had finality to it, but I didn't want her to hang up.

"Wait! Can you give me her grandmother's phone number?"

"She doesn't have a phone."

"She doesn't have a phone?"

"No, she lives a life of seclusion."

"Well, what's her grandmother's address?"

"I'm sorry, what did you say your name was?"

"Daniel. Daniel Gaskins. I'm a friend of Cami's from California. I just need to talk to her."

"That's out of the question." I heard her hang up. If it would have been possible to reach through the phone line and slap her, I would have. Fine, she won't give me the address over the phone; maybe she'll be more willing to give it to me while I'm standing at her door.

Six hours later I was on an eastbound plane. I shook my head at myself. This was stupid. Cami was an adult, and if she didn't want to talk to me, she didn't have to. I had been pretty hard on her, but that's how we were with each other. If she thought I'd done something stupid, she'd be the first person to tell me. If I believed she was just avoiding me, I never would have boarded the plane. Something was wrong. I could feel it. She needed me.

As I transferred planes in Atlanta, I turned on my phone to see if Cami had called me back. I was surprised to hear a voicemail from my father: "Daniel, I need you to call me as soon as you get this."

He never called to visit, usually only picking up the phone when someone died. I dialed his number while I walked to my next gate. "Hey, Dad, you wanted me to call you?"

"Daniel, where are you?"

"Why, what's wrong?"

"You aren't in Charleston, are you?"

"Uh, no. Why would I be in Charleston?" I got a strange sensation. I hadn't told anyone but the lady at the ticket counter in the airport where I was going. What the heck was going on?

"Well, where are you? I phoned your boss, and he said you took a vacation."

During the summer, I worked as a lifeguard on the beach in Carlsbad. My boss looked at me like I was crazy for wanting to take some vacation days. My job was every single guy's dream, but finding a replacement for me was a piece of cake, so he told me to have a great time. I didn't want to own up to flying to the east coast to check on Cami, "You assumed I'd take a vacation to Charleston?"

"No. No, it's not important. I just want to know where you are."

"Uh, Dad, why did you call me in the first place?

"I received a call from Camille's stepmother. . . it doesn't matter. So where are you?"

"Cami's stepmother called? What'd she say?" I wanted to add: How would Cami's stepmother have your name and number?

"Daniel, I've told you. Camille is off limits."

"We're just friends, Dad. I've never looked at her sideways. Something's wrong, I can feel it. She needs me."

"Leave it alone, Daniel. You don't know what you're getting yourself into."

I'd made it to my gate, and the plane was already boarding. I was sure he could hear the intercom paging flights in the background. "I gotta go, Dad."

"Daniel! I don't' know where you are, but you'd better get back here now."

I hung up the phone. Maybe he'd think we got disconnected or something. How in the heck did Gretchen know I was on my way there? Better yet, how did she know how to get in touch with my dad? Something was definitely wrong, and Gretchen was trying to cover it up. I handed my boarding pass to the ticket agent and knew a team of wild horses couldn't stop me from getting on that plane.

After a short forty-five minute flight, the plane touched down just after midnight. The right thing would have been to get a hotel then give her new family a visit in the morning. But I was never known for making the best choices. I got in a rental car, plugged the address into the navigation, and decided they were going to have a visitor tonight whether they liked it or not.

My phone buzzed again; my dad was calling me. I hit "Ignore." I'd only driven fifteen minutes before the navigation told me I'd arrived at my destination. In front of me stood a very large, very secluded estate, with enormous centaur statues flanking the driveway. It looked like every light in the house was on. "Huh, that's odd." I looked at my watch: almost 1 a.m. As I pulled up the driveway, I noticed a man with his arms crossed standing just in front of the steps. It looked like he was waiting for somebody.

I stopped the car and walked up to him, stuck out my hand and flashed my friendliest southern California smile, "Hi, I'm Daniel. I'm looking for Cami."

"I know exactly who you are. Did your father not tell you to return home?"

I could feel my eyebrows raise when I answered, "He did, but I was already halfway here. Where can I find Camille?"

"You can't find her. Go back where you came from."

"Look, I don't know what your game is. She came here for a couple days. I haven't heard from her since Monday night. That was three days ago. I just want to know that she's all right, and then I'll be on my way."

"Gretchen already told you, she's staying with her grandmother in Florida."

"Fine, give me the address."

He leaned in, nose to nose. I knew he was trying to intimidate me. Truthfully, he had me by several inches and at least fifty pounds. I didn't know why he was being so hostile, "You have no business with my daughter. Return to your family before you put mine in danger."

"In danger? I just want to know that she's okay."

"You're not welcome here. Let your father explain why. On your way – now!" He flicked his hand like he was dismissing someone beneath him. I was way past pissed. I don't know what possessed me to do it, but I took a half a step in his direction, and my fist connected hard with his jaw. I'm not sure what I expected to accomplish. I hadn't punched anyone since Billie Kennedy on the playground in third grade. This didn't look like it was going to turn out any better than that time.

William Strayer looked at me. I saw his pupils change from normal to huge – it was the first time I'd felt unfettered fear in my whole life. My punching him in the face stunt didn't make him flinch but seemed to pour acid in his voice. "Out of respect for your father, and only him, I'll give you this single warning. You've been told Camille is off limits. If I see you near her again, I'll kill you myself. Stay away from Camille. Stay away from my family. Keep to your own kind."

"My own kind?"

He turned his back on me and went inside the house. I was furious. I let my emotions get the better of me when I started pounding on the door, the windows, yelling at the top of my lungs, "Cami! Cami, can you hear me?! Where are you?! I just need to know that you're okay!" I don't know how many choruses I yelled, but my throat was going raw, and I was hoping the jackass would call the cops soon.

To my surprise, a younger version of William Strayer stepped outside onto the porch. "Hey, Daniel. Let's go for a ride, okay?"

"I'm not going anywhere with you! I wannna' see Cami, now!"

"Hey, Slugger, she's not here. You're about a heartbeat away from being stomped to death by my dad. We don't have to go anywhere, we can just sit in your car, but you need to get off the porch before he removes you from it."

"I'm not leaving until I see her."

His voice was kind, and for some reason, I believed him when he told me, "Daniel, my name's Beau. I'm her brother and I promise you, if she were here, you could see her. C'mon, just step down and I'll tell you what I know."

We got in my rental and Beau sat down in the passenger seat. "Look, I'm not sure what's going on either. All I know, I got home from work Wednesday night, and Mom and Dad were freaked. Her grandmother took her to Florida. Her car was abandoned a few blocks from here."

"But, that doesn't make any sense."

"Not to me either. I know Mom and Dad won't talk about it with us, but they were fighting like crazy last night."

"Didn't your mom want Cami here?"

"Are you kidding me? Mom loves Camille. We all do. She was yelling at Dad, telling him he needed to go get her. Something bad was going on there."

"But he didn't go?"

"He went this morning, but her grandmother put a sp . . . I mean, the estate was locked down. Camille's grandmother won't let Dad set foot on the place."

"How do you know she's okay?"

"That's the thing, we don't."

"So call the cops!"

"Dad already tried that, and they threatened to put him in jail."

"So, no one can talk to Cami because there's no phone? No one can get there because the gate's locked? If she's in trouble, we have to do something."

"Dad says he's got a friend who is working to get her out, but Dad was essentially escorted to the state line earlier today and sent home."

"Give me the address. I'll go."

Beau looked down at the floor board, "Yeah, you need to talk to your dad first."

"My dad? What does he have to do with this?"

"Look, I can't go into any detail, but . . . there's no easy way to say this . . . Camille's special."

"You think I don't know that?"

"I mean, there are things her mom never told her about her family."

"Angela told Cami that she didn't have any family. I knew her mom really well. She wouldn't have lied to Cami without a reason. Sounds like Angela knew something like this could happen."

"We all want her back as badly as you do, but if you try to go there, I don't know what her grandmother would do to you or her. It'll be better for Camille if you don't try to find her. Let my parents handle it."

"What's her grandmother's name? I just need to know she's okay."

"She's Zandra Chiron. Zandra won't hurt her. I may not know much else, but I know that."

I liked Beau. Cami had told me about him, and I trusted him. It didn't mean I would follow his advice, but I believed him.

CHAPTER 26

Camille Benning – Florida – Friday

I had four assigned guards who rotated their shifts. I was never left alone – even while asleep, watchful eyes were there. Each remained under strict orders not to speak with me, not to answer any questions I asked, and above all, not to let me out of their sight.

My first week was the toughest. Each time I attempted to go to an area of the house that I was forbidden from, I found myself in some sort of physical pain as a deterrent. One guard used pressure points; he was by far the most humane of the four. The other *day* guard was quick to grab me by the nape of my neck and shove me in the direction of his choosing. Although none ever left a mark, it was clear that each one took his job very seriously and had no intention of letting me go farther than I was allowed.

That first week I fought them at every turn. I refused to dress in the elaborate outfits to go sit in a formal dining room by myself for dinner. After several days, the only conclusion I could draw was that if I didn't dress for dinner and make my way downstairs when directed – I wouldn't eat. A couple mornings I had tried to sleep late; Aragon tipped the entire mattress up so that my body spilled out onto the floor. In protest, I grabbed a blanket and a pillow and curled up on the floor. I was not willing to go to the garden for another lesson from Zandra – Aragon carried me in my pajamas to the garden and set me down on a bench.

By the afternoon of my seventh day, I knew no one was coming to rescue me—I had to plot my own escape. The frosted window in my bathroom was small, but I was sure I could squeeze through it. It had been nailed shut, but that didn't stop me. I kept a butter knife from a breakfast tray and used it to pry the nails loose. The sound of the running water masked the complaints from the nails as I pried them free. I opened the window only to see there was no ledge to step onto. The bathtub was full and I was fully clothed. I needed a rope or bed sheets or something. When I emerged from the bathroom, the guard made eye contact with me but quickly looked away. I walked over to the side of the bed and grabbed my book, "You might as well get comfortable," I motioned to the chairs, "I'll be in there a while."

A change of sheets was lying on the corner of the bed; I was able to grab one without the guard realizing. I tucked it close to me and balanced the book so it would obscure that I was carrying the sheet if the guard happened to look my way. The guard didn't flinch. Once back in the bathroom, I ripped the sheet into thirds, then knotted it every foot for added strength. I secured one end to the claw foot on the bottom of the ancient bathtub and threw the rest of it out the window.

I scraped both of my hips pulling myself through the window, but I didn't care. It was my first taste of freedom in almost a week – I could feel my heart racing. The height of the window scared the crap out of me, but the sheet allowed me to get ten feet closer to the ground. I dropped and rolled onto the lush grass. I knew I'd never make it on foot, so I crept around the house toward the garage. I sneaked around each corner, careful not to let anyone see me. I made it all the way to the garage door; when it swung open, I heard, "Out for an afternoon stroll?"

Zandra stood just inside the garage with a very large man I'd never met before. Not wasting one bit of the adrenaline coursing through my body, "You can't keep me here!" I spat out, refusing to be any more of a victim than I'd already been.

"Can't I? Camille, I am your guardian. You don't get to simply decide to leave."

"I just did."

"Ahhh, I see." She gracefully crossed her arms in front of her and quietly responded, "It would be a shame for you to leave before I believe you're ready. It might even be considered disrespectful. If I were to be disrespected by you, in this community, you can be assured a debt would be owed."

A debt? What kind of a debt would I owe her? Smearing her reputation couldn't result in a blood debt, could it? "You kidnapped me! You've kept me here against my will. I just want to go back to my family."

"I *am* your family, you ungrateful nag. You decide: do you want one of your half brothers to pay your debt for leaving my estate without permission, for stealing one of my cars, for tarnishing my good name? I can see now you do not possess the strength your mother had. She would never have allowed another to pay her debt. I still believe that if Kyle Richardson had demanded a blood debt when he was wronged, she would have returned to pay it herself."

My stomach cinched tight. I couldn't stand the thought of Brent, Bart, Bruce, Ben or Beau being penalized for my actions. I wanted to leave this place, but not at their expense. I put my head down and took myself back to my room without another word. I hated it here, I hated this woman, but I would never fall into her trap. I'd become a model prisoner and pray for an early release.

I found myself wishing I had never called Will. I wished I had stayed hidden in California, working my job as a cashier, living in a shoebox of an apartment, free to go to the ocean or the mountains – whenever I chose. My father's home had been more like a fairy tale, something dreamt up by Disney himself: a family who loved me, an ancestry I never knew, and endless possibilities for life. Meeting Will, Gretchen, and my brothers seemed like a blessing – truly a life that I had always craved. But reality was I had known their joy for a week. I kept watch on the front gate, hoping Will would come driving through to take me back to his house. He never did. Did he even know where I was?

Shortly after my attempted escape, I found myself prying at that loose baseboard in the closet. The thing jammed into the plaster was a diary; written in flowing calligraphy across the front was the name *Angela Chiron.* The diary's cover was made of leather and was locked with a key. Sure that my mother would want me to read whatever she had written, I used a wire hanger to pry the lock open. The first entry was written in smooth flowing handwriting: I recognized it instantly as my mother's.

Entry One Sep 21 – My engagement was just announced – Kyle Richardson. I didn't care who she chose. Living with the devil himself would be better than my mother. She's got it in her head that I won't go through with it. She has no idea how deep my hatred is for her and this prison. Father came to my room last night and gave me this diary. He said it would be better for me to write my words down than to say them to my mother. Just once, I wish he would stand up to her. Just once I'd like for him to tell her to go to hell where she belongs.

The next several entries were of little value, so I flipped a few pages and found:

Entry Twelve Oct. 2 – I met Kyle today. Truthfully, I had expected a monster. It didn't take long for him to decide mother was completely unstable. He wanted to return home to try to convince his father to speed up our wedding date. He told me if it was within his power, he'd marry me today and get me out of here. I'm sure he felt sorry for me – the wounds on my neck were scabbed and bloody again from her tirade this morning. I knew I looked a fright. Trying to cover my neck with a scarf didn't do any good as the blood seeped through the bright yellow material. He said he'd be back every day until we were married.

This entry threw me for a loop. I wondered if she was some sort of a vampire? Why would my mother's neck be scabbed and bloody? Zandra was so wrapped up in Greek Mythology but had never mentioned vampires, werewolves or any creatures from the night. My imagination began running wild.

Entry Thirteen Oct 3 – Angelo was at it again today. He's as evil as mother. I overheard that he'd attacked a woman in town. I sat all day looking out my window, hoping the authorities would come take him away – no one ever came. Kyle stopped by again today. He's so kind. When no one was looking, he gave me some medicine for the wounds on my neck. Less than a month, and I'll be able to leave this place with him – and never look back.

The guard knocked on my closet door and about made me jump out of my skin. "Just a second, I'm getting dressed!" I answered before he could open the door and catch me with the diary. I tucked the book behind the drawers, inside the dresser, and pushed the baseboard where I'd found it, back securely against the wall.

I found a long forgotten crayon that lay dusty in a corner. On the inside of the closet, near the floor, I made a series of tick marks – one for each day I'd spent in this place. I didn't know how long I would be kept here, and knew I needed some method to keep track of the time. I didn't know why my mother ran away or why she had given up everything that was her birthright, but hopefully the diary would reveal truths to me that I couldn't find anywhere else.

I couldn't be sure, but from their strength, I believed the guards to be Centaurs. The servants didn't talk to me either; I wasn't even sure if they spoke English, but I wasn't as frightened of them, so I assumed they were human.

Each morning, no matter the weather, Zandra and I met in her gardens. She taught me about Greek Mythology with the same reverence my high school Civics teacher taught me about Democracy. The first few weeks were all her telling me stories, but eventually she waited to tell me a new story until after I had repeated the story to her from the day before. There were never conversations; she didn't spend time with me anywhere but the gardens and only for an hour each morning.

There was no telephone, no television, and no internet – there were plenty of servants, but the only person who would speak to me was Zandra. I had read enough about Stockholm's syndrome to know I would eventually feel some sort of a bond with her, just because she was the only one to show me even the smallest sliver of kindness by speaking to me. The solitude of Zandra's home was deafening. The only part of the day I looked forward to was my garden time with my captor and the few moments I could steal in my closet reading my mother's thoughts in her diary.

The lesson on my twentieth day was by far the most helpful of anything she'd taught me. While we sat in the sun, I silently wished for a notebook, doing my best to commit her words to memory. The mythology she had been teaching me was interesting, but this day's lesson was centered on Centaurs and specifically Centaurides' skills.

She began, "There were seven mares on the pasture of Thessaly when Kentaros arrived, each one part of the world's oldest breeds. The centaurs born of these mares each had very distinct markings and temperaments. Many centaurs born of Kentaros and the respective mare took on a family name closely tied to the mare's breed.

An Andalusian mare bore Centaur children, and they took the name Andalcio. Their women were able to move objects with their minds.

A Schwieken mare bore Centaur children that kept the breed's name as their family name; these Centaurides could read people's thoughts.

A white Arabian mare's descendants became Owens; they communicated with spirits.

A Barb mare took the family name Barber; her children could see the future.

A Fjord mare also kept her breed's name as the surname for her bloodline. Her daughters could communicate telepathically with others.

Centaurs born of a Tahki mare took the family name Tak. Their power was unique, the ability to plant ideas in another's consciousness. They could make others believe an incident had occurred, and were known for their deceit and ruthlessness. The Tak bloodline offended Zeus, so he eventually cast them out; Zeus barred them from ever returning to Thessaly. He also forbade all other Centaurs from fraternizing with the Taks. Their bloodline did not survive.

The Chiron family descended from a black Arabian mare, and when Zeus bestowed his gifts on all the female Centaurides in all the bloodlines, he looked most favorably on Chiron's descendants. We were given all the collective powers bestowed on each bloodline – except, of course, the Taks'."

"But I've met Centaurides who have more than one skill."

Zandra nodded and smiled. "Inbreeding would be catastrophic for our race. We would have long ago perished. A Centauride typically possesses the skills of the two dominant bloodlines that run through her body."

"So if someone is a Centaur, their last name can only be one of the six from the original herd?"

"No. Over the years, many opted to take on names other than their family names. This was done so that the family names would not become too obvious to the humans."

"How many Centaurs are there in the world?"

"Pure-blooded Centaurs? One in ten thousand, possibly more. Half-breeds that have Centaur blood but are unaware they are something more than human – five in one thousand.

I asked my next question cautiously. This had been one of the few times she openly answered my questions. "How does one Centaur know another?"

"Centaurides can feel each other in their minds: it is a familiarity with a stranger, a kinship. Centaurs sense other Centaurs through their warrior sense. I'm told it is a tingling in their chest, a silent warning, useful in battle, I assume."

"Zandra, I don't have any skills." Truthfully, I could read minds through touch, but I'd only successfully done that with one person. I could read the images from Drake's mind, but that was a far cry from simply reading another's thoughts. "What's wrong with me?" I had opened myself up and expected her to give me a kind response, encourage me in some small way.

I shouldn't have been surprised when she responded, "You were born out of wedlock. You are an amalgamation." The hatred in her words cut me deeply when she added, "You should not exist. My daughter did this to you: she allowed you into the world and she taught you nothing. Her responsibility is now shouldered by me, and *you* are not worthy to carry my name."

I had been here for so long. I'd had almost no contact with anyone but Zandra, and this was the first time she had openly told me she was ashamed of me—that I didn't belong. I had fooled myself into believing that this elaborate kidnapping had somehow been done for my protection, that she wanted me to join the Centaur kingdom as a full-fledged Centauride – eventually she would see her daughter in me. There were no words to describe the utter despair that enveloped me. Choking back the tears, I pleaded, "Let me go home. I won't tell anyone we're related. I'll never breathe a word to anyone." I knew I was a pathetic mess as I saw her angry words grow into a look full of disdain. I pleaded, "I won't ever tell a soul. Just let me go home."

"It is too late for that. Because of the idiocy of your father, others know of you. You must learn your heritage so that you may embrace it. We must call to the magic in your blood; I can feel it in you. I can also feel your denial of who you are."

A man walked up and leaned down to kiss Zandra's cheek. I had to look at him twice; his face was masculine, but he looked eerily like my mother. He had the same brown eyes, bushier eyebrows, dark curly hair, and the same pointy nose. The biggest difference was I rarely saw my mother without a welcoming smile, and this man seemed to have a permanent scowl. "Good morning, Mother. You're looking well." I was so used to everyone on the property ignoring me, except Zandra, that I was shocked to see him make eye contact with me.

Zandra's voice softened as she answered, "Angelo, I'm so glad to see you've returned from your trip. I have a surprise for you."

He took me in with the same disgusted look Zandra had just bestowed on me, "Word reached me, Mother. I came to see for myself. Are you certain she isn't a half-breed? I wouldn't have put it past Angela." He had her eyes, their eyes – this was my Uncle Angelo. I had just read the entry about his attack on a woman in my mother's diary. His presence made me want to shrink into a corner. He looked so much like my mother in his features, but where she exuded happiness, love and joy—this man gave off hateful, menacing vibes. Even without reading her diary, instinctively I would never wish to be alone with him.

Zandra shook her head and continued talking as if I weren't there. "No, she clearly is the spawn of Angela and William Strayer."

"Where's her brother?"

"I'm sure he's tucked away somewhere. I've looked through her thoughts many times; she has no recollection of him. Shame. I've dispatched a team to tear Angela's past apart. He'll turn up."

Zandra's words still stung, and I was too frightened to ask what they were talking about. A brother? Why did they think I had a brother? This question had escaped me before I caught the thought in my head and hid it behind my mind's brick wall.

Zandra did the same thing Gretchen had done to me. I didn't have to ask the question out loud. She was only too happy to answer my thoughts. "Every Chiron Centauride who gives birth, since Kantaros walked the earth, has always given birth to a set of fraternal twins. You have a brother somewhere in the world. We need to find him."

My eyes widened, and I felt dizzy. "A brother? I don't have a brother. I mean, I've got five half brothers, William's sons." She had to be wrong. There had to be some kind of mistake.

Angelo shot me a glare. "Of course, you've got a brother. Did you not listen to your grandmother? Things haven't changed since the beginning of time. You are a worthless excuse for a Centauride, but that doesn't surprise me. Your mother was pathetic, too. The Chiron bloodline is dominate; we were favored by Zeus."

He wanted me to challenge him; I could feel it. His words were hurtful. I couldn't argue his slanderous comments about me. Even I was embarrassed that I was unable to do what every other Centauride could do without effort, but I wouldn't allow him to attack my mother, "My mother was not pathetic. She was wonderful. She worked hard her whole life, and she treated everyone with kindness and respect."

"Ha! And she's dead. Were you not listening? I am Angela's twin. I felt her leave this world. I feel her spirit lurking here now." Angelo stopped looking at me and shouted out, "Angela, keep hiding in the corners! Spend your death the same way you spent your life! Camille is part of our family. Mother will not be as soft on her as she was on you!"

One of the marble statutes began to weave. I saw it sway twicc right before it toppled over. Angelo was fast and jumped free of the statue before it could fall on him. He shouted, "You've got to do better than that, Angela! I'm not surprised to see you are as weak in death as you were in life. Go to the pastures; leave Camille in our care. We'll see that she pays your debts!"

I looked in all directions. I needed her to tell me how she escaped. I needed to be away from this place. Why couldn't I see her?

Zandra answered me, "You can't see her because you choose not to see her. Imagine her disappointment in you. I can see her. I can see you fell short in her eyes, and you continue to do so by refusing to use the gifts you were born with. You need only open your mind to find your twin."

Without thinking I blurted out, "Angelo, if you had this connection with my mom, how did you never find her?"

Angelo's teeth were mashed together; his lips were thin angry lines and his eyes blazed when he answered, "She was cloaked by magic. When her spirit left her body, I felt it go. I knew she had died."

I was intrigued. Not only had my mother escaped, she was able to completely hide from everyone, even Angelo who should have had Centaur GPS connection to her. "But your twin connection did not work before her death?"

Zandra must have read my thoughts because she turned her attention to my uncle, "Come, Angelo, we have much to catch up on."

The two of them left me in the garden. My heart hurt: I felt like I didn't belong, that I was inadequate, that I would never have the life I wanted. Angelo said I'd pay for her debts. What did that mean? To think I was excited when today's lesson began, and in this moment I couldn't imagine a fate worse than the one I was living.

I thought back to times as a teenager. Mom always knew when I was up to something I shouldn't be. I remembered I'd stayed at a party all night on the beach. I'd arranged with a friend to cover for me; if my mom checked on me, I was staying at her house. When the sun rose and I knew it was time to go home, my mother's car was waiting for me in the beach's parking lot. I didn't know how long she had sat waiting for me. Most parents would have flown off the handle. She didn't. All she said was, "I'm disappointed in you, Camille." I think I would have taken any punishment in the world if it meant I wouldn't have heard those words.

Another time when I'd "borrowed" a sweater from her after she'd told me I couldn't, I sneaked into her room and jammed it deep into my book bag. I tried to get to the front door when she stopped me. She took it out of my book bag before I left for school that morning and scolded me for lying to her. All my friends noticed it, too. I was the only one who could never get away with anything. I'd never put it together before.

She really was a Centauride. I was her daughter and if what Angelo told me was true – I had a twin brother somewhere in the world that I'd never known. I thought back to Mom's treasure box in her closet, the photograph of two babies. Was Zandra right? Maybe as a Centauride and as a daughter, I was a disappointment to my mother.

Thankfully, Angelo departed the same day he came. He was like Zandra, evil to the core, with no thought for anyone but himself. I felt horrible for my circumstance. I wanted to run away. I wanted to talk to someone. I needed human contact.

I read the whole diary in short bursts; there weren't that many entries. From what I'd read, she really didn't care for Zandra and was thrilled with the idea of marrying Kyle Richardson and getting the heck away. I wish there had been something that talked about how she made her escape. A secret passageway? Maybe her father finally came through for her? But I didn't find any clues in it, other than to know Zandra had always been a vile person, and her brother Angelo was mean to her his whole life.

Entry Eighteen Oct Demo – Kyle stopped by again today. I can't wait to get married and get away from this place. Dad refuses to stop Angelo's constant threats. I can't believe we are related, let alone twins. Angelo warned Kyle I'd run the first chance I got, and that Kyle needed to talk to mother about keeping me under control. When Kyle told Angelo that he wasn't worried, Angelo offered to show him how to slice my Achilles' tendon, to keep me from running. Kyle pretended he thought that Angelo was joking, but he stayed with me all day and offered to camp out in the backyard if I wanted him to. Two more weeks and this hell is over.

By my forty-second tick mark on my closet wall, I began to wonder if I'd ever be permitted to leave or speak to another human being. I was thankful Bianca had taught me how to protect my thoughts so the hatred I felt for Zandra was masked from her view. I did broadcast the loneliness I felt growing each day, hoping it would ebb away at Zandra's resolve to keep me a prisoner. Those lonely thoughts gave way to the longing for relationships that might never be. I felt myself thinking often of Will, Gretchen, and my brothers, how all of them had willingly accepted me into their home, their lives and their hearts. The fun-loving brothers I'd only known for a mere week had been abruptly stolen like a prized toy. The knowledge that somewhere in the world I had a brother that I'd shared my mother's womb with was crippling because I didn't know if he was dead or alive. The father who was full of love, who I'd been denied my whole life, was robbed from me. I thought of Daniel all the time. I knew he would be worried sick by now. The solitude proved unbearable, and the guards witnessed me in emotional turmoil nearly every evening, but none offered even one word of comfort. They looked on as my hopelessness threatened to envelope me.

As I stared at that forty-second tick mark, I made up my mind, no matter what Zandra chose to do to me, it couldn't be worse than the utter hopelessness of being denied human contact – or Centaur contact. When she joined me in the garden, she waited for me to repeat the lesson from yesterday—I rebelled the only way I knew how, "Zandra, when can I see Dad again?"

"Your father is very busy. He'll see you when he chooses to make time for you." She was lying. I couldn't read her mind or her thoughts, but I could feel the truth. She was keeping me from him.

"Does he know where I am?"

"Of course, he knows where you are."

"Then why hasn't he come to see me?"

"I'm afraid I don't know."

"Bullshit!" The look on her face was worth every penny in my bank account, and I would have gladly handed it over. I'd rattled her.

"I think we'll skip the lesson today. I'll see you tomorrow." She stood and walked away. I felt that initial panic that I had wasted what little human contact I was afforded by my belligerence. The panic gave way to seething anger; I made myself a silent promise that I would not relent. I watched as an alligator that had been sunning along the water's edge dove into the water – even that beast with prehistoric ancestors had more freedom than I did. I wouldn't give up, and I refused to politely sit through one more of her lessons.

I was done. Nothing in the world was worth this isolation. When I heard the door to the house close, I knew my human contact was over for the day. I was wearing blue jeans, a sweatshirt, and my favorite sneakers – perfect traveling clothes. I stood up and started walking toward the large iron gate. I could hear my guard's footsteps behind me. I had gone thirty feet when I heard his voice for the first time in six weeks, "Stop!"

I ignored him and picked up my pace.

His voice was loud and menacing, "Camille, I said *stop*!"

I didn't even glance over my shoulder. I had spoken to him on several occasions and was ignored. I wouldn't give him the satisfaction of a response. Instead I let loose into a sprint for the gate. Two vice grips for hands grabbed my shoulders, throwing me violently to the ground when I was less than twenty feet from the gate. I hadn't expected the impact. I lay on the ground weighing my options. I could easily make it into the swamp with a hope that this man couldn't swim and the alligators I watched every day would not attack me. I sat up from the ground, brushed the gravel off of my face, and glared in his direction.

His face was angry when he demanded, "Go back to the house."

"You go back to the house. I'm going home."

"This is your home, Camille."

"No, this is her home. I'm leaving." I stood up, brushed the last of the gravel from me and looked at the gate. I could reach it and be over it in less than thirty seconds. The problem was, I knew the guard was even faster. Where's a man-eating alligator when you need one? I took a step toward the water, deciding this would be my best shot at freedom. When I did, the guard heaved his whole body at me. The weight of his frame knocked the wind out of me and covered me in gravel a second time.

The guard anticipated what I was about to do. He was done talking to me. His palm gripped my neck at the base of my skull, and he forcibly escorted me all the way to the front door.

The anger inside me welled up with such fervor that I was sure it would spill over and poison those around me. I knew I needed to hold the anger, but I also needed to get it back to a slow boil. I did what I knew would bring the anger under control, but in doing so would make my heart ache all over again.

I closed my eyes and imagined the day on the yacht with Drake: how his skin felt as I held his face in my hands. I saw the surprised look on his face when images of the two of us flooded from his mind. I remembered how overcome I was by the images, so much so that I kissed him without warning. I sat in my room for what felt like hours, reliving those precious few moments with him, trying to remember what we had said to one another.

Drake was my island oasis. I could feel the molten anger subsiding. It didn't go away – but I felt I had it under control again. Thoughts of Drake had somehow become my escape. I thought of my easy friendship with Bianca and wondered if she'd been able to convince Drake to break their engagement after I'd been taken away. I wondered what they knew of my disappearance. Did they think I'd hopped a plane to California? I tried not to think of Daniel, but knew he was probably a nervous wreck; we'd been friends since I knew what a friend was. Even when I'd gone away to summer camp, I had never gone longer than a week without talking to him.

The morning of tick mark forty-three, I again met Zandra in the garden and asked her the same question as the day before. She refused to answer and gingerly walked away for a second time. It was in that moment that I realized she was manipulating me in one of the most sadistic of manners. She withheld what little human contact was afforded to me. I was stronger than she gave me credit for, sharper still for noticing it, and then it hit me – I wasn't alone. My mother's spirit was undoubtedly here with me. I just needed to figure out how to communicate with her. By Zandra's own admission, this was a gift bestowed upon me by Zeus himself; no amount of manipulation would inhibit this gift.

CHAPTER 27

Camille Benning – Florida – Six weeks following her abduction

I looked at my guard; it wasn't the same one who had tackled me yesterday. "I know you're forbidden from talking to me. I don't need you to say a word, but I do need you to help me. My guess is you don't like her any more than I do. Blink your eyes once for yes, twice for no. Do you understand?" The guard's eyes darted from left to right to ensure no prying eyes could see. He blinked once. My heart did a cartwheel in my chest.

"Does my father know where I am?" His eyes blinked once, again. "Has he tried to see me?" Again, one single blink. "Do you know how long she plans to keep me?" This time he blinked twice. "Will you help me get out of here?" He blinked twice again. What little hope I had felt when the guard blinked his answers disappeared in front of my eyes.

I heard my mother's voice for the first time since her hospital room, "*Listen to his thoughts.*" I looked in all directions to see if she had miraculously appeared, but I couldn't see her. I smelled her perfume, and a warm glow overtook me—she was with me. I concentrated with everything I had on this guard standing in front of me. I looked at the lines around his eyes, the way the red vessels showed through the white, and the light caramel brown of his eyes. My concentration did not waiver. I was sure he had to feel me tugging at his thoughts. It was as if a thin membrane separated them from me.

The guard did nothing to impede me. I looked in all directions to see if Zandra was anywhere close. I visualized the membrane separating his thoughts from me, and with near surgical precision, I cut a big gaping hole in it. I saw the guard's knees weaken for a moment; he recovered quickly and looked away. I asked him my question with my thoughts, "*Can you hear me?*"

No reaction. "*Can you hear me in your head?*" Again, nothing. He had to have known I was there, but he couldn't hear my thoughts, so I whispered, "What's your name?"

His answer came to me loudly, through his thoughts, "*I am* Phineas."

"Phineas, I can hear you." His eyes glistened and a smirk appeared on his face. I was thrilled to have someone who would talk to me. I talked aloud and he through his thoughts. He must have been suspicious that Zandra was closer than either he or I could see because he instructed, "*Keep your voice low. I am a close friend to your father. I told him of your tantrum yesterday. He was pleased.*"

"I wouldn't call it a tantrum, more of an assertion of independence."

"*Call it what you want, she was furious when Aragon told her you tried to escape. Have you seen your future?*"

"Uh, no. How do I do that?"

"*I don't know how, but all Chiron Centauride's can see the future; very few can see their own. Zandra saw your future and locked you away to keep it from happening. Gretchen is not as powerful as Zandra but believes you are at a crossroads. You are capable of several destinies.*"

"So Zandra is trying to change my future by keeping me locked up here? She can do that? Change someone's destiny?"

"*She can influence it, but she cannot preclude one that has been selected.*"

"What'd she see?"

"*I don't know, but whatever it was, it really shook her up. Your father hoped that she would use this time to teach you the things your mother didn't, to bestow her maternal gifts on you.*"

"The only thing I need from that woman is an exit. So how do I get out of here?"

"*Your father is still working on that. Because you aren't married, it is within her rights to remain your guardian. Your father wants to know if you have spoken with your mother's spirit.*"

"Funny that you should ask. She spoke to me for the first time a few minutes ago, telling me to delve into your head."

"*She may be able to help you, more than I can. If I am caught aiding you, Zandra will seek retribution on my family. I've already put them at great risk.*"

I was so pleased to be talking with someone, I didn't think of the implications for him. "Thanks, Phineas. Let my father know I'm okay."

"*I will.*"

"Why hasn't he come to see me?"

"*She's put a spell on the gate, so none of your blood relatives can enter. William said you need to ask your mother about the night they met. He said you needed to know something about that night.*"

"I will. Tell him not to worry." When I stood up, Phineas followed me, just as he had during his shifts since the first day I came to Zandra's home. He neither made eye contact nor shared another thought with me. Unsure of whether Zandra would be able to know if he were communicating with me, I silently closed the hole I had opened in the membrane of his thoughts. It was quiet again, but bearable. At least now I knew I wasn't alone – I had an ally.

That evening, I sat by myself, the same as I had done every evening, to a lonely dinner in an empty formal dining room. My evening guard had relieved Phineas, and I was feeling sorry for myself again. It was Aragon, who was extremely loyal to her; he was the one who stood guard in my bedroom nearly every night. I hated the idea of being watched while I slept, and I especially hated that he was the one watching me. Zandra walked into the room and saw the food I had pushed around on my plate. She looked at me with her usual disapproving glance, then announced, "I have a gift for you."

I was startled by her voice initially. This was the first time she had talked to me outside of the garden. My heart leaped at the idea that I might be leaving soon. She withdrew a wooden box from inside a linen bag. When she opened it, purple velvet lined the interior and a shimmering necklace lay waiting. "This was your mother's. I sense you are eager to leave my estate. I wanted you to have it."

I nodded enthusiastically, pleased that all our lessons and this dreadful prison were soon going to be a part of my past. Zandra motioned for me to stand, and I held my hair away from my neck, allowing her to clasp the exquisite necklace to me. It was made of platinum and unbelievably large sapphires. I had never experienced wearing jewelry made of platinum before and had no real appreciation for how heavy it would be. When Zandra secured the clasps, I felt a short burst of energy encircling my neck. She said, "This necklace's weight is meant to remind you of your obligations to this bloodline, to your family."

Zandra had given me a gift that belonged to my mother, acknowledging for the first time that I belonged. I was her flesh. I was thrilled, and without thinking, I blurted out, "When can I see my father?"

An electric shock so powerful shot through my body from the necklace, it brought me to my knees. I knelt on the floor crumpled from the energy, wondering what had just happened. Zandra's wicked voice calmly responded, "You will not see him until your wedding night,

Camille. Each time I feel your belligerence or you initiate a quarrel with me, you will be reminded of your place in my home. Do you understand?"

I nodded my head in horror. A second ago, I had felt like a princess. What I realized was that in addition to my 24 hour guard watching my every move, my grandmother had given me the Centaur equivalent of an electrified shock collar to curb my outbursts. She smiled widely, in an effort to project her dominance, "Your mother wore that same necklace. She, too, was headstrong and threatened to run away at the first opportunity. I mistakenly removed it from her before she could marry the Centaur I selected for her. I will not make the same mistake a second time."

"Zandra, I can't be married. I can't choose. Mr. Richardson had me swear an oath that if his son was still not chosen by the time he was twenty-nine, I would choose him."

Her smile widened, giving me goose bumps. "You won't have to wait five years, Camille. I have already chosen Gage Richardson for you. You will be married in a month."

I shouted at her, "But I don't even know him!" Another electric charge rocked my body. My body shook in a mixture of adrenaline and desperation. I gritted my teeth, knowing that I would bring on the brutality of the device with another outburst, but I didn't care. "He is about to be chosen by another Centauride." The electric charges seemed to grow in intensity and length with each zap, as I braced myself when the third shock hit me.

Zandra shook her finger at me, as if correcting a small child caught in a cookie jar. "I'm afraid that won't happen. I've already spoken with my dear friend, Kyle. After your mother's stunt, he and I have developed a healthy respect for one another. You and Gage will be married in one month. Preparations are already underway."

I put my hands to the torturous device in an effort to move it away from the delicate skin around my neck, "I won't marry him." The fourth shock hit me so hard that I felt the flesh around my neck scorch, my fingers went numb, and I couldn't help but scream out in pain.

Zandra seemed to be enjoying the brutality of her present, "Have we learned our lesson yet? I can assure you, you have no alternatives."

I didn't think I could make my voice work without releasing sobs instead of words. The smell of burned flesh was thick in the air, and I knew she would continue to batter me until I relented or went up in flames. She stood in front of me, "Do not try to remove my endowment. It is your legacy. It can be removed by me or by your husband. I will only warn you this one time: should you try to remove it, the pain will be unbearable and the scarring a permanent reminder of your insolence. Attempting to leave my estate has similar results. You will learn your place. You will be obedient to me for the remainder of your stay, and you will not run away from your obligations. Goodnight, Camille. "

With her final threat, the tears that I had held for the last forty-three days of loneliness, and the last fifteen minutes of brutality, let loose. She had won. I was a sobbing mess, and as the salt from my tears streamed down my face, several down my neck and into the now open wounds, the sting was a horrific reminder of how utterly horrible my existence had become. I finally understood my mother's diary entry: it hadn't been some vampire. My own grandmother had put this device on my mother. From her description in the diary, it could do far more than scorch my skin.

Sleep didn't find me that night. The pain of the raw, charred skin on my neck didn't permit me to find any sort of position that would dull the pain. I asked the guard if he could get me some Neosporin, but he looked forward, with no acknowledgement to my request. I watched the sun pour in through the window, praying that my nightmare would be over soon. Why was she so set on me marrying Gage Richardson? She had set up a similar arrangement with his father and my mother—but my mother was able to escape. Waves of sadness washed over me as I imagined my mom growing up here with this lunatic. No wonder she told me her family was dead. No wonder we never traveled outside of California. I was furious with myself for not having run away to a remote jungle to escape this crazy woman when I had the chance. But at this point, running away was no longer an option.

In one short month, I would be married, married to a man whose heart would forever belong to Bianca. She told me no decision I ever made would drive a wedge into our friendship. Marrying the man that she loved might qualify as a wedge. Three heavy knocks hit my bedroom door with such force that the wall shook. I stared at the door, not willing to utter a syllable.

"Camille, could you come out here?" It was a man's voice. I didn't recognize it, but someone was talking to me. It was someone besides Zandra.

CHAPTER 28

Camille Benning – Florida

At this point I would relish any visitor that was not my captor. I stood up gingerly from my bed, carefully put a sweatshirt on over my nightshirt and grabbed a pair of jeans. My guard didn't flinch. I turned the doorknob cautiously to be sure it wasn't some sort of a trick.

I recognized him from the pizza place the day Bianca hatched her "brilliant" plan. It was the man who would become my warden in a month. His voice was confident and his expression told me he was pleased to see me, "I thought I'd stop by to acquaint myself with my fiancé." He looked handsome. He wore a black t-shirt, a size too small for his biceps, his jeans were well worn but clean, his goatee and mustache were nicely trimmed, and he gave me a willing smile.

"Hi, Gage." I found the strength to mumble, "Nice to see you again."

"I thought we could get to know each other. Maybe go for a drive or something." He gave a startled look at the guard who had spent the night standing at attention. I could tell Gage didn't know what to make of him, so he added, "We could take your escort along." He had recovered quickly from his surprise, as if every single Centauride just happened to have a guard posted on her 24 hours per day.

I shook my head, "I'm not permitted to leave the estate."

"Even with an escort?"

I shook my head a little more vigorously. When I did, the necklace rubbed one of the sores on my neck, and I winced. Gage saw me wince, but I'm sure he didn't know why. "How about a walk in the garden?" he offered.

I looked at the guard to see if he would object. He continued focusing his attention onto the opposite wall. "Okay."

Gage seemed nice. He complimented the gardens that I also once thought were beautiful, the statues of the Greek gods that lined each section. The guards hadn't changed over like they normally would have. I began to wonder if something had happened to Phineas. He should have been here by now. Could Zandra have found out that he shared information with me? He said she would go after his family. If she was somehow listening to us yesterday, what would she have heard?

"Camille, did you hear me?" Gage was staring at me.

"I'm sorry, my mind was wandering. What'd you say?"

"I asked if you had chosen the gardens for our ceremony?"

"Uh, Zandra hasn't told me where."

It was obvious that Gage was trying to be charming, "If I get a vote, I'd like it to be next to the statue of Zeus."

My spirit was nearly broken, "I'll ask her if she minds."

"Camille, is there something wrong?"

I couldn't answer him. His question was wrong, on so many levels. When he realized I had no intention of answering him, he said, "Camille, you're supposed to be excited. We'll be united in a few short weeks. You don't seem the least bit interested."

I had cried my eyes out last night until nothing was left. I knew there was no escape, and I would be forced into exactly the life my mom never wanted and had carefully sheltered me from, hiding me away for twenty-two years. All her sacrifices for me had been made in vain. Gage grasped both my hands in his, "Do you not want to marry me?" There was a hopefulness in his voice, and I was too emotionally drained to try to figure out if it was hopefulness that I did or did not want to marry him. It didn't matter what I wanted. It wasn't my choice. I had no options.

"I . . . just had a rough night last night. I'm sorry if . . . I don't seem into it."

My lack of enthusiasm didn't diminish his, "I think Dad and Zandra are enthused enough for both of us. The invitations will be going out tomorrow." My only response was a solitary tear dripping down my cheek. I tried to wipe it away quickly before he could see, but Gage was far too perceptive.

"Talk to me, Camille. There is something bothering you." If I hadn't been subjected to the last two months, the kindness in Gage's voice wouldn't have had such an effect on me. But the absence of any human contact, other than Zandra, combined with the emptiness of emotions and the horrible night last night left me broken. It left me needing comfort. I leaned fully into Gage, sobbing silently against his chest as he gently wrapped his arms around me. He told me it'd be okay, and I got the impression he had no idea why he was comforting me, but he held me anyway.

When my emotional meltdown had subsided, I looked up at him with blurry eyes and tear-stained cheeks. I could see he was at a loss, unsure what to say. Finally I took my eyes off of him and found a very interesting patch of grass to concentrate on while he still held me in his arms. The words were out before I realized they had come from me. "What about, Bianca?"

Gage let go of me as if my skin burned him. He took a step away from me and said slowly, "I don't want you to mention Bianca to me, ever."

I was confused, "But she loves you. Why would you agree to marry me?"

His voice was harsh and his eyes angry, "Bianca is engaged to another Centaur. Never speak of her to me."

"But, Bianca is my friend . . . I don't. . ." the necklace must have decided my question constituted disobedience because the wounds that had been caked over with scabs overnight were just reopened by the new zap of electricity. I fell to the ground on my hands and knees and screamed like a Banshee. Gage stood, dumbfounded.

The necklace of horrors was hidden from view under my sweatshirt. The freshly opened wounds seeped blood through the sweatshirt as Gage's eyes watched helplessly. I saw him look at the guard, who paid no attention whatsoever to me writhing in pain. Gage knelt down beside me and saw the streaks of blood from the freshly opened wounds. He instantly tried to remove the necklace from me, but that only resulted in a second zap to us both and a shriller scream from me.

The guard seemed to have no problems talking to Gage, "The necklace is enchanted. It requires her obedience to Zandra and to you. You will be permitted to remove it from her after you are married," he added sadistically, "if you choose to." The guard's voice held no sympathy for me. His comment, "If you choose to," wasn't lost on me either. I'm sure if I had been betrothed to this guard, he would never remove it.

Gage's voice was full of volume when he yelled at the guard, "Are you insane? She's bleeding!"

"She is fully aware of the power of the enchantment. As your fiancé, she should have listened to your warning. The necklace does for you what you are too kind to do to her. She will not run away. She will not change her mind. She will be an obedient wife."

I could see the horror on Gage's face. He commanded, "Guard, leave us."

"I'm under orders from Zandra. You two are not to be left alone. I serve as her guard and her escort while you are on the premises."

Zandra appeared from around the hedge closest to the house. I knew she had witnessed what had happened or at least pieced it together. She flashed Gage a warm smile and held out her hand to him, "Gage, so glad you could stop by this morning. I'm afraid Camille has lessons in the garden every morning. You'll have to come back later to acquaint yourselves with each other."

"Miss Zandra. I believe Camille needs a doctor." I could see he struggled momentarily for the right words. "Her necklace has rubbed her neck raw."

Zandra's warm smile broadened when she said, "The necklace teaches her lessons more effectively than either you or I could teach her. She is not in need of a physician. Camille is in need of better manners. I believe she'll find them soon, don't you agree?"

Gage reached down, took my hand in his and politely asked Zandra, "It's really a beautiful day, and we've hardly had time to acquaint ourselves. Would it be all right if we spent some time getting to know each other now?"

Zandra eyed him suspiciously. "Very well. Do not leave the gardens." The polite tone she used with Gage disappeared when she addressed me, "Camille, we will continue our lessons tomorrow morning. I suggest you use this time to fine tune your manners."

Gage showed no fear, but an overt respect for her authority, "Uh, Miss Zandra, would it be possible for her escort to give us some privacy? I understand that we need to stay in clear view, but I'd like to get to know Camille a little better. Could he watch us from the garden's entrance?"

Zandra agreed and motioned for Aragon to move the fifty feet toward the elaborate entrance, in between two marble centaurs. Gage still held my hand but motioned for me to sit down. "What has she done to you?"

"She's been teaching me about Greek mythology, mainly."

"What's the story with the necklace of horrors?"

"She didn't like some of the things I had to say, and I tried to escape. The next thing I knew I was going through some twisted version of electric shock therapy."

"I'm going to have to leave for a few hours, but I'll be back, I promise. Is there anything I can get you?"

"Could I . . . I mean could you . . . I'd really like to see . . . Never mind."

"Who? Your dad?"

"I can't say her name."

Quietly, he nodded that he understood. "I'm saying this for the necklace's benefit more than yours, okay?" He waited for me to nod, then said, "You may say anything you want to me. An opinion or a question is not disobedience. You should not be punished for being inquisitive. It pleases me that you have a strong spirit."

"Thanks." I was so embarrassed of the position I was in, it was hard to look him in the eye.

"So, now that is out of the way. Why did you choose me for your husband?"

"Zandra chose you. She didn't tell me why other than she really wanted my mom to marry your dad. Mom ran away before the ceremony. I just found out that we were engaged last night."

"Last night? But she and Dad have been talking for over a month. You had no idea?"

I shook my head, still nervous about talking out loud. Gage breathed a huge sigh of relief. I wasn't sure why, and he didn't explain. "Is there anything I can bring you when I return?"

"A cell phone. I haven't talked to anyone in like forever."

Gage nodded. He stood and took both my hands in his as I remained seated. "I'll do my best to smuggle it in, although mine was confiscated when I arrived this morning. I was told that the marriage was your idea. You're saying that isn't true?"

I started to answer but stopped myself before I could say the word. Telling him the truth might be construed as disobedience to Zandra. I shook my head in response.

He bent down and kissed my hands. It sent shivers through my body. I'd had more human contact with him in the short time he spent with me than I'd had the whole time I'd been here. It felt good to be with someone who wasn't trying to manipulate me, someone who didn't believe kindness to be a character flaw.

"I'll be back soon," he promised.

As I watched him walk away, I wondered if he'd really be allowed back. Zandra could change the enchantment on the gate to ban him as well. I wasn't sure if I could make it another month living like this. I looked back at the guard and wondered where Phineas was.

CHAPTER 29

Camille Benning – Florida

I was surprised to see Gage back before dinner. He wasn't alone. Bianca and Drake were both with him as he stepped through the massive entryway. Bianca ran to me, threw her arms around me, and squealed, "Camille, I've been so worried about you!"

I was so excited to see the friendly faces that I couldn't make a coherent sentence. Drake stepped through the entryway and brought in suitcases. I looked questioningly but couldn't peel myself away from Bianca. I could feel his eyes on me; they were heavy and I couldn't read his expression. My mind jumped to our lunch at Andolini's, the last time all four of us had been together. The excitement of that day seemed so long ago. I wasn't sure I was even the same person anymore. I felt weak, frightened, broken – a far cry from the euphoria from my last day of freedom.

Zandra walked down the staircase, suspicious of the people who had arrived without an invitation. "Gage, so lovely to see you again. I see you've brought friends."

"I spoke with my father this morning and told him how well Camille and I had hit it off. I knew Camille and Bianca were good friends, but as you know, Bianca is betrothed to Drake Nash. It would not be appropriate for me to travel with another Centaur's fiancé. My father recommended that I bring Bianca and Drake for a stay with you until we are wed."

"Your father suggested this?"

"Yes, Miss Zandra. He knows Camille is new to the Centaur way and thought having the three of us to keep her company may make her transition into our society less . . .problematic."

Zandra's expression was stern, but she did not argue. "If it is at your father's request, I can hardly deny you." She looked at my guard, "Aragon, take their luggage upstairs. There are several open bedrooms in Camille's wing. Notify the staff that Camille will have company for dinner this evening." Without another word, she turned and walked away. The guard looked perplexed. I had not been left unguarded since the day I set foot here.

Aragon looked at the suitcases, then at me, then back to the suitcases. Gage could see the guard's internal struggle as clearly as I could. "Aragon, Camille will be safe with us. She won't bolt out the door. If Miss Zandra wants you to take our luggage upstairs, I wouldn't neglect her direction." He made a motion with his hands around his own neck, emulating the necklace I wore. The guard agreed and took the suitcases.

As soon as the guard was headed up the stairs, Bianca whispered, "Gage told us. Don't worry, we'll find a way to get you out of here."

"I can't believe you're all here. How long are you staying?"

She answered conspiratorially, "As long as it takes. Drake works for his dad, so it was easy for him to take the time off. Gage told his dad what he'd seen, and Kyle said to do whatever it took to keep you safe."

We knew watchful eyes were on us. Bianca, Drake and Gage were full of excitement, funny stories, and a real love of life. It was therapeutic just to be in their presence, and I was more grateful than I could have ever expressed to any of them, to have them near me after so much loneliness. After we had eaten dinner and spent several hours together, Bianca announced, "Okay, I'm exhausted. Drake, will you walk me to my room?"

"I'd be happy to. Good night, Gage. Good night, Camille. I think I'll turn in, too. See you both in the morning." The two walked arm-in-arm up the stairs, leaving only Gage, me and my guard in the sitting room. Gage walked across the room, sat down beside me on the sofa and whispered, "There is nothing you could do or no action you could take that would be disobedient to me." He pressed his lips to my forehead. When he stood up, he moved his hand to my cheek and looked lovingly in my eyes, "I need a word with Miss Zandra. Will you accompany me?"

Reeling from our tender exchange, I wasn't sure how to react. Was he testing my necklace to see if I would refuse? I didn't. We found her in an art studio, working on a beautiful oil-painted landscape. Gage cleared his throat, "Miss Zandra, good evening."

"Hello, Gage, Camille. How are you two getting along?"

"Very well, thank you."

She looked at her watch; it was after 11:30p.m. "You're up rather late this evening."

"We were both going to turn in. I had another request that I hoped you'd consider."

Zandra set her paint pallet down and looked at him. She seemed to have all the patience in the world for his requests. "Camille tells me that her guard is posted in her room while she sleeps. Although I'm sure it is for her protection, she hasn't been sleeping well. As her fiancé, I'm none too thrilled that another man is permitted in her room while she sleeps."

"You are correct, Gage. The guards are for her protection. It is not negotiable."

"I was afraid you might say that. Well, thank you for your consideration. I need to phone father tonight and let him know that we arrived safely. I'll escort Camille to her room then step outside the gate to retrieve my cell."

He had just threatened her. I didn't have a clue what sort of power Gage's dad had over Zandra, but her eyes widened and she stammered, "You know, as her fiancé, I'm sure you have her best interests at heart. If it pleases you, her guard will remain outside her room while she sleeps. We do have a phone in the house that you may use. There is no reason for you to have to brave the mosquitoes and the bats walking to your car; her guard will show you where it is."

"How very kind of you, Miss Zandra! I'm so pleased. I will definitely relay to my father how accommodating you have been." Gage held out his elbow for me to hold as he escorted me to my room. When we were outside my bedroom door, he pressed his lips to my forehead a second time and said, "I'll see you in the morning, Camille. I had a lovely evening and look forward to tomorrow. Sleep well." Gage turned his attention to the guard, "Please alert me if you are concerned for Camille's safety. Do not enter her room without me. Do you understand?"

"I understand, Mr. Richardson. Have a good evening."

Gage's smirk was undeniable. I had no idea what he was up to, but I was pleased that he seemed to have far more influence in this house than I did. I turned in for the night, and although I hadn't mentioned to Gage that I hated the idea of being watched while I slept, I was thrilled that he somehow knew it to be true. I crawled into bed and was excited for the first time in a long time; there was a ray of hope for my future.

I heard a ruckus out in the hallway about an hour later. I was sure I had heard Gage's voice, something about a bat in his room. I saw a blur by my door but was half asleep and paid it almost no attention, at least until I realized I wasn't alone. The illumination from the windows brightened the room. I felt a gentle hand caress my cheek, and heard a low whisper. "Camille, it's me. I had to see you." I knew who was kneeling beside my bed when those beautiful ice blue eyes came into focus.

CHAPTER 30

Camille Benning – Florida

"How did you. . ."

Drake held his finger to his lips. "Gage created a diversion to get the guard away from your door."

"But, I thought you and Bianca . . ."

Drake shook his head at me before I could even get the words out. "I brought you something." He took some salve from his pocket and motioned for me to sit up. He continued kneeling beside my bed, his fingers gently putting the cooling ointment on the wounds around my neck. His touch was light; if I hadn't felt the relief I wouldn't have known he was touching me. I had become so accustomed to the burning sensation on my neck that the cool from the ointment was indescribable. As my body concluded it was Drake's touch it felt, a new fire began to spread from his touch.

Once he had used his healing hands on my neck, he brought the full force of his stare on me. "I've missed you, Camille." My senses went into overload: I could feel my hands trembling, my heart picking up speed, alone in a room with someone who not only wanted me, but was eager for my touch as well.

I reached my palm to his jaw. He closed his eyes, as if savoring the feeling. I felt the stubble on his cheek, the warmth of his skin, and felt my island oasis here in the flesh. Drake put his hand over mine, opened his eyes, and his stare held me motionless as I tried to find the words. He was the first to recover, "I've thought of you every day." The hopefulness in his eyes wouldn't let me go.

I knew I couldn't take the heartache. I couldn't profess feelings for someone I knew I could never have. Doing so would be the thing that actually broke my spirit – it would leave me a ghost of a person. I tried to speak but nothing would come out. I tried to look away, but my eyes refused. Instead I sat there, my hand remaining on his cheek, memorizing the feel of his skin, drinking in his scent, knowing this was the final farewell.

"I can't read your mind, Camille. I won't make you read mine." Before I could protest, his lips were on mine and his arms pulled me tightly to his chest. My rapidly beating heart tried to lunge from my chest, and I couldn't breathe. His breath was hot. I felt my whole body aching for his touch. His lips found their way to my ear as he whispered, "Run away with me. Tonight, right now. We'll leave and never look back."

I hadn't uttered a word since he arrived, and I knew he was waiting for me to say something. My only answer, "Drake, we can't."

He wasn't deterred, "Yes, we can. Gage set it up perfectly. He's willing to take the heat. All we have to do is leave. Come with me, Camille."

"I can't. The necklace won't let me leave."

"Gage said he took care of it. He gave you permission to do anything you want tonight." As he said the words, Drake's hands found my flesh and began softly caressing the small of my back, sending goose bumps all over my body. Until he said it, I had been so wrapped up in Drake that it didn't occur to me that kissing another man had to be some sort of crime for the necklace, yet nothing had happened. A small ray of hope emerged, and I thought for half a second that I might actually be able to run away.

"That was only part of it. I can't leave."

"I can take it off." I knew he wouldn't be able to, but the thought of running away, being free, overwhelmed the self-preservation side of my consciousness. As Drake's fingers touched the clasps of the necklace, a powerful electric charge rocked us both and sent Drake flying into the wall and me back onto the floor. I could tell each electric charge continued to get stronger and shock me for longer periods of time. I didn't scream out like before. I knew the "warnings" I had been given initially had been painful, but they were just that – warnings. This latest singed the barely healing skin around my neck, cut off my air and opened the scabbed wounds all over again. I wasn't sure how many more warnings I would be afforded. The device could prove fatal if I didn't follow its rules.

Drake ran back to me as soon as he had his bearings. "I'm so sorry! Are you okay? Camille, talk to me!"

"Keep your voice down. I'm fine," I whispered. We both listened for the footsteps outside my door. I didn't hear any and was able to take a breath.

Fresh blood trickled down my neck as I watched the revulsion on his face. "Does she know what that does to you?" He asked horrified at the results.

"Of course, she knows. She put it on my mother when she was supposed to marry Gage's dad. She already told me it stays on my neck until I'm married."

Drake held me tighter, his body pressed hard into mine, "Camille, I can't lose you. Not to Gage, not to anyone." I stood up, clinging to Drake, absorbing his warmth, pulling all the comfort from him that I knew I'd need to survive another day. He said more to himself than to me, "We'll figure something out. I promise."

It was an empty promise. Zeus himself wouldn't be able to deliver on this one. Drake spent the night holding me. I felt stronger in his arms and reveled in the dream that we could run away. But my reality kept reminding me—that dream was never to be.

As the dawn arrived, I wasn't sure how we were going to get Drake out of my room. He must have noticed my increasing nervousness. Without releasing me from his hold, his lips found their way to the skin not scorched from my torturous device on my neck and my ear. He whispered, "I'll be waiting for you in your closet tonight. Gage will keep you downstairs long enough for me to get into position."

"You're going to hide in my closet?"

"Unless you have a better idea. Gage can't come up with a distraction every night; it would cause too much suspicion."

"So, Gage, he doesn't mind?"

"Are you nuts? Gage knows how I feel about you. So does Bianca."

I could hear my heart pounding in my chest, scared that I might ruin the moment, but more fearful of not knowing the answer, "How *do* you feel about me?"

Drake gave me the strangest look. Sarcasm oozed from his voice when he said, "I'm fascinated by your threshold for pain. How do you think I feel about you?" His lips found mine in an aggressive and needy way. His hands clung to my flesh as if it would be the last time he would hold me for a lifetime. I didn't know what would happen the rest of the day, and in that moment, the earth could have stopped spinning and I wouldn't have given it a second thought.

I heard a light tapping on my door, "Darling, it's Gage. Ready for breakfast?"

I looked wide eyed at Drake, and whispered, "Darling? Are you sure he's okay with this?"

Drake rolled his eyes. "It's an act, Love. He needs to be convincing or your lunatic grandmother will ban him until your wedding night, which means I'd have to go, too. Go spend the day with your fiancé. I'll be waiting for you tonight."

I called toward the door, "Gage, I just need five minutes to freshen up."

"All right. I'm starving. Hurry up."

Drake and I were both on our feet. The pangs of adrenaline started to grip me when I realized I'd be able to see Drake again tonight. I had just spit the last of my toothpaste into the sink and rinsed when Drake came up behind me. I looked at the reflection of us in the mirror. His arms wrapped around me as he seemed to be transfixed by the couple in the mirror, too.

His lips were at my ear, while his eyes were glued to the mirror. He confessed, "I started to believe I'd never hold you again."

I couldn't respond. I felt my welled-up desire for him begging to be released. I turned my body so that I faced him, slipped my hands up under the back of his shirt and rested my head on his chest. I felt his hands stroke my hair as he waited for me to say something. His lips kissed the top of my head as I confessed, "I never stopped thinking of you. I don't want to wake up without you next to me. I don't want fantasies anymore. I want you."

Drake placed his hands gently on either side of my head and pulled my face away from his chest, so I was forced to look in his eyes. "I need you, Camille." His lips were on mine: they weren't gentle. Our bodies were tight against each other and our breaths were erratic. I lost myself in him again until I heard a tap at the door that brought me back to reality.

"Drake, I gotta go. Gage is waiting." I didn't want our moment to end, but knew I couldn't take a chance on the guard coming in. "Get in the closet. I'll see you tonight."

Drake looked like he was in pain, "I can't let you go, Camille."

"You have to or we'll get busted and there won't be a tonight. Go!"

His lips found mine one last time before he dashed toward the closet. As soon as I'd seen the closet door closed, I opened the door to an awaiting Gage. Gage took my hand and walked me down the hallway with my guard in tow. As we hit the top step, he commented, "You look absolutely radiant this morning, Darling. Having the guard outside your room must have done wonders for you." I looked at him as he wore an enormous smirk.

"It did. Thank you for speaking with Zandra on my behalf. I'll need to give her my thanks as well."

Zandra was waiting at the bottom of the steps and had heard our conversation. "Ah, it's good to see you two getting along so well."

Charm oozed from Gage when he said, "Who could not fall under the spell of such a beautiful creature?"

She smiled sweetly at Gage and asked me, "You slept well, Camille?"

I wanted to laugh but instead put on my most thankful expression and answered, "Yes, Grandmother, I did. Thank you for allowing me some privacy." It was the first time I had referred to her as "Grandmother," and I watched her reaction as I spoke.

She was pleased. "I'm glad you slept well, Camille. Are you ready for your lesson this morning?"

"Yes, Grandmother."

Gage interrupted, "Miss Zandra. I was hoping we might be able to tour your estate this morning, that is, if you don't mind."

"With an escort?"

"I was hoping you might consider escorting us."

Zandra looked surprised, "Me?"

"It would give us both a chance to get to know you better. Camille was telling me how much she will miss the beauty of your estate." Okay, that was a little on the thick side, but Zandra seemed to physically soften in Gage's presence. I had come to think of her estate as a prison and had no desire to ever set eyes on it again once I was paroled.

"I believe we could skip your lesson one more day, Camille. I'd love to show the two of you around." Gage continued to play his role as my doting fiancé, perfectly. He opened doors for me, held my hand, smiled as Zandra told us about nearly every blade of grass. Thirty minutes into our tour, Bianca and Drake strolled hand-in-hand onto the expansive grounds and found us near a fountain depicting Aphrodite. As the five of us walked together, Drake purposely brushed his arm against mine then caught my eye for a fraction of a second. I nearly jumped out of my skin. He was like the forbidden fruit, daring me to take a bite.

Several hours later as our tour drew to an end, Bianca spoke up as we approached the front door to Zandra's mansion. "Miss Zandra, thank you so much for giving us such a wonderful tour. Drake and I have some wedding plans to finalize. Do you have an escort you could provide us while we drive into town?" I felt the hairs on the back of my neck prickle.

"Don't be silly, child. I'm sure Gage would love an opportunity to escort you two."

Gage shook his head, "Miss Zandra, if you don't mind, I'd like to spend the afternoon with Camille. I thought a dip in the pool might be fun." I cringed when I thought of chlorine on my neck but found a way to force an adoring smile at Gage.

Zandra had transformed before my very eyes. No longer the hateful captor that I had loathed for weeks, she was now the accommodating host. "Very well then. I'll have Camille's guard escort you two into town. Gage, I'll change and join the two of you by the pool. I would very much like to know how your family is doing." The rest of the afternoon was a tremendous bore, but Gage really turned on the charm, and by dinner time Zandra was treating me as though I were her long lost granddaughter rather than a blemish on her otherwise noteworthy family tree.

Bianca and Drake returned early that evening. Zandra, having immensely enjoyed her time with Gage and me, politely asked them, "Did you two take care of all your arrangements?"

"We did. Thank you for the use of an escort, Miss Zandra," Drake answered sweetly. "Bianca and I are excited to start our life together. I think we're both regretting that we put the wedding off for so long. Watching Gage and Camille together makes me jealous that we'll have to wait so long."

Zandra raised her eyebrows. "Really? Well, you can always move the date forward."

"You know, we might just do that." Drake leaned over and kissed Bianca's cheek, "I don't believe I can wait much longer for you." Bianca giggled, and I wanted to barf. The hair on the back of my neck stood on end, and I had trouble hiding my instant jealousy. Drake gave her another tender kiss on the cheek, while I dug my fingers into my knees.

Gage realized that I was at a low boil and leaned over to me, whispering only loud enough for me to hear, "It's only an act, Darling." Gage's comment did little to soften my impending implosion.

"Bianca, I think I'll turn in early tonight," Drake announced with an adoring look at her.

Bianca took Drake's hand in hers, "I'm a little worn out myself. Would you walk me to my room?"

The two excused themselves, which left Gage and me alone with Zandra, again. Having them out of the room did wonders for my self-control. Gage and I spent another hour with Zandra, Gage the perfect guest, and I, quiet but attentive. An hour after Bianca and Drake had gone upstairs, Gage looked my way, "Darling, you look exhausted. Are you tired?"

I hadn't been paying attention to their conversation, but realized this was Gage's "get-out-of-jail-free" card for me. I yawned, "It's been a full day. I think I'll turn in, too."

"I need you well rested for our adventures tomorrow. Miss Zandra, will you keep me company or am I on my own this evening?" Zandra had always struck me as a wicked person, but super perceptive. I had to wonder if she'd see through all of Gage's fake charm. So far she seemed to be soaking it up like a sponge, but I made a mental note to tell him he needed to tone it down a little.

"I'm an old woman, Gage. You get your rest. I'm sure Camille will be ready for an adventure with you tomorrow." She looked at me with a warmer expression than I had seen her wear in the last two months, "Camille, I had a lovely day with you today."

Her thoughtful comment nearly rendered me speechless; I was able to choke out, "I did, too, Grandmother. I look forward to our lesson tomorrow." If Beau could see me now, he'd never again question my acting abilities.

She gave me a thoughtful smile. I was worried I may have put it on too thick, but she seemed genuinely pleased with me. "We may suspend your lessons for a while. Gage is an excellent influence on you, and I'm sure you'll want to spend the day together. The weather should be exceptional. Get your rest."

"Thank you, Grandmother. Goodnight."

Gage held out his arm for me, and my guard followed in tow. We were halfway up the steps when Gage turned to the guard, "I need just a minute with my fiancé." We stood in full view of the guard, but he was unable to hear Gage's whisper. "There is nothing you could do or no action you could take that would be disobedient to me. Sleep well, Camille." Gage pressed his lips to my forehead. I knew this was his way of reminding the necklace that my time with Drake was done with his blessing. Gage held my door for me as I slipped into the dark room. He shut the door behind me. From the shadows under the door, I could see that the guard had taken his position in the hallway directly outside my room.

CHAPTER 31

Camille Benning – Florida

I took a deep breath and walked the few steps to my closet. I had no sooner put my hand on the door knob than it swung wide with Drake on the inside. He took me in his arms and swung me around like a child. When my feet touched the ground, I was fully wrapped in Drake's arms. Careful not to alert the guard, Drake exhaled the words, "I missed you so much, I thought I'd burst today, Love."

My mouth opened on his, and I felt like I was spinning again.

When we stopped to breathe, Drake's excitement shone on his face, "I bought you a gift today."

"A gift? Why?"

"It might have been more of a gift for me." He wore a mischievous grin, and I felt my heart doing its sprint just like it had last night. He reached behind him and pulled out a cardboard box, "I saw it today and have been dying to see what you'd look like in it." He motioned for me to go into the bathroom, and I could only imagine what I would find in the box.

As I stood in front of the mirror wearing the ivory satin nightgown, my nerves began taking control of my body, and I wasn't sure I had the courage to go out half-dressed. The length was only to mid-thigh, the front was cut low: I looked like a mannequin at Victoria's Secret. I saw my shorts and a t-shirt that I normally slept in lying beside the sink. I nearly switched into them when I caught my reflection in the mirror. If my shorts and t-shirt were enough to make his heart speed up, his arms wrench tight around me, and his throat murmur those deep sexy sounds—I couldn't wait to see his response to this ensemble. After the last six weeks, I wanted to be wanted. I wanted to see Drake's eyes pop out of his head. I wanted to hear the groan of desire I knew would come from deep within him.

Drake made me feel beautiful, sexy even, but walking out to his waiting eyes – I wasn't sure I could. I found a bathrobe hanging on the back of the door and wrapped it around myself before I stepped back into the bedroom.

Drake's hands found me in the dark as his voice exhaled, "Did you wrap yourself up in that robe like a present for me? Are you trying to torture me?" He stood in front of me wearing only a pair of shorts. His shirtless body called to me. The moonlight through the window shimmered off his muscular shoulders and tight abs. The sight of him, even in the moonlight, took my breath away.

I wanted to feel his skin on mine. I buried my face in his chest as my arms wrapped around him. He smelled wonderful, he felt incredible – his muscular frame and warm skin invited me to lose the robe. I loosened the tie and let the robe fall to the floor. Drake took a couple steps back, taking me in. He leaned in toward me, scooped me up in his arms, and carried me to the bed, his lips pressed lightly to mine. I didn't know how far he intended to go, and I wasn't sure I possessed the willpower to put any brakes on.

Drake lay me gently on the bed and slid in behind me. His hand stroked my arm, from the top of my shoulder to the tip of my fingers, up and down, countless times. His touch generated goose bumps all over my body while he kissed the back of my neck just under my hairline all the way to my shoulders. His caresses were tender, and without words I could feel the turmoil in his touch. I could hear his breathing was heavy, and I felt like he had poured an accelerant on me—I was on fire. When I thought I could take no more, he exhaled a warm breath by my ear, "Remember that day at Andolini's?—I told you I would combust? That was me being sweet." I did remember his words just before I drove away, and his admission made me smile. Drake added, "I'm not being sweet. I seriously feel like I'm going to combust."

"Oh sure, *you're* going to combust?"

His breath was haggard, his voice strained, "I had intended to be a perfect gentleman, but intentions sometimes go by the wayside."

"You *will* be a perfect gentleman. I'll go switch this getup for some sweatpants if I have to. We both know my fiancé is across the hall." I tried to be funny, but missed my mark by a long shot.

His lips froze in position on my shoulder. I knew my words struck a nerve. "We need to figure out how to get that damn necklace off you. I want to disappear with you, Camille."

"I'm all ears if you have an idea."

"If you could, would you run away with me?"

I didn't have to think of my response. "Faster than an Olympic sprinter."

Drake hugged me hard from behind. It felt like his arms were a vice, and I was so tight against him, I could feel his muscles flex behind me. I had found my heaven right here on earth in Drake's arms. I was surprised when he blurted out, "Break your engagement with Gage."

"You know I can't. I'm not the one who set it up to begin with."

"It's still your choice. Choose me."

"Drake, you hardly know me."

"What do I need to know that I don't already know?"

"Lots of things." I struggled, before my mouth started spewing random things about me. "I like to sleep in the middle of the afternoon. I like to snow ski on the bunny slope, and I'm terrified I'm going to fall off the lift chairs. I hate baseball, not dislike—hate. I miss Starbucks White Mocha Latte. I can't ride a bicycle. You don't know anything about me."

"You think because I didn't know that, I don't know you well enough to marry you?"

"I think if life were fair, I could choose to go back to my old life: no mind reading, no knowledge of the future, no magical powers. I'd be free to go to the movies, lay on the beach, laugh at YouTube videos, and do everything I used to love."

His voice was pleading, "We can do that, Camille."

"That's the thing, Drake. Why does it have to be all or nothing? I'm being forced to marry a guy I hardly know, who is in love with someone else. You're asking me to break the engagement I never wanted, so I can choose to marry you. I'm twenty-two. There are too many things I haven't done yet."

"So we'll do those things together."

"What if I want to do them myself?" I could see my words stung him. I tried to lessen the hurt by explaining, "Maybe it would be different if I had grown up knowing what I was or at least what was expected of me. But I didn't. I grew up my way. I couldn't care less if my family's bloodline doesn't go on. I don't need someone else to be happy; I just need not to be a prisoner."

Drake eased himself away from me. He didn't look at me when he answered, "But you couldn't be happy with me?"

I shook my head. "Maybe you. Or maybe a high school history teacher, or maybe a commercial fisherman. Life can't be scripted, Drake." It felt good to say to Drake what had been boiling under my skin since I found out about all these crazy traditions. "I'm willing to make a deal with you."

I knew I'd hurt him, but it was only fair he know the real me. "If we get out of this mess, we'll date. . . my way. No escorts, no supervision, none of the crap everyone's been trying to shove on me. We'll go to the movies. If we have a good time and we both want to, we'll go on a second date, then a third. If – and that's a big if – years later we both get to the point that we can't live without each other, then we talk about forever. Deal?"

"I don't need years to know you're the one I want, Camille."

"That sucks, Drake, because I do. I want time. I want to. . ." I squeezed his arms that had gone slack around me, "savor you. Get to know you. I want something more than just a physical attraction. I don't want you to miss me while we're apart. I want your whole body to ache, to go through withdrawals for me. When we get to that, if we ever get there, that's when we'll know we're right for each other."

"If that's your measure, my body aches right now, and it has since the first day I saw you at Bruce's wedding."

"Have you heard anything I've said? I don't know anything about you. I'm all for running off with you and disappearing for a while, but I'm not ready to marry anyone. Unless I'm forced into it with Gage, it's not going to happen."

"Camille, we'll find a way to get you out of this betrothal." He waited a long minute before he continued, "I'll go along with you. We'll do things your way. But I don't need years, or months, or weeks – if I could get you to see through my eyes, to feel through my heart, you'd understand why I think the process you just laid out is ludicrous. I know my heart. When you decide that I really am the one, trust me, I'll never let you regret it. We'll stay like this forever, fused as one."

His words were like a drug, and I, an addict, desperately in need of a fix. I rolled over so that we faced each other; my hand swept his face. I studied him, worried that he, like everyone else in my life I cared about, would soon be taken away from me. I traced his lips with my finger, touched his face with my palm, and ran my fingers into his hair. Drake was beyond attractive: his ice blue eyes held me in a trance. I said nothing. I wanted to take him in, memorize everything about him.

I didn't want to end our moment, but the self-preservation side of me took over. I knew if we kept this up, he was right: I would fall in love with him. It wouldn't be a crush or blind lust; it would be the rip-out-your-heart, falling-off-a-cliff love that comes once in a lifetime. I would be devastated on my wedding night to Gage, a hollow shell of a person losing someone forever whom I could never have. "What are we doing?" My question caught him off guard.

Drake smiled at me as he whispered, "We're acquainting ourselves with each other, Love." His voice was happy, content, but it turned amused when he added, "Unless you have a better activity in mind for this evening."

I could feel the hopelessness of the situation seeping in. Making plans to date was ridiculous when any hope for a future other than the one forced on us wasn't possible. "I'm marrying Gage in a few weeks, and you're marrying Bianca. There's nothing either of us can do to stop it."

"Break your engagement with Gage."

"This stupid necklace would take my head completely off if I said that out loud."

Quietly, he said, "Camille, we need help. There has to be some way to get it off."

"How? We're out of options, Drake. All we're doing now is making the heartbreak worse—putting off our own goodbye."

He turned my face to him so I was forced to look in his eyes, "I can't give you up. Even if it's just a few nights together, I want them." I looked away, knowing his words cut clear through to my soul. "It's better than a lifetime of regret for ignoring what little time together we were afforded. I'll take what I can get, Camille."

"So, this is it? I lie here with you, praying that we'll have one more night tomorrow, and the next after that. We're going to run out of tomorrows. We can't wish the dawn away."

"For now, live in the moment, Love." This time his voice was heavy with the same desperation I was feeling. He tried to comfort me by pulling me closer, and I tried to be comforted by drawing him in. The feeling wouldn't go away. Our nights were numbered, and our time together nearly over after it had just begun.

I wasn't sure if he was trying to convince me or himself. "Gage is one of the most cunning men I know. He may have a plan he hasn't shared with me yet. Don't give up on us; we'll find a way." Drake drifted off to sleep before I did; he spoke to me while he was sleeping. I don't know how many times I heard it before I drifted off with him, but I fell asleep to the sound of Drake's whispers, their own soft lullaby: "Choose me, Love, choose me."

The next morning was much the same as our first, with Gage knocking on my door. He didn't come in, nor did he allow the guard entry to my room. I hid Drake in the closet, although I could hardly tear myself away from him. I would have welcomed an eternity in Zandra's prison if it meant that I could spend every night with Drake. I stole one final kiss as I closed the closet door.

Gage and I were already seated for breakfast when Zandra joined us. I didn't wait to be spoken to. My night with Drake gave me strength for another day with my captor, "Good morning, Grandmother. I hope you slept well."

"I did, Camille. Thank you for asking." She turned her attention to Gage, "Is there something you'd like to tell me, Gage?" It was such a strange sensation. She was warm to me, but when she spoke to Gage, her voice had turned to ice.

Gage realized something was wrong. His charm began to waiver as he shakily responded, "I can't think of anything pressing to tell you. I spoke to father last night. He sends his best."

"Hmmph," was her reply. She was frustrated with something and announced, "I think we all need to go to the garden this morning." She motioned for us to stand up; Gage and I did without hesitation. I desperately wanted to read his thoughts to find out what caused the change in Zandra, but I didn't want to do it in front of her. I had only successfully done it once before, and I hadn't seen Phineas since. I worried I had done it wrong, and maybe our conversation had been discovered by Zandra.

We took a seat on the bench together as Zandra pulled up a chair. "Have either of you heard the teaching of Aphrodite and her gift to Unice?"

I shook my head that I hadn't and sat up straighter. I hadn't taken a shock from the stupid necklace in a day and a half and wasn't about to start today with one. I had a strange feeling that unlike the other stories she had told me, I needed to pay close attention to this one.

CHAPTER 32

Camille Benning – Florida

"Unice was a Centauride. She was exquisite: long flowing blonde hair, bright blue eyes, a kind smile and a soft heart. She roamed the pastures of Thessaly with the other Centaurs. Unice had the voice of an angel and often sang as she galloped along the countryside. Her voice would entice strangers, beckoning them forward in search of the angel on earth who sang to the heavens. One day a human, a man, happened upon her pasture. Her body was obscured by a large boulder, so he only saw the human half of her beauty and heard the magic of her voice. The man's name was Winfield. He was so taken with her that he sat perfectly still, content to listen to the beautiful songs she sang."

"Winfield came to the meadow for weeks. Anytime he tried to come closer than his perch, she would disappear behind the rocks. When the weeks turned into months, Winfield confessed that he was deeply in love with Unice. Unice was sure when he found out what she was, the lust he felt for her would disappear. She stepped out from behind the rocks she had hidden behind and showed her whole body to Winfield."

Winfield cried out to her, begged her not to leave, and professed his love for her. The two spent their days and nights together, deeply in love but unable to be together. Unice wept one evening and Aphrodite saw her tears and felt her heartbreak. Aphrodite took pity on the couple that was so deeply in love and changed Unice to a human. Unice was the first Centaur to be changed from a Centauride to a human, years before Zeus gave his gift to the Centaurs."

Zandra looked squarely at Gage, "Has your father ever shared that story with you?"

He nodded, "Yes, he has, many times."

"Do you know why the story of Unice and Winfield is so important to your family?"

"It's just a legend, Miss Zandra. It is a fable for lovers who think their challenges are insurmountable, that love can conquer all."

"No!!" Zandra screamed. "It is not a fable. It is your heritage, Gage."

Gage said nothing. Zandra was furious with him when she continued, "Imagine my elation when I find out my granddaughter, one of the few living Centaurides in Chiron's bloodline is going to marry a Centaur in the Winfield bloodline?"

"That's right, Miss Zandra. I believe my father is pleased with our betrothal for the same reason."

I was interested in the story, partly because the story tied to a living breathing person. I directed my question to Zandra, rather than Gage, "So is Gage a pure-blooded Centaur?"

Gage looked embarrassed by my question. I'd meant no offense, but after all her lessons over the last six weeks; I didn't know what to make of the story. Zandra answered, "Winfield was human. Aphrodite's magic transformed Unice to a woman, but the bloodline remains Centaur, and it retains Aphrodite's magic."

I smiled at Gage, who I worried might have been offended with my question on his ancestors, and ribbed him good naturedly, "So you have *love* magic. Am I under your spell?"

Through clenched teeth, Gage answered, "As much as I am under yours, Darling." He wasn't offended. He was trying to maintain his composure, hiding the humor behind a stoic expression.

Zandra interrupted our private joke, "So, tell me, Gage. Why is it that this morning I saw a woman, other than my granddaughter, slip from your room when she believed no one was near?"

Alarm spread on Gage's face; he stayed silent. Zandra turned her attention on me, "Did you know that Bianca spent the night with Gage?"

I should have denied it. I should have played dumb waiting for Gage to think of a reasonable excuse. I knew I needed to choose my words wisely, as I was acutely aware that the necklace was unforgiving. I kept my voice even and strong, "Grandmother, I was aware. They spent the night together with my blessing." Gage's expression moved from alarm to shock. I think he believed my honesty would enrage the necklace.

Zandra screeched, "What?! You allowed this?" I could feel the necklace pulsing with energy. It had to have reacted to her fury, but I didn't receive a shock. I strained the muscles in my neck in anticipation of the electric charge, but nothing happened.

In a gentle tone, careful to be absent of any hostility, I answered, "Bianca is my dear friend. She tried to choose Gage, but her mother wouldn't permit it. Gage has accepted your invitation to be my husband, but until we are bound by marriage, he has my blessing to see Bianca."

She turned her rage on Gage, "It is you! You are the one who interferes with Camille's destiny. I have put the necklace of obedience around my granddaughter's neck, and it was you whose fate was fallible. It is your unwillingness to commit that leaves her destiny undecided!"

"Miss Zandra, I will honor my commitment to Camille. I am ashamed that you so easily read my desires for Bianca and misinterpreted them as intentions by Camille. Camille will make a good wife, and she does not deserve to wear this necklace of obedience you have put on her."

Zandra eyed him suspiciously. "You mean to tell me, you have hoped for another woman while staying at my estate, then brought that woman here? That is why I keep seeing a man other than you in Camille's future?" Gage was definitely braver than I was. I checked my mind's brick wall – it was intact. There was nothing to contradict Gage's confession or augment it with one of my own.

Zandra glared at both of us. She stomped out of the garden and slammed the door to the house. I asked tentatively, "Now what?"

"Now, we wait. Why would you tell her it was with your blessing?"

"It was the truth. The necklace didn't zap me."

"You knew we were getting together?"

"I assumed you and Bianca had the same arrangement as Drake and I did. You choreographed the perfect arrangement for both of us. Thanks, by the way."

Gage chuckled at me, "Well, our midnight rendezvous may be over for a while."

"Did you mean what you said to Zandra?"

"What part?"

"That you'll honor your commitment to me. You're still going through with it?"

"We don't have recourse, do we?"

"Ten minutes ago I would have said that we didn't, but given her reaction, I wonder if there isn't a shred of decency in her."

Gage looked surprised by my statement, "How do you mean?"

"She didn't seem pleased about her decision to put this stupid necklace on me. If we can get her to take it off, I'll leave. Not just the estate, I'll leave the country if I have to."

"Zandra would find you."

"She never found my mother." I wondered if Gage knew our parents had once been betrothed. "My mom ran away on her wedding night and was never found."

"I knew that much, but I think that had more to do with my dad protecting your mom than anything else. He really loved her. He's told me about Angela my whole life. Even my mom doesn't mind him telling the stories."

CHAPTER 33

Camille Benning – Florida

I felt my eye muscles flex, "No way!"

"Yeah. She told Dad her greatest wish was to be free of Centaurs. She said she wanted to be human. He thought her wish, left ungranted while it was within his power to honor it, could destroy Aphrodite's magic. Dad set her free then put a protective spell over her. You should have seen him the night that he found out she'd had a child with another Centaur after he gave up his most powerful magic to protect her – he was pissed!"

"Was that the night of Bruce's wedding, when I met him?"

"Yeah, I think so. You have to understand, he seriously loved your mom. But your mom was so freaked from growing up with Zandra that he couldn't force her to marry him. It just wasn't in him. The night of the wedding, he told her he'd protect her from Zandra—gave her a plane ticket, an apartment, cash, a new identity and sent her away."

"I don't believe it."

"He wouldn't have any reason to lie to me about it. It's the only explanation for why Zandra never found her. Dad has Aphrodite's magic. Protecting someone he loved with her magic was the only thing that ensured her safety."

"So that story Zandra just told us is true?"

"My dad thinks it is. I mean, don't get me wrong. I know he has powerful magic, but he wasn't willing to use it against your mom. It seems like it would have been a lot easier on both of them if he had used it to make your mother fall in love with him. Whether it came from Aphrodite or the Wicked Witch of the West isn't all that important. He knew where she was her whole life. You, on the other hand, were a real surprise. He didn't know anything about you."

"Why would he agree to let you marry me? You'd think it would open old wounds or something."

"I think he thought I'd be more charming or something, who knows. Dad and Zandra do have one common goal; they definitely want us to marry. I don't think there's anything either of them wouldn't do to make it happen." He took a breath, then explained, "Zandra is by far the most powerful Centauride. Her power comes from her lineage. Dad is in the same boat. He loaned a chunk of his magic to your mother, but since your mother's death. . .sorry, Aphrodite's magic has returned to him. They have this crazy idea that if we marry, our children will be kind of a Centaur Super-Race. We have the only two ancestors who were touched directly by the gods."

"So how do you feel about it?"

"About marrying you?" I nodded. "When Bianca chose Drake, I didn't care about much of anything. But when word spread that you had come to your father's house, I thought my dad might try to work something out with your dad. Let's face it; it's not hard to look at you." Gage's smile was shy. He had been so larger-than-life since I met him that it took me aback. "I thought maybe you and I could start out as friends and maybe grow into something more—eventually I'd get over Bianca. When I showed up the other morning, and you were wearing the same stupid necklace Dad had told me about, that had been worn by Angela, I knew I couldn't force you to marry me any more than he could your mother. I told my father about the necklace, and he wasn't happy. I told him I thought if I could bring Bianca and Drake back with me – history wouldn't repeat itself."

"Does he know how you feel about Bianca?"

"Sure he does. But he knows engagements are almost never broken. The fact that we were both betrothed, it wouldn't have occurred to him or anyone else."

"I'm ready to disappear, deep, deep undercover and never see another Centaur for the rest of my life!"

"We aren't all bad. In fact, I know one who would follow you to the end of the earth."

"Drake?"

"Well, yeah. He's been infatuated with you since the night of your brother's wedding. When his engagement to Bianca was announced, he didn't show even a hint of excitement. He spent like thirty seconds with you that night, and he was ready to sacrifice his bloodline."

"You weren't even there that night. How would you know?"

"Bianca told me, and I see it on Drake's face. You should have seen him the other night when I told him how we were going to smuggle him into your room. You'd have thought he just won the lottery."

"You could have clued me in a little ahead of time."

"Right, the next time I try to sneak my fiancé's lover into her bedroom, I'll make sure to send word ahead of time."

"So, what do you think Zandra's going to do to us?"

"I don't know, but knowing her, it'll be something dramatic. She might send me away. Are you going to be okay here without me for a few weeks?"

"As long as I know I'm getting out of here, I'll be fine."

"Good, sorry Bianca got us busted. I told her to use her microwaves or whatever power she has to make sure the coast was clear."

I patted Gage's hand, "I'm sure her thoughts were elsewhere."

We didn't have to wait long. I had no sooner gotten my words out than Zandra emerged from the house. In as kind and thoughtful a voice as I had heard from her, she said, "There's no reason to send you back to your father's, Gage."

"Miss Zandra, I deeply apologize for my indiscretion. It won't happen again."

That wicked smile that had been reserved for me reappeared, "I know it won't. The problem has been dealt with. There will be no more distractions."

Horror gripped me when I saw the crimson on her hands. "Grandmother, what's on your hands?"

In that same sweet voice she had just used with Gage, she answered, "Camille, that is the blood of your enemy. Her heart no longer beats." She turned to Gage, "As a gesture of my goodwill, I also stopped the heart of the man who lusted after your betrothed. *Your* competition is also no longer a concern."

"Noooooooo!" was the only response I could get out. I grabbed hold of Gage, trying to steady myself. He pushed my hand away and ran into Zandra's mansion. I was behind him, but he topped the stairs before I took the first one. My guard was in chase and grabbed my arms, holding me in place on the third step from the bottom.

CHAPTER 34

Camille Benning – Florida

It was Phineas. I hadn't seen him in several days, and in the back of my mind I knew I should have been concerned. He did the unthinkable and whispered aloud to me, "Be quiet child, before the necklace does her dirty work." He stood behind me with my arms cinched behind my back as the tears rolled down my cheeks. I heard Gage scream out as if someone had completely squeezed the life out of him. I heard furniture being thrown into walls, glass break, and then stillness.

Several minutes went by, and my sobs were nearly uncontrollable. Zandra had stepped into the hallway and eyed me suspiciously. I stood slack with Phineas still holding me in position. I saw Gage emerge from the upstairs hallway. He walked toward me with heavy steps, a defeated man. He took the steps slowly, his head hung low. He paused in front of me and gently brushed his fingertips to my cheek. I saw blood on his hands and on his clothing, tears streaking his face, "I promise I'll be back for you on our wedding night. . . I can't stay."

Gage continued his march down the steps as Phineas allowed me to fall to the floor. He addressed Zandra with authority, squeezing the emotion completely out of his voice, "I'll notify their families. This is a debt I hope you are forced to pay before the sun sets tomorrow."

"No Chancellor or Magistrate will find me guilty – you may want me to hold my tongue. I'm sure your family would be none too thrilled with the circumstances of their deaths. I will be here the night you return to marry Camille and meet your destiny."

Gage gave me one final sorrowful look before he walked out the door and shut it behind him. Zandra turned her attention to me. "I understand she was your friend, but I did it for your own good. No Centauride should ever share; it goes against nature." I didn't respond. I couldn't. I was in shock. She continued, "Her fiancé had feelings for you. Were you aware? I could see it through his deceit. I couldn't allow for him to interfere with your destiny either. I'll give you the remainder of the day to mourn." I hadn't collected myself fully when she said, "It was done out of love, Camille."

My body shut down: I felt it go slack as everything went black.

As I awoke, I saw that it was dark outside, and for the slightest fraction of a moment, I reached out for Drake. When I came up empty, the events flooded over me again. My eyes were swollen shut: I must have been sobbing in my sleep. My throat was on fire, and I felt like I would be sick. I pried myself out of bed, splashed cold water on my face, hoping it would help my eyes enough so that I could open them.

Drake was gone. We knew we'd never be able to have more than a few precious weeks together, but being robbed of what little time we should have had together felt cruel, even more cruel than the betrothals. So much no longer mattered. Drake was no more than a shooting star in my life; I didn't realize how much of an impact he'd had on me until he was stolen away. In that moment, I knew I had lost the love of my life. I knew why Kyle Richardson had hidden my mother from Zandra all those years ago. I would have wished for any fate for Drake other than death, even if his fate never allowed me to see him again. That's what love is. I was in love with him and didn't know it until he was gone. I would never have the chance to tell him. My heart ached, and I wondered if I'd ever be able to escape the pain.

Bianca had been the truest of friends, an ally. I hated love-triangles – but she was the first person I'd ever known to advocate for a love-square. She was deeply in love with Gage and willing to take nearly any risk to be with him. I couldn't fault her for her crazy plan – love makes you do things you wouldn't dream of—even befriending the woman who is supposed to marry the love of your life. There would never be another Bianca.

I saw the two feet standing on the other side of my door: still a prison, but now, one of indescribable horrors. When I lay down on the bed, I realized it still smelled of Drake. If I closed my eyes and lay very still, I could imagine him with me. I let my mind wander. I had been so focused on my own circumstances that I didn't know anything about him: not his family, his interests, hobbies, political persuasion , what his job was other than he worked for his father. The only thing I knew was every time I closed my eyes, I could see his ice blue eyes staring back at me.

I stayed in my room. There was no need to leave. I had taken every lesson that I would allow Zandra to teach me. I didn't need food, and I could get water from the bathroom sink. From time to time I would see a guard open the door – I guess checking to see if I was swinging from the rafters. I never once acknowledged one of them, and none ever uttered a word to me. I found the small tube of salve that Drake had gently put on my neck to help the healing. I would be rid of this stupid necklace very soon, and when I was, I wanted no reminder that I ever wore it, that this time ever existed.

By the third day with no food and only water for sustenance, I felt lethargic. I had difficulty determining what was a dream and what was reality. I had decided that when Gage came to take me from this house of horrors, I would ask him to let me go back to California—back to the uncomplicated life I had led before I met my father or any of the others. I knew he wouldn't be over Bianca and may even hold me responsible for her death. I was pretty sure he would be happier with me out of his life than he would with me in it.

The door opened slowly. It was Zandra. I turned away from her and looked out the window. I'm sure she said something to me, but I was too weak to waste the energy to listen. Whatever she had said, the lack of a response from me must have been some sort of an answer she was seeking because moments later I was again alone.

DANIEL

I stood outside the gate, a state policeman on my flank, leaning up against the steel gate, wondering what kind of a prison Cami was in. It took several hours to convince someone even to accompany me out to Zandra Chiron's property. After we got there, I was expecting the police to help me. I got the distinct feeling they were humoring me.

When the policeman had spoken to her through the intercom, I'd expected him to be polite, but firm. I was thoroughly pissed off when I heard him say, "Good evening Miss Zandra. This is Officer Westcott from the Florida State Police. If it wouldn't be too much trouble, could I have a word with you?"

I expected the massive gates to swing free, maybe I'd see Cami goofing around, and I could give her hell for not calling or texting me or her family. I didn't. The place was large, completely surrounded by a swamp that acted like a moat, and the gates didn't budge. An elderly voice answered back through the intercom, "Officer Westcott, so nice of you to drop by. I'll be down at the gate in a few minutes."

I turned to him and said, "We need to get in there."

Officer Westcott shook his head, "We don't have a search warrant, and Miss Zandra is well regarded in the community. You can ask her permission to speak with her granddaughter, but don't go off half-cocked."

"Half-cocked? My best friend is being held prisoner in there."

"So you say. Maybe she ran away from you."

"She didn't run away; she was taken!"

"By a little old lady? You ever met Miss Zandra?"

This guy was about as helpful as a mall cop. I could see a golf cart driving toward us. The lady on it had to be Zandra Chiron. She had long silver-white hair, wore a large brimmed straw hat, and gave us both a warm smile. "Hello, Officer Westcott, so nice to see you again. To what do I owe this pleasure?"

Officer Westcott tipped his hat, "Good evening, ma'am. We're sure sorry to bother you this evening, but this young man is worried about your granddaughter, Camille. He asked us to come out here. We obliged to make sure there wouldn't be any trouble."

"Trouble? Trouble from me? Certainly not."

"Oh, no, we didn't think you would be any trouble at all, Miss Zandra. We wanted to make sure he wasn't a nuisance to you."

"How very thoughtful of you." She gave him a thin smile, almost daring me to say something to get me handcuffed and escorted away.

I straightened my posture, returned her smile and asked, "Mrs. Chiron, I'm Daniel Gaskins. I was wondering if I might see Cami for a few minutes."

She lowered her chin and raised her eyelids. The look was thoughtful, sincere, and to anyone who'd grown up around actors – it looked rehearsed. "I'm sorry, Daniel. Camille is under the weather. I'll be happy to tell her you stopped by."

"Mrs. Chiron, I'm sorry to hear that. I've flown here from California because I hadn't heard from her. Is there any chance I could see her?"

More firmly than her first refusal, but still an Oscar-worthy performance, "I'm afraid not. I will tell her that you inquired about her."

"Could I stop…"

I was interrupted by Officer Westcott's hand on my shoulder as he said, "She's not feeling well, son. Time to get going."

I yanked my shoulder away from him and on reflex shared my best glare, "I'm not leaving until I see her."

Mrs. Chiron, still with the sweet voice, "Officer Westcott, you know how I feel about trespassers on my property. I'm an old woman and fear he may return when you aren't here to protect me. Is there anything you can do?"

I couldn't believe my ears. Was she trying to get me thrown in jail? I just wanted to know that Cami was fine. "Listen, I just want to see her. Just for a second. Once I see her, I'll go."

"I've already told you, Mr. Gaskins, she isn't well enough for visitors."

Officer Westcott interjected, "Miss Zandra, thank you for your time this evening. I hope we weren't too much trouble. Daniel, let's go."

Although it sounded like a request, his big beefy hand cinched tight around my arm as he led me back to his squad car. I couldn't believe this was happening. I could see the house off in the distance. If Cami was in there, I didn't understand why I couldn't see her.

Maybe what Dad had told me was true, it wasn't just his family – all full-blooded Centaurs would see me as nothing more than human. I would never be worthy to be in her life – not even as just her friend. I had given up hope of anything more years ago when he first told me about his family and why I was different from other humans. I was thirteen and had my very first crush – Cami. She was really tough, not just for a girl, but like, "bite steel and spit nails" tough. She never picked fights, but she was always the first person to step in and shut someone down if they were picking on someone else around school.

At thirteen I thought she was beautiful – my dad picked up on it right away. He told me she was different, that she wouldn't want to be my friend in another couple years – that she'd outgrow me. He discouraged our friendship, but never outright forbade it. I'd seen her date one loser after another. As her friend, it bothered me, but whenever my dad heard about it – he would get pissed off. Yet now that she was with the rest of her family and no one would let me see her, he didn't seem to care at all. None of it made sense to me.

I wished I understood the whole Centaur thing. My dad told me enough to pique my interest, but fell short on actually answering questions. Dad and Cami's mom were not at all friendly; there was always this weird tension between them, and any time there was a school function where both had to attend, I could count on them to be at opposite ends of the auditorium.

I was lost in thought when I felt the squad car come to a halt in front of the Jacksonville Airport. "My return flight isn't until tomorrow." My overnight bag was in the back seat of the car. I hadn't even checked into a hotel before I went to ask for the police's help.

"Son, my advice to you is, you get in there, get on a plane, and get out of here—tonight. Miss Zandra's an influential lady. She knows judges, lawyers, politicians – you name it. She isn't someone you want to cross."

"I just want to see Cami. I don't know what the big deal is."

"The big deal is, you asked nicely and she said, 'no'. You get caught over that way again, you won't get the option to go home – and the last place you want to be is in a jail, here, with her as the complaining witness."

I couldn't be mad at the guy. He may have strong-armed me into the car, but I could hear his sincerity, and he was right. My dad had told me not to come, Beau had told me not to come, and Cami still wasn't returning any of my calls. Maybe Dad was right after all: maybe she really had outgrown me.

CAMILLE

I remained in that "almost" dream state for another full day. By then I had visibly lost weight that I didn't need to lose. My cheeks were sunken into my face, and any hint of color from the sun had bleached itself off my skin from the dark room. Large purple circles hung thick under my eyes. I had eaten crackers and fruit that were left for me just inside my bedroom door – not because I wanted them but because I couldn't be dead when Gage came back. I needed to live. I didn't think his spirit could take one more loss – no matter how painful my presence might be for him.

I caught myself talking to Mom lots of times, "You never should have given me Will's name. . . Why can't I see you? . . . Are you here?" I never once got a response or even saw her outline.

I knew I was a little over a week away from the wedding. Although pleased with the idea I would soon find my escape, I didn't welcome the celebration that came so close to the tragedy. Phineas stepped into my room at close to 3 a.m. and saw that I lay there awake. "Camille, you will be able to leave soon. Tomorrow morning I will bring you breakfast. I want you to eat it, do you understand?" I nodded that I did, but I wasn't sure my feet were planted in reality or if I were dreaming the conversation. "Have you contacted your mother?" I stared at him blankly, not fully processing his question. Phineas put his hands on both of my shoulders, "Camille, your father wants you to contact your mother's spirit. She needs to tell you something."

The physical contact was the first I had had since he kept me from collapsing down the steps. It awakened something inside me. I remembered: Phineas had told me to contact my mother, then Gage and the others came. How long ago had that been? Two weeks and I still couldn't speak to her, or at least she never spoke back. Then it hit me, I would be able to talk to Drake, to tell him how sorry I was, to tell him I loved him. For the first time since Gage left, I felt a glimmer of excitement again. I was weak, too weak from allowing myself nearly to starve to death. When Phineas brought me food the next morning, I wasn't hungry, but I found the strength to eat – not much because my stomach wasn't able to hold much, but enough to jump start my body again. He came back at lunch time with more food, and I ate a second time. I could feel my mental faculties slowly returning. I still had difficulty concentrating, but I tried talking to my mother all the time. I told her about everything; something told me she was with me, but I couldn't see her and I couldn't hear her.

"Mom, do you remember when you forced me to ride a bicycle? You thought it would be fun to ride by the ocean? I begged you not to make me do it. I pleaded with you to let me sit on the beach. You wouldn't take no for an answer. You worked double shifts for weeks so you could buy us matching bikes. I still remember looking at it in the store: the pink tassels, the big white banana seat. It was so beautiful at the bike shop. I wanted you to be proud of me, but I was terrified when you took them both out of your van in Carlsbad. I knew everyone was watching me, and I was scared. Do you remember what you told me?"

I waited, hoping she'd answer me, hoping I could hear her just for a second. "You said bravery is measured by how hard you try, not by whether you actually succeed. We went home from the beach that day with my skin gone on both knees, both elbows and my cheek. I never did learn how to ride it, but you still told me I was the bravest person you'd ever known."

I looked for her face, begging her to show me the same grainy image of herself that she'd shown me at Bruce's wedding. I confessed, "I don't know how to be brave unless you're with me. I need you to show me how to be brave again."

When my mother didn't show herself, I believed it was because my heart longed to see Drake. She knew me better than anyone on the planet, and she must have known that it was Drake I needed to see. Her loss had broken my heart, but his death was my fault. Zandra had killed him because she knew *he* was who I wanted.

I needed to tell him how sorry I was. I'm sure Phineas could hear me through the door, but I didn't care. I sat on the edge of the bed, feeling the place where he'd lain. I smoothed my hand over the pillow that had cradled his face. "Drake, I don't know if you can hear me. I hope you can. I was just scared, okay? When I found you, you were everything I'd ever dreamed of. No one's supposed to get everything they want. No one is supposed to be perfect. It seems like every time I feel a sliver of happiness, a machete comes from out of nowhere to remove whatever I love most."

I felt hot tears dripping down my cheeks, my vision clouded, my throat was tight. "If I'd broken the engagement like you asked me to, maybe you'd still be here. Or maybe I'd be with you right now. You told me my plan was ridiculous, you didn't need to know me better – the truth is, I didn't need to know you better, either. You were the one."

I took my palms and wiped the moisture from my cheeks, drying my hands on my jeans. "I know I don't deserve a do-over. I should have seen you for what you were when I had the chance. I'm so sorry." My voice lost its volume. I whispered, "I love you, Drake. I always will. There'll never be another." I buried myself in the pillow he used, trying to drink up whatever scent was left.

I slept, wishing for dreams of Drake, wishing to touch his skin, to feel the stubble on his face one more time. I wished I had known how I felt about him while he was still alive. I tried to communicate with my mom's and Drake's spirits all the time. I kept thinking of it like a television station that was just outside the range of my digital receiver. Nothing worked. I never heard, saw, or felt either of them.

My guard detail of four had dwindled to two. I wasn't sure when it happened, but sometime during the time that I'd nearly starved myself to death, the other guards were gone. Aragon kept his post in the hallway during his shifts at night. Phineas began standing his watch inside my room during the day. He knew I was close to a mental breakdown and did everything he could to keep me from losing it.

Phineas openly spoke to me, trying to nurse me back to health. Although he seemed to be more comfortable stationed at my door, he occasionally took a seat in one of the chairs in my room. He was a constant reminder that I was coming back; I would be *me* again soon. I still wore the hideous necklace: not so long ago I had thought it beautiful. I no longer felt that way. I hadn't felt even a flicker of energy from it since Zandra's last visit to my room, but I didn't tempt fate either.

"Have you contacted your mother's spirit?" It was always the first question Phineas asked me. Although I missed her, I was secretly expending most of my energy desperately trying to contact Drake. If spirits chose to stay earthbound, maybe he had chosen not to stay with me. I couldn't blame him. What little time we had spent together wouldn't have obligated him to me. I tried to speak with both as often as I could get my brain to focus, but even though I gathered strength, I had no luck whatsoever.

Friday at noon a seamstress brought a beautiful dress to my room. She put it over me and pinned it for the last of the alterations before tomorrow's wedding. I caught a glimpse of myself in the mirror: I had lost too much weight. The last couple days with Phineas had done me good, but I still looked sickly compared to the person I'd been just weeks ago. My hair had lost its luster, my skin looked dull, and my bones were nearly visible under my skin.

Phineas and I were having our usual dinner chatter when there was a soft tap at my door. Phineas immediately came to attention and in three large strides had opened it. Phineas excused himself and allowed a woman to step through the door and into my world.

CHAPTER 35

Camille Benning – Florida

She had kind eyes, ice blue, exactly the same shade as Drake's. Her hair was shoulder-length, smooth and straight. She wore expensive cologne; I couldn't place the scent but knew I'd tested it at Dillard's. "Hello, Camille. I'm Hallenjah Nash. Is it okay if I speak with you?"

My heart stopped. This was one of Drake's relatives. She looked almost too young to be his mother, but I could see so much of Drake in her, I didn't know who else she could be. Would she, too, blame me for his death? I answered, "Of course."

"I am Drake's mother. I was hoping to speak with you about my son."

"I can see the resemblance. He had your eyes. I'm sorry for your loss."

"I can see that you are. Maybe you can help me find him?"

I gave her a questioning look but didn't know how to phrase it. Hadn't Gage told her what had happened? She continued, "You see, obviously, I am a Centauride—just like you. If my son were dead, he would have answered my calls to the spirit world. He has not."

My mind was strong, but I didn't understand what she was telling me. I confessed, "I've tried to speak with him as well, but I'm afraid I'm not very proficient."

"Your proficiency has nothing to do with it. He is not in the spirit world. I fear he is hidden somewhere in this fortress. I felt his presence when I stepped on the grounds. He is here: he is *alive*."

I yelled for the first time in weeks, "Phineas!!!" The door bolted open as if he were ready to do battle. "This is Mrs. Nash. She says Drake is still alive. Where is he?"

Phineas hesitated for only a second. He stepped inside my bedroom and closed the door. "I don't know for certain, but two of your guards were reassigned to the guest quarters, the day that. . . when Gage left the estate. I haven't spoken to the guards, and the estate staff are not permitted entry."

"You didn't think that was odd?"

"Truthfully, I was too worried about you. I was pleased that I was left assigned to you. It didn't occur to me to be curious."

I couldn't be angry with him. If it weren't for Phineas, I wouldn't have had the strength to even speak to Drake's mom. "How do we get into the guest quarters?"

Phineas answered sternly, "You don't! You stay put. I will try to get into the structure this evening."

"I want to see them."

"Camille, I don't know if they're there. If they are, I don't know their condition."

Hallenjah responded, "He's alive."

I threw my arms around Drake's mother. This was the first time I had felt joy in weeks. I felt her body stiffen at my unexpected show of emotion. Once she'd regained her footing, she returned my embrace. I asked her, "Why would Zandra pretend they were dead?"

"Why, indeed. I was hoping you could shed some light for me on that one."

I didn't know how much Gage had told her, and the last thing I wanted was to dime anyone out, so I only shared, "She's nutso, that's why."

"That is one explanation. Do you know my son spoke of you to me?"

Drake, talked about me? To his mother? What had he told her? When had he talked to her? "No . . .I wasn't aware. I mean, I met him. . . before. . .you know."

"You spent the day with him on your father's yacht. It must have been some afternoon." Her tone wasn't accusatory, but she was politely making me aware that my infatuation with Drake likely had a hand in why Zandra faked his death. "Do you know that after he spent the afternoon with you, he asked his father and me if we would support him breaking his engagement to Bianca?"

"Uh, no. I wasn't aware of that either." I took a deep breath, almost scared to hear, but knowing I couldn't not know, "What'd you tell him?"

"We told him Bianca was a lovely Centauride who would make an excellent wife." She watched my eyes, and she seemed perceptive enough that she probably saw the glossiness I wasn't willing to let free. "I also told him to follow his heart, that if he was happy, we were happy. He was so nervous at the time that I believed he wished to break his engagement with Bianca to pursue a human. That was until Gage filled in the missing pieces for us when he delivered the news of Drake's death."

"And you came to meet me?"

"I came to find my son. Zandra knows I am here. She will also be aware that I can feel his presence. It is only a matter of time before she owns up to not murdering them and sets them free, or makes good on her fabrication and slays them."

A rush of emotions shook my body. "Phineas, take Mrs. Nash to the gate. Get her out of here."

"Camille, I can't leave you."

"I'm going to find Drake and Bianca. You get her to safety and catch up with me after."

"I can't let you do that."

I stood my ground. I didn't feel weak. I felt energy surge through my entire body, my necklace buzzed to life and I could feel the energy once again pulsate through the device. "I'll be fine. Get her out of here before Zandra catches her here."

Phineas shook his head, "If anything happens to you, I won't be able to face your father again. I'm here for your protection."

"Dammit Phineas! I don't need your protection right now. I need to get Drake out of here. Take care of his mom. I'll find them and get them to the gate."

"Zandra is on the estate. How do you plan to find them? She will know you've left your room. She will sense your excitement."

I shook my head. "If she senses my excitement, she'll interpret it that I am excited for the wedding. My thoughts have been blocked from her since my arrival."

Hallenjah nodded, "It's true, Phineas. None of her thoughts have escaped since I've been here. She has blocked all of them from me. If I cannot read her thoughts, neither can Zandra."

Phineas reluctantly agreed and motioned for Mrs. Nash to follow him.

Before she left, Hallenjah said, "Wait! Why do you wear a necklace of obedience?"

I nearly spat out the words, "Zandra thought it would be an exceptional engagement present."

"Come here for a minute." Hallenjah put her hands on either side of the necklace. I cringed, anticipating the electric shock that rocked me when Gage and Drake had done the same thing. She spoke loudly, "As matriarch of the Nash herd, I absorb your magic. This Centauride has proven her obedience; she is free of your enchantment." I felt the same pulse of electricity run through it that I felt while Zandra was near, but no painful shock followed. A few seconds passed, and the pulse faded away completely. I reached up and touched the clasps: it came off easily.

"I'm free, I can take it off!"

"If you intend to convince Zandra that you haven't spoken with me, you may want to keep it on."

I did as I was told and left the necklace in place while I bolted from the room. After not leaving it for weeks, I had become immune to the stale air inside. Phineas and Hallenjah followed me down the steps. When we reached the outside, we went in opposite directions. I passed the garden where I sat on the bench so many mornings with Zandra. As I ran toward the structure at the far end of the property, I soaked up the last of the day's rays. I forgot just how incredible the sunlight felt on my skin. The air was thick with the smell of the swamp, lush and green. I heard the sounds of the swamp and tried to concentrate on them to calm my nerves.

I saw the guard standing in front of the guest house's door. I stood just outside his view, allowing the foliage to camouflage my approach. I was able to stay away from his view and went around the back. I found a window opened, allowing breeze from the swamp to enter. The open window had steel bars on it. They had been installed recently, likely in a rush. A pile of more metal bars lay haphazardly below another window a little further to my right. That window was closed. I could see it had been nailed shut. A forgotten tool pouch was buried under the stack of metal bars on the ground.

I found a crow bar in the tool pouch and wedged it under one of the bars on the window. The screw securing the bar in place complained, but I didn't relent. I kept angling and re-angling the crowbar until I heard the screw fly free from the structure. I went to work on a second bar. As I had disengaged the second, I heard a squeal of excitement from inside the house. I looked up to the window and saw Bianca. I put my finger to my lips in the international signal for, "Be Quiet." She nodded.

The next time I glanced up at the window, I saw two sets of eyes staring down at me. I let out a harsh whisper, "Block your thoughts!"

Both nodded, neither uttered a word.

In five minutes I had removed five screws, which were enough for Bianca and Drake to slip through the opening. Bianca was on the ground in seconds. Drake's frame was much bulkier than Bianca's, and he was halfway through the bars when Phineas joined us. I could see the desperation in Drake's eyes when he saw Phineas. He slid free of the final bar on the window, then charged Phineas.

My whisper was louder than it had been just seconds before, "Stop! He's helping me."

Drake stopped his assault. Phineas grinned, eyeing the metal bars hanging loosely on the window's frame, "Clever. What now?"

CHAPTER 36

Camille Benning – Florida

Bianca had given me a quick hug. I was thrilled to see her, but it wasn't her embrace that I'd longed for. The reunion I'd never hoped for, never thought possible—happened. The thrill of seeing him in front of me rendered me speechless. Drake scooped me up into his arms. I didn't care about anything else in the world. He was alive. I could hear Phineas filling Bianca in. I was so wrapped up with Drake that I didn't think he was listening, either. He whispered, "I never thought I'd see you again. Not until after you belonged to Gage. Not until there was no chance for us. I need you, Camille. Don't marry him. I swear I'll wait for you for as long as it takes, but don't marry him."

"I won't." I couldn't get anything else out because Drake's lips were on mine. There was nothing discreet about us, and I didn't care if the entire world saw us. I pulled my lips from his and said, "Leave with me, now."

Drake's eyes drifted to the necklace I still wore. His hand reached for it in a silent reminder to me that I couldn't go. I couldn't contain my smile. "Your mom was here." I reached up to the clasps of the necklace and took it off.

Drake's eyes grew to the size of quarters. "You took it off!"

"Your mom fixed it. It turns out any Matriarch can remove it. I thought I was going to have to marry Gage to get it off."

I was still cradled in his arms, his voice heavy, "You were going to go through with it? You would have married Gage?"

"I didn't know you were alive until your mom told me a little while ago. As far as being bound to Gage, I didn't think I had much of a choice. If I had refused to marry him, I would have stayed a prisoner here. I'd already planned to go back to California, to my old life. I figured Gage would let me divorce him." Some of my darker desires included convincing Gage to return to Zandra's estate to exact revenge for the killing of Bianca and Drake. Now that I knew the truth, I didn't think I'd share that one with anyone.

"There's no divorce for Centaurs, Camille. It can't be done. A couple united can be parted by death, but the surviving Centaur cannot marry again. They cannot be bound a second time." Drake finally eased me onto my feet but kept his arms wrapped around me.

"Anything is possible. I was born of two Centaurs that weren't married. That isn't possible either."

"Camille, you don't understand. You're the only one. There are no others."

"What do you mean there are no others?"

"You're the only Centaur child to be born out of wedlock. Gage would never have agreed to a divorce. He would have been shunned by his family. He would have lost his livelihood. He would have been disgraced." Drake still held me in his arms, the warmth I never thought I'd feel again encircling me.

"Well then, it's a good thing Bianca isn't dead. He can marry her." I was all smiles and wasn't sure gravity still worked because I felt like I was floating. I brought myself back to earth when something that had bothered me for a long time came to mind, "But wait—Gretchen said she gave Will permission to be with my mom if he wanted."

Drake eyed me curiously, "Your father shouldn't have been able to . . . you know . . . with your mother. Gretchen may have given him permission because she didn't know what to make of it. I've heard of no bloodlines from the pastures of Thessaly that can break a bond."

"So maybe he was from a different pasture."

Drake stopped, arguing with himself more than with me, "There couldn't be. It's not possible."

"What's not possible?"

"Something I need to talk to my parents about when we return."

Phineas cleared his throat. He wore a grin that stretched from the side of the house to the window. "What are you two waiting for? Let's go." Phineas led us straight to the garage, where we all piled into a sleek black Mercedes. I saw a rack of fresh vegetables setting by the door to go into the house. "Give me a second." I grabbed eight tomatoes out of the pile and went to the Bentley. I shoved each of them into the car's gas tank, one right after the other, replaced the gas cap, and jumped back into the sedan.

Bianca asked, "What was that for?"

"They'll be able to go thirty miles before the engine seizes. They'll be stranded, and it'll give us a better head start. Drive Phineas!"

We raced down the driveway, Phineas pressed a button, and the foreboding gates opened wide for us. We were free. As we sped down the two lane road, it felt like we had wings instead of wheels. Bianca told me they'd been held in the guest house the whole time. It didn't occur to me that the guard staff had changed—the staff of four rotating their watch over me had changed to two—but I was so out of it from the grief of losing them both, I hadn't noticed.

The sun was just setting over the horizon when we pulled into Will and Gretchen's driveway. It was a marvelous homecoming. Everyone but Beau stood outside awaiting our arrival. Gage arrived within minutes and grabbed hold of Bianca, the same reunion Drake and I had shared just hours before. No one said a word, as they had pushed all pretense aside, holding each other tenderly, ready to finally begin their life together, regardless of who had been betrothed to whom. I expected William to say something about rules, commitments, bloodlines or something, but he didn't – he looked relieved.

Drake pulled me close to his side and addressed my father. "Camille has had a horrific ordeal. She's not ready to make her choice, but when she is, she'll choose me." Drake looked down at me as if he were waiting for me to argue what we both already knew. "As her unofficial fiancé, I will protect her to the death, and I will not leave her side."

Will nodded, "Gretchen agrees with you; it's only a matter of time."

My eyes darted to Gretchen. She bowed her head slowly, and I blurted out, "I thought if you told someone their future, you jinxed it or something?"

Gretchen stepped closer to Drake and me, in a tone that left nothing to interpretation, "Camille, your destiny has been fluid. I've seen so many different outcomes for you in the last two months, I'm still not certain. What I do know: If you choose a Centaur, Drake is the Centaur you'll choose—when you're ready. Your heart has already made the choice. You just need to give your mind time to accept your heart's decision."

Drake was standing behind me when Gretchen said he was my future. I felt his arms wrap around me as he lovingly kissed the top of my head. Drake whispered, "There's no rush, Camille. Take your time, but know that I won't allow anyone to separate us."

I crossed both arms over Drake's arms that were wrapped around me and leaned back fully into his warm embrace. It felt like things were going to be okay, even if I only got to savor that feeling for a couple minutes. I didn't miss Gretchen's words, "If you choose a Centaur." I'd said from the beginning that I wasn't sure I wanted anything to do with being a Centaur – but that was before I knew how I felt about Drake.

Drake spoke to my father, "It's only a matter of time before Zandra catches up to us."

Will nodded, "Get some rest. I can forbid her entry into my home. You'll be safe here. Welcome to our family, Drake. Thank you for bringing Camille home."

We climbed the steps to my room. So much had happened; I hardly knew where to begin. With all the weird rules and strange traditions, I half expected someone to jump in front of us and send us to separate rooms. No one did. While we walked into my room, Drake said, "You know she'll be here soon."

"Uniting the bloodlines is no more than a pipe dream for her now. Gage and Bianca are going to make it official – he's off the market. Once he's chosen, officially, by Bianca, my blood debt is paid."

"Gage has a brother, Camille."

"What?"

"I can't believe he never told you. Brandon is eighteen, and if Gage is out of the picture, Zandra could do the whole thing over again. Gage's dad and your grandmother are serious about uniting their two bloodlines."

"What's the big deal?"

"I think they're trying to find immortality."

"Immortality?"

"Chiron was an immortal who willingly gave up his immortality. Unice was made a human before Chiron, and had immortal blood in her veins, as well. I think Kyle and Zandra are trying to make Centaurs immortal again or at least their bloodlines. They aren't going to give up just because Gage and Bianca are together; in fact, Bianca is probably in as much danger as we are."

"Does she know?"

"The three of us talked about it while we were all at Zandra's estate. They know to go into hiding. They can use Aphrodite's magic to hide if they need to. We already know that works."

I thought of what Gage told me, how his dad was really in love with my mom, how he hid her and protected her. Gage could do the same thing for Bianca, and I might never see them again. "I need to talk to Bianca."

"They've already left."

"Do you know where they went?"

"I have an idea, but nothing specific."

"How do we get in contact with them?"

"That's the point, Camille. We don't."

"Gage won't break contact with his family, will he?" Growing up with just Mom and me, it was hard to imagine willingly giving her up, let alone a whole family.

"He's not sure how far his dad'll go. He's not taking any more chances with Bianca."

"Maybe Mr. Richardson isn't so bad. Maybe it's just he and Zandra together that are the problem."

"She's power mad, Camille. She'll hunt us down with or without Gage's dad."

"She's an old woman, Drake. I doubt she'd stand a chance against us."

"You are still unfamiliar with our ways. Don't confuse age with power or strength. The only reason you and your mother were safe for all those years was Aphrodite's magic protected you both. That protection is no longer there. Zandra is a Centauride scorned: she will seek her revenge."

"So what are you saying? We need to go into hiding?"

"We need more than a good hiding spot. We need magic of our own."

I could see Drake was just as exhausted as I was. We slipped into my bed, his arms wound around my body, and I felt tingles all over my skin. I didn't want to talk about Zandra, going into hiding, or finding our own magic. I only wanted to feel Drake's body against mine, savor the rhythm of his heart beating against me and listen to his breathing. We melted into each other and drifted off together. It felt like I'd only just blinked my eyes when an arm shook me.

"Camille," Will's voice was an urgent whisper, "wake up. Quickly, wake up."

I wiped the sleep from my eyes, squinting into the darkness. I felt the warmth of Drake's body against mine as his muscles flexed beside me. "What's wrong, Will?"

"Camille, Zandra is on her way. It's worse than we thought. You need to get up. We need to get you out of here."

"I thought you said we'd be safe here?"

"You've got an hour, two at best and her forces will be upon us. You'll be safe inside my walls, but I can't offer you protection outside the house, and you couldn't stay inside forever."

"Where will we go?"

"I've chartered a plane. You'll need to get to the Monck's Corner Airport where a plane is waiting. Go now, Sweetheart. It's your only chance."

Drake tugged me hard. He didn't need to hear anything else. "Camille, I'm not losing you again, let's go."

I turned to Drake, "But where? Won't she find us wherever we go?"

"I've got an idea." Drake turned to Will and asked, "How big of a plane is it?"

"It's a jet, son. Go. Everything you need is waiting on the plane." Will pulled me into a tight embrace. "Be careful. If you need us, we're a phone call away. I'll stay here long enough to throw her off of your trail. Don't go near San Diego."

Drake nearly pulled me out of Will's arms. "I'm sorry, Love, we need to go." I started to struggle against him when he murmured, "I can't lose you again." That was all it took. I knew if I lost him a second time, I wouldn't survive – I couldn't fault him for feeling the same. "I'm going to give my parents a call. We need to go in five minutes."

I looked around the room. There wasn't much of me here. As I packed clothes, I saw my cell phone by the night stand, exactly where I'd left it several months before. Neither Will nor Gretchen bothered to unplug it while I was gone. My voicemail box was full. I saw the call log. Daniel had called every day for the last two months. I needed to call him and let him know I was okay. But what would I tell him?

Drake peeked in through my bedroom door, "Ready, love?"

"I guess so, but I need to know where we're going."

"Ireland, at least that's where we'll start."

"Ireland?"

"Ireland's our first stop. Our history is unreliable; too many fables are mixed in with truths, so I'm not a hundred percent certain where we'll end up. Do you have a passport?"

"Well, yeah, but not here. It's at my apartment in California." Spring break of my senior year was in Cabo San Lucas. I had only that single stamp in my passport, although I had fantasies of traveling the world. Not in my darkest nightmares could I have imagined a deranged grandmother coming into my life then chasing me around the planet.

"Looks like we'll need to make a detour."

"A detour, for a passport? Drake, did anything happen to you that I should know about while you were captive in Zandra's guest house? A big knock on the head or something?"

Drake stepped through the door, was in front of me in four strides and looked into my eyes, "Yes. Something did happen. I fell hopelessly in love with a woman with a death sentence on her head. Now grab your backpack. Let's go."

"I think this is great and everything, but what kind of magic are we looking for? I mean, is it bigger than a breadbox? Are we going to need a crane?"

"I'll tell you everything once we're in the air."

We didn't go to the airport I'd flown into. We went up to a sleepy runway in Moncks Corner. I hated the idea of leaving my beautiful sedan in the lonely little parking lot. The car had fewer than three hundred miles on it, and it seemed like a huge waste of money considering how much I'd been able to use it.

As I shut the trunk, I looked at the small control tower in front of us. It was only two stories, with open-ended hangers spread out along the outskirts of the runway. It looked like maybe twenty small planes called this airport their home.

"So which one of these are we taking?"

"None of those. Your father sent a jet. It should be here somewhere."

We walked the fifty feet from the parking lot to the airport's terminal – I use that term loosely. I didn't know airports existed that didn't have TSA. No x-ray inspection, no displays announcing arrival and departure flights: this looked closer to a car rental agency than a real airport. A man looked over a counter with a headset on. "You Mr. and Mrs. Nash?"

I froze, but Drake didn't miss a beat, "Yes. We're here for a pickup."

"Your pilot just radioed in, should be on the ground in about five minutes. He's already filed his flight plan and says he doesn't need fuel. Once he's on the ground, you can go out to the tarmac. You're all set."

We saw a sleek, black jet making its approach to the airport. When it touched down, it looked seriously out of place with the privately owned Cessnas and crop dusters that hid under the open bay canopies. After it landed, we stepped out onto the runway. The aircraft's engines were whining quietly as we walked out toward it. The hatch opened, and a set of stairs materialized from its fuselage. Drake led me by the hand to the stairs as a man wearing a headset, loud surfer shorts, and Oakley's yelled down to us, "Drake and Camille Nash?"

Drake answered, "That's us."

"Come on up. Sorry we're late." Once we were inside the cabin, the man said, "We were fixing the passenger manifest. For today's flight to New York, you're "Fred and Wilma Rubble."

I smirked at the man, "A little obvious, don't you think?"

"Naw, obvious would have been Fred and Wilma Flintstone. When we fly international, our manifest will have to match your passports."

"My passport's in California."

"Already taken care of." I cocked my head to the side, wondering how they'd had a chance to get my passport. Before I could ask, the man lifted the stairs behind us and closed the door. It was remarkably quiet inside and not like the commercial airplanes I'd been on. "I'm Chip. The bar is there, under the television. There should be some snacks in the cabinet under it. If you're really hungry, there are some frozen meals in the freezer. There's a bedroom in the back. Help yourself to anything you want."

"You're the pilot and the steward?"

"Co-pilot, and this is more self-service, if you know what I mean." The engines began throttling up and Chip smiled, "Sounds like that's my cue. The pilot must be ready to go. We shouldn't be stopping along the way. FAA says I have to give you a safety briefing. If we lose cabin pressure during the flight, there are oxygen masks in the storage compartment over your seats. If we have an emergency landing, you can open either of the two doors by pressing and pulling the handle up. If the captain and I become incapacitated during the flight, pucker up and kiss your asses goodbye."

My eye muscles flexed and Chip laughed, "Just making sure you were paying attention. Sit back, relax, watch a movie or do whatever you like. If you need anything, just hit the intercom on one of the seats."

"Thanks, Chip. How long a flight will it be?"

"We're going up to New York. We'll get a full tank of fuel there and head to Dublin straight away. Mr. Strayer had us stop in North Carolina to pick something up for you. It's in that envelope on the seat."

CHAPTER 37

Camille Benning – Charleston, SC

Drake opened the envelope. Inside were two passports, two credit cards and a stack of Euros. I opened the passport and saw myself staring back. It said my name was "Angela Chiron." I looked at the other and it was "Gage Chiron."

"He couldn't have chosen less conspicuous names?"

Drake smiled, "He's helping us out a great deal. Nash is a well-known bloodline from the original pasture, but it doesn't carry the same weight as the Chiron name."

We felt the plane lift up off the ground, and I watched us climb higher and higher, "The original pasture?"

"Right, we're going back to Thessaly."

"Thessaly? You're serious?"

"Of course, I'm serious."

"Thessaly is in Ireland?"

"I think so. So much myth is rolled up with legend, we may find out it's somewhere else."

"So we're flying halfway around the world, and we aren't even sure we are flying to the right country?"

Drake gathered my hands in his and brought them to his lips, "Think of it as a honeymoon."

"A honeymoon? Just because the pilots think we're Mr. and Mrs., I'm still single. If it were our honeymoon, you would not be getting away with taking me to Ireland in search of a pasture where ancient Centaurs used to breed."

"It was more than a breeding ground, Camille. It was where our race was born. It's sacred, and it has a magic all its own."

"So we're going to do what, dig up some soil or something?"

"It won't be that easy. We need to find your great uncle Zethus."

"My great uncle? I've never heard of him."

"He's Zandra's brother. The stories I've heard say that he lives at Thessaly. He's as much a direct descendant of Chiron as Zandra – but he was favored by the gods and has something that we need."

"What?"

It wouldn't have been possible for the pilot or co-pilot to hear us, but Drake whispered anyway, "Hercules' arrow."

"You're not serious!"

"I am serious. We need the arrow. Having it will be enough of a deterrent. The tip still has the blood of a Hydra."

No one could be more surprised than me that after everything she'd put me through, I didn't want her dead, "But that'll kill her."

"We aren't going to shoot it through her heart. If we can get the arrow from Zethus, the tip of the arrow pricking her skin will drain her of her magic. She'll live out her life, but we won't have to look over our shoulders."

"Are Zethus and Zandra close?"

"I don't know, but I don't have any other ideas, Love."

Once we had started the second leg of our trip, New York to Dublin, I stood up and held my hand out to Drake, "Come with me." I led him to the rear of the aircraft and found the bedroom that Chip had pointed out. I didn't want to think about her chasing us, where her brother's loyalties might lie, if we could find the pasture, or even if the arrow existed.

I was exhausted and hoped this flight would take three days. I was sure I could spend that long in bed—longer, knowing Drake was not only alive but with me. Drake snuggled in close, and it only took minutes for his breathing to slow down. All those conversations I'd had with his spirit, or so I thought, I'd confessed everything. I swore if there was any chance ever to tell him how I felt, I wouldn't hold anything back. "Drake?"

His eyes were closed, his lips turned up in a content grin. He looked like he was seconds from drifting off to sleep, "Hmmm?"

"I love you." I'd never said those words to anyone but Mom, and I knew I'd never feel them for anyone else.

Drake's eyes snapped open and his grin morphed into a wide smile. He leaned toward me on one shoulder as his free hand caressed my arm and his lips crushed onto mine. When he pulled his lips away, his ice blue eyes were staring directly into mine. "Say it again, Camille."

I couldn't help beaming back at him, "I said, I love you, Drake."

He wrapped both his arms around me, pressing himself into me and whispered in my ear, "For how long?"

I cocked my head to the side, "What do you mean: for how long?"

"How long do you promise to love me?"

"Always, Drake."

Before I could blink an eye, Drake had pulled me up to a sitting position on the bed. My legs were draped over the side of the bed and he was kneeling in front of me. "Camille, I promise to protect you. I promise to always put your needs before mine. I promise I'll never let you go to bed angry, and you'll never wake up alone. I promise to love you the rest of my life, and when this life is over, I'll spend my eternity in the pasture with you."

I was speechless. Luckily, Drake didn't wait for any kind of a response from me. He pulled me into his chest, "I've never wanted anything more than you to love me back." He crushed his mouth onto mine again. I didn't have to say the words. He knew I'd made my choice.

We both gave ourselves over to the exhaustion. Hours later I awoke from the deepest sleep I'd had in months. My hands traced the chiseled lines of his chest, his arms stayed wrapped around me. I knew Zandra wouldn't fade into the background. Before I came to South Carolina, I'd never given much thought to my future; I caught myself now thinking of the possibilities. Somewhere between awake and asleep I smelled my mother's perfume. My eyes snapped open. I saw her sitting on the edge of the bed; she was so beautiful—her skin almost glowed. She held her finger to her lips, silencing me, pointing at the sleeping Drake beside me. "Be careful, Camille. Centaurs are not what they seem. Most are like Rupert, more beast than man."

"You mean Drake?" I shook my head at the absurdity. "But, I love him."

"I know, Camille. But do you love him enough to save him?"

"Save him from what?"

"No one is safe with you right now. The Lost Herd seeks you. I had to give up Kyle for the same reason, it was the only chance he had at life. They still found me."

I'd never gotten a straight answer from Gretchen and I wasn't able to ask my father. Mom might be the only one I could ask right now. "Brent says we're part of the Lost Herd. Are we?"

"Trust yourself, Camille. Know that you and you alone can find what you seek. If you love Drake, do not put him in danger. Do not allow him in your life."

"Mom, I can't . . . I can't give him up." I looked at him sleeping peacefully beside me, muttering more to myself, "I almost didn't make it without him."

"I know it's hard, Camille. But if you love him, you'll send him away. Take the fight to your enemies and give them nothing to hold over you. Drake is your only weakness. They will exploit him and you will fail."

"But you never fought your enemies: you went into hiding. Gage told me all about it."

"You're right, if I had it to do over again, I would have fought. I did not see what would happen to you. You, too, will have a son and daughter one day. You need to make the choice now, before it's made for you. The Lost Herd will find you. When they do, you and your descendants will never be free."

I could see pain welling up through her eyes. "Your father. . ." Her lips moved but her words were muted. I saw her figure fading into the background.

"Mom! I can't hear you! Mom!" I reached out to where she had been sitting and felt nothing but air. Everything seemed to be in slow motion. "Mom, don't leave!" The sound of my own voice startled me. I awoke to the dark bedroom, trying to figure out if she had been there or if I'd just dreamed her. I took in a large whiff hoping to catch even a faint hint of her perfume – but I smelled nothing. She wasn't there.

I struggled to go back to my dream, but I didn't have any luck. All I found was a dreamless sleep. I awoke hours later to Drake's arms still around me. I didn't want to flinch because it still felt a little euphoric to be there with him. My mind began to wander. Did I really have a twin brother somewhere in the world? Mom said I'd have a son and daughter; Zandra must have been telling the truth about twins. What would Zandra do if she saw me again? How would we know Bianca and Gage were okay? Did my mom really appear in a dream or was it my imagination? Why couldn't I see or hear my mom? What did I have to fear from the Lost Herd? What did Drake mean when he said we needed to find our own magic? Could I share any of this with Daniel?

All these questions were sailing through my mind when I heard Drake murmuring in his sleep: the lullaby that broke down my defenses at Zandra's, "Choose me, Camille. Choose me." I snuggled in closer to him, pushing the questions to the back of my mind. I'd worry about all of that later. For now, I would live in the present – savor the love of a man I thought I'd lost forever. Mom's warning was probably just a dream; after everything we'd gone through, my mind wanted to believe that real happiness was finally mine.

FROM THE AUTHOR

I hope you enjoyed Blood Debt! I would love for you to write a review on Amazon. It doesn't have to be long, just let others know what you thought of the story. Here is the link: www.amazon.com/review/create-review?ie=UTF8&asin=B008L79YRO

I am an independent author, which means I do not have an agent, a publicist, or a publishing company backing me up. I DEPEND on word-of-mouth advertising. If you enjoyed *Blood Debt*, it would mean the world to me for you to recommend it to a friend (or ten friends!). If you recommend it to someone who tells you they do not have time to read, let them know it is also available as an audiobook!

If you would like to chat with me, here are the best places to find me:

Amazon author page: www.amazon.com/author/nancystraight

Facebook: www.facebook.com/nancystraight.author

My blog: www.nancystraight.com

Twitter: www.twitter.com/NancyStraight

Goodreads: www.goodreads.com/NancyStraight

Email: nancystraight@gmail.com

I read and respond to every message I receive. (Sometimes a day or two late, but I do respond to everyone who reaches out to me). I hope to hear from you!

If you wish to receive free promotional items, notification of book signing events, and upcoming book releases, you can join my subscriber's list here: http://eepurl.com/bDtmDL

Happy Reading,

Nancy

ACKNOWLEDGEMENTS

Blood Debt would not have been possible without the support of several incredible people. Linda Brant, my aunt, has painstakingly edited and polished *Blood Debt.* Rebecca Ufkes, Kris Kendall, Charles Young, Melissa Balentine and Jennifer Nunez volunteered to be Beta Readers—their feedback was invaluable.

Interestingly enough, I didn't pick the title for this book or this series – I let friends and fans do that for me. Many thanks to Keren Spencer for naming the book *Blood Debt* and to Bridget Howard for naming the series *Touched.* It was quite an amazing feat when neither had read it, and I think you'll agree they could not have come up with two more appropriate names!

The beautiful cover was designed by Amber McNemar at e-Think Graphics.

I wish there were a way to single out each of the independent authors out there who have helped and inspired me along the way, but a thank you to each one would be a book in itself. A few that I cannot leave out are: Shelly Crane, Rachel Higginson, Charlotte Abel, Amy Bartol and Shannon Dermott – each one has been an incredible inspiration to me and I highly recommend their books!

Book bloggers are the unsung heroes for indie authors. There have been many that I feel indebted. One that deserves a special place on this page is Mandy at: http://www.twimom101bookblog.blogspot.com She has become a dear friend and is a true indie advocate.

Finally, my husband, Toby, has been supportive of my every adventure. Thanks for all the nights you made dinner and did homework so that I could follow my dream!

All my love,

Nancy

www.ingramcontent.com/pod-product-compliance
Lightning Source LLC
Chambersburg PA
CBHW070638310726
48982CB00001B/324

* 9 7 8 0 6 9 2 7 9 8 5 9 1 *